BLOOD OF 1

THE RUTHLESS BOUNTY hunter Brunner is scouring the land of Bretonnia for the notorious highwayman Gobineau. After a series of deadly encounters, the chase leads Brunner to the blighted ruins of the accursed and evil city of Mousillon. But when Gobineau manages to lay his hands on the legendary Fell Fang, a relic that is rumoured to have the power to summon dragons, Brunner and his allies must fight their way through arrogant nobles, rogue wizards and even a vampire in order to get their mark.

A WARHAMMER NOVEL

Brunner the Bounty Hunter

BLOOD OF THE DRAGON

C L Werner

To Jess and Dean – the brothers of the dragon.

A BLACK LIBRARY PUBLICATION

First published in Great Britain in 2004.

Paperback edition published in 2004 by
BL Publishing,
Games Workshop Ltd.,
Willow Road, Nottingham,
NG7 2WS, UK.

10 9 8 7 6 5 4 3 2 1

Cover illustration by Clint Langley.
Map by Nuala Kennedy.

A CIP record for this book is available from the British Library.

ISBN 1 84416 095 5

Distributed in the US by Simon & Schuster
1230 Avenue of the Americas, New York, NY 10020, US.

Printed and bound in Great Britain by
Bookmarque Ltd, Croydon, Surrey

See the Black Library on the Internet at
www.blacklibrary.com

Find out more about Games Workshop
and the world of Warhammer at
www.games-workshop.com

THIS IS A dark age, a bloody age, an age of daemons and of sorcery. It is an age of battle and death, and of the world's ending. Amidst all of the fire, flame and fury it is a time, too, of mighty heroes, of bold deeds and great courage.

AT THE HEART of the Old World sprawls the Empire, the largest and most powerful of the human realms. Known for its engineers, sorcerers, traders and soldiers, it is a land of great mountains, mighty rivers, dark forests and vast cities. And from his throne in Altdorf reigns the Emperor Karl-Franz, sacred descendent of the founder of these lands, Sigmar, and wielder of his magical warhammer.

BUT THESE ARE far from civilised times. Across the length and breadth of the Old World, from the knightly palaces of Bretonnia to ice-bound Kislev in the far north, come rumblings of war. In the towering World's Edge Mountains, the orc tribes are gathering for another assault. Bandits and renegades harry the wild southern lands of the Border Princes. There are rumours of rat-things, the skaven, emerging from the sewers and swamps across the land. And from the northern wildernesses there is the ever-present threat of Chaos, of daemons and beastmen corrupted by the foul powers of the Dark Gods. As the time of battle draws ever near, the Empire needs heroes like never before.

Couronne

Pale
Sisters

Forest
of
Arden

Gisoreux

Montfort

Mousillon

River Grismerie

Bastonne

Forest
of
Châlons

Bordeleaux

The Massif
Orcal

Aquitaine

N

Brionne

BRETONNIA

CHAPTER ONE

IT HAD BEEN *nearly a year since the affair of the Black Prince and my parting with the bounty hunter, so it had been quite unexpected when I had encountered him, his raiment caked in the mud and dust of travel, armour sporting the beginnings of rust not uncommon among warriors on the march, making his way along the narrow winding streets of Parravon. Yet, somehow, though unexpected, it had not been surprising to see Brunner again. And despite the events that caused me to forsake the Tilean city of Miragliano for the quiet Bretonnian township of Parravon, despite the treachery and ruthlessness that permeated Brunner's hunt for the Black Prince, despite even the violent and menacing aura that surrounded the man himself, I found that I was quite pleased to see my old collaborator again.*

My name is Ehrhard Stoecker, originally of Altdorf until events surrounding my notorious history detailing the infamous vampire count Vlad von Carstein made it prudent for me to emigrate from the lands of my birth. However, even in exile, I found it impossible to keep my mind idle and my pen from parchment. In Miragliano, I began recording the exploits of the adventurers I would come upon in that city's many taverns and wine shops and none of those exploits had been so bloody or so fascinating as the career of the bounty killer Brunner. Now, forced by the requirements of an empty belly to pen the atrociously bloated and self-aggrandising family history of the Duc of Parravon, I found myself drawn more than ever to the violent, often horrific journeys of Brunner. It was with great enthusiasm that I invited my old confederate to join me at the inn where I had made my abode, eager to learn more of his travels and the dark deeds that accompanied them.

Brunner spent some time regaling me with tales of his time among the Tilean city states following my abrupt and hasty retreat from Miragliano. I heard many things that disquieted me and made me ever more pleased that I had forsaken the south for the safety of Bretonnia and the protection of its valiant knights. The bounty hunter told me of the horrors that lurked beneath the slopes of the Vaults, the unclean vermin who now claimed the halls of the old dwarf lords of Karag-dar. He told me of dead things that stalked the nighted streets of Miragliano itself, and I shivered as I recalled the experience that had made me flee Altdorf so long ago. He told me too of the corruption that was rife throughout the Tilean countryside, of dread emissaries from the realms of the Dark Gods and the zealous madmen who opposed them, the infamous Inquisition of Solkan. I hastened to record every detail of Brunner's accounts, my pen darting across each page as the bounty hunter piled horror atop horror. When he had finished, Brunner leaned back in his chair, sipping at a tankard of mead, watching me as I hurriedly completed my notes.

I looked upon my companion and was once more struck by his imposing figure. He wore brigandine armour about his lean, yet somehow powerful frame. Over the cloth and metal was fixed a breastplate of gromril, that fabulously strong metal whose secret is known only to the dwarfs. Steel vambraces and greaves protected arm and leg, blackened to prevent any betraying shine. Upon the table, the bounty hunter had set his helm of blackened steel, the dark shadow of its empty visor staring up at me with a menacing gaze. Beside it rested a small crossbow, a weapon which I knew my companion would be able to employ in the space of a breath should he have need. I knew that there would be other weapons ready at hand, the array of knives that crossed his breast in a worn leather bandolier, the wicked hatchet that swung from his hip, or even the expertly crafted pistol holstered across his belly. Two weapons in particular had a certain notoriety attached to them. The first of these was the huge knife with a serrated edge which Brunner had morbidly termed 'the Headsman', and it was the last thing many a wounded outlaw had seen in this life.

The other was a long sword, its slender blade crafted long ago in the forges of the Reikland, its golden pommel and hilt fashioned in the shape of a winged dragon. Drakesmalice it was called, and I had seen for myself the skill and felicity with which the bounty hunter could employ it. The sword itself had some history in the region, until the utter destruction of the line by the Viscount de Chegney it had been the traditional heirloom of the barons of the house of von Drakenburg. Given the unspoken animosity which my collaborator had always displayed toward the viscount, it was somehow fitting that the weapon of that villain's vanquished enemy should find its way into Brunner's hands.

I roused myself from my study of the bounty hunter, forgetting once more the deep gashes and dents in his armour and the stories that lay behind each one. I looked into the man's harsh features, meeting his icy blue eyes.

'That accounts for your exploits in Miragliano,' I told him, dipping my pen once more into the ink well. 'But it has been two seasons since you brought down the Black Prince and I cannot believe that a man such as yourself has been idle for all that time.'

Brunner leaned forward, the legs of his chair rapping against the floor. He set the tankard of mead down upon the table and favoured me with a grim smile.

'Oh, I have been anything but idle,' he told me. 'You need not trouble yourself on that score.' Again, that unsettling, wolf-like smile came upon his face. 'You have perhaps heard rumours, stories about trouble in the east?'

The breath caught in my throat. There had indeed been stories in recent weeks, tales of destruction and horror that had spread like wildfire, unsettling the knights of Parravon, making them restless. It was expected that any day the duc would announce some campaign against the source of these troubles, a quest to destroy the beast who ravaged the eastern dukedoms. Indeed, if there was any truth in the rumour, knights all across the kingdom were already riding to test their mettle against this challenge, to prove their bravery and their embodiment of the old virtues.

'The dragon?' I gasped. 'You had something to do with that?' My mind exploded with a thousand questions, and my hand was unsteady with excitement as I strove to write down the bounty killer's responses. 'You have seen it? It is real?'

Brunner nodded his head slightly and his voice fell into a low whisper. 'It is real,' he told me. 'And I have seen it.'

There was a haunted quality to Brunner's voice that had never before manifested itself in our conversations, the echo of lost tomorrows and vanished yesterdays.

With a final sip from his tankard, Brunner began his account…

SICHO CRANED HIS neck about within the ring of coarse rope that encircled it. Was it not bad enough that they were going to hang him, did they have to drag it out as well? The rope was chafing his skin to the point where it was becoming unbearable, an itch that his hands, tied behind his back, couldn't scratch.

The poacher and sometime bandit looked over to where the warden continued to drone on and on about his crimes, the despicable nature of his soul, and how he was deserving of an end far more terrible than the simple hanging proscribed by the duc's law. Sicho rolled his eyes, turning his attention to the muddy, manure-strewn square and the ramshackle hovels that passed for the thriving hamlet of Veleon. The crowd that had gathered was much larger than he had anticipated, there were perhaps fifty people in the onlooking mob, far more than a puddle of pig piss like Veleon could support. Most likely the duc had declared a holiday so that the peasants of the neighbouring villages and hamlets might have the opportunity to see his execution. Most considerate of him, considering that Sicho's death might be the most exciting thing to intrude upon the dull drudgery of their lives for years. Of course, the duc was motivated more from hopes that seeing Sicho swing might throw cold water on the ambitions of any fledgling poachers and bandits among the peasantry.

Better to die quickly than take a slow death like those idiots, Sicho thought to himself. I'll wager half of them have never even tasted meat, the bandit added as he found a particularly wretched crone gawking at him with a mouth completely devoid of teeth. Sicho twisted about as much as he was able and glared at the bloated figure of the warden. The man was droning on now about an incident Sicho had nearly forgotten involving the theft of a knight's bones from a village outside Brionne.

'Can you hurry it up?' the bandit snarled through his split lip and bruised face. The militia men who had captured him had been quite enthusiastic in their work. The warden rolled up the leather scroll from which he had been reading, slapping it against his meaty palm. 'At the rate you're going, we'll be here half the night.'

The rotund official shook the rolled scroll at the condemned man, taking a menacing step toward the bandit. 'You might show a bit of contrition for all your filthy crimes, you snivelling cur!' the warden spat. 'For you'll answer to the Lady and the gods for your misdeeds, brigand! When that rope goes tight and the air is strangled out of you, the time for repentance will be past.' The warden looked past Sicho, locking eyes with the two brawny militia men who held the other end of the rope tied about the outlaw's neck. Between them stood the old signpost over which the middle section of the rope had been thrown.

'At least I'm an honest thief!' Sicho cursed. 'Tell me, what lets you keep that fat belly of yours full? Not, millet and gruel I'd wager.'

The warden bristled under the insult, as much for its truth as the venom with which it was voiced. The fat man's face darkened until it was nearly the same hue of red as the worn leather tunic that struggled to encase its girth. 'We've been about this long enough, dog!' he hissed back. The warden looked again to his two men. He lifted the hand that held the scroll. 'When I lower my hand, pull the rope and send this animal to the gods.'

As the fat man's hand began to fall, however, there was a sharp snap and the sound of splintering wood. The downward descent of the official's hand was arrested, the scroll it gripped fixed to the wall behind him, pinned in place by the dull steel of a crossbow bolt. Gasps broke out from the crowd and the warden turned away from a fruitless attempt to free the proclamation. The fat man's eyes went wide with surprise and apprehension as he saw the figure regarding him from the back of the milling mob of peasants.

The man was an imposing sight, his upper face hidden within the blackened steel of a foreign-style helmet, a suit of weathered brigandine armour enclosing his slim figure, a breastplate of dark metal encasing his chest. It was like looking at some shabby imitation of the knights the warden served, some crude and base mockery of the shining plate and colourful tabards of Bretonnia's great warriors.

Even the horse upon which the man was seated was dark and grim, a far cry from the noble and valiant chargers of the knights.

But the warden saw these things only in passing, his attention fixed upon the strange weapon the warrior held at the ready. The warden had never seen a crossbow, though he had heard such a weapon described for him by a relative who had once travelled to Couronne. The curious, almost box-like device set upon the weapon puzzled him, he couldn't imagine how such a weapon might work. The fat man turned his eyes back to the expressionless steel face of the stranger's helm.

'I need to have a few words with that man whose neck you are about to stretch,' the warrior's cold voice told him.

The colour returned to the warden's features as he noted the assumed authority in the stranger's tones.

'You dare to interrupt an appointed representative of the Duc de Vertain in the execution of his official duties?' the fat official snarled. He might never have seen a crossbow before, but he had a good idea of how they worked, and this stranger had already fired his missile. He looked over at his militiamen. The two soldiers hastily tied off their end of the rope and began to stride forward, hands resting easily on the hilts of their swords.

The strange weapon gripped in the rider's hands jerked and the groan of the steel bowstring firing sounded again. The two militiamen froze as a pair of bolts dug into the ground at their feet. The warden looked with horror from his subdued men back to the rider. He staggered back, cowering against the wall as he saw the repeating crossbow swing in his direction.

'Next time I aim higher,' the rider told him. 'But if you'll oblige me, I'll have a few words with your prisoner and then be on my way.'

The warden nodded his head slightly, slinking behind the nearest of the dirty, muttering crowd.

The bounty hunter urged his horse forward, pushing his way through the peasants until he looked down upon Sicho.

'You're a little late to collect the price on this head,' the bandit sneered, spitting a blob of phlegm into the dust. Brunner gave the condemned man an icy smile, reaching his gloved hand forward and letting his fingers grip the rope rising behind Sicho's neck. The brigand rose to his toe tips as Brunner pulled slightly at the noose.

'I had hoped you might be more co-operative,' he told Sicho, pulling once more on the rope, enough to make the bandit's next breath turn into a gasp. 'Maybe I'll have them cut you down after you've hung a bit. See if that loosens your tongue.' Brunner released his hold on the rope, leaning back in the saddle of Fiend, his warhorse. 'If that doesn't work, we can always try it again. As often as we need.' The bounty hunter reached beneath one of his vambraces, removing a rolled scrap of leather. 'They're going to hang you, Sicho. How many times they hang you, that's your decision.'

Sicho rotated his head in wide circles, trying to loosen the grip of the noose about his neck. The bandit curled his lip, snarling back at the bounty hunter. Then his eyes fell upon the object held in those gloved hands, and the portrait that had been drawn upon the wanted poster. The hostility drained away, replaced by a peal of laughter.

'Gobineau!' the condemned outlaw cried out. 'You are looking for Gobineau!' Tears were running down Sicho's grimy face as he continued to laugh.

Brunner rolled up the poster, stuffing it back into its place beneath his armour. He looked back at the laughing prisoner. 'You sometimes ran with Gobineau. I want to know where he could be now. When did you last see him?'

Sicho's face contorted into an ironic smile. 'When did I see him last?' he scoffed. 'He is the reason I am here! Trying to outrun this bloated toad and his half-witted swamp cats! The warden and his men were on our trail after we relieved a horse breeder of a few stallions he didn't need. Gobineau was worried that they would catch us on the open road, so as we were riding he reached over and slashed my saddle, dumping me into the road. Of course, this idiot,' Sicho gestured with his chin at the scowling warden, 'was so happy to catch me, he completely gave up chasing Gobineau.' The bandit spat into the dust once again. 'I'll be waiting for that bastard at the gates of Morr!'

'Tell me where Gobineau was heading and maybe I can give him your regards,' Brunner told the prisoner. Sicho's smile broadened and his features lit up as he contemplated how well his treacherous ally would fare with the notorious bounty hunter on his trail. The thought of such a revenge warmed the condemned man's doomed soul.

'We were stealing the horses to outfit a new band Gobineau is gathering together in the hamlet of Perpileon in the realm of Montfort,' the bandit provided. 'I am sure, if you were to hurry, you'd catch him there.'

Brunner nodded his head, turning Fiend away. 'Oh, I'll catch him,' the bounty hunter assured Sicho. 'You've troubles enough without worrying about that.' The bounty hunter walked his horse slowly back through the crowd. He glanced over at the warden as he passed the still subdued official. Brunner touched a finger to the brim of his helm in a clipped and somewhat nonchalant salute. 'Thank you for your consideration, warden. I won't be needing anything else from your prisoner. You may see to your duty now.'

THERE WERE MANY trails that wound their way between the pastures and fields of Montfort, skirting the edges of the forests and detouring around the scattered patches of moor and swamp that dotted the realm's landscape. The largest and most prominent of these were the roads that connected the more important towns and villages to the few cities that rose amid the green farmlands and savage wilds of Bretonnia. Though little more than dirt paths by the standards of more cultured lands such as the Empire and Tilea, the roads of Bretonnia served the same function, moving people and goods from one place to another, nurturing the few tradesmen of the kingdom, assisting the devotions of pious pilgrims and facilitating the wanderlust of the knights out to earn their colours and their name, and those who employed them to darker pursuits.

The road that wound past the holdings of the Marquis de Galfort on its way to the distant Grey Mountains and the fortified city of Parravon was well known to be the haunt of highwaymen and brigands. Bretonnian peasants called it 'the Widow's Way' and did not deign to travel its course, instead detouring through the many game trails and cattle runs that meandered through the wooded hills. Still, there were some few, strangers to the district or aristocrats secure in their own aura of invulnerability, who were foolish enough to tempt fate and travel along the ill-rumoured length of road.

It was for just such foolish prey that three men had concealed themselves within the thick bushes that fronted upon a bend in the course of the Widow's Way. They were kindred spirits, members of a cruel and lawless breed, their faces as brutal and bestial as the filthy furs they wore about their lean, wolfish frames. The leader among the three openly flaunted his contempt for the rulers of the land and their laws, the torn tabard of a knight of the realm tied about his waist like the loin-wrap of a Southlands primitive.

The tall bandit leader grinned as he saw the small mule-drawn cart plodding toward them upon the road. It had been several weeks since they had eaten the last of their horses. No matter how humble, whatever loot the cart might hold would be most welcome.

Dogvael looked over at his companions, motioning for them to draw their swords. The brigand leader stared at the notched, rusty blade in his hands. It was at times like this that he most missed the reassuring feel of the powerful hand-cannon he had liberated from one of the Viscount de Chegney's foreign mercenaries. But it was no good brooding on more pleasant times. Now, a bit of mutton would be exotic enough for the bandit's tastes.

The three men waited until the mule cart was only a few yards away before they exploded from behind the bushes. The man to Dogvael's left rushed forward and seized the bridle of the animal while the other two bandits menaced the man seated on the cart behind it with their swords.

'Stand and deliver, scum!' Dogvael snarled. It was all traditional, of course, like reciting lines in a play. Dogvael had no intention of letting his victim live, no matter how forthcoming he was.

The man seated on the cart drew back in horror, dropping his whip in his fright. Dogvael smiled at the peasant's cowardice.

'Bandits!' the man shuddered. 'Whatever shall I do?'

Dogvael's eyes narrowed as he noticed the almost comic extreme of the cart master's fear, the curled hands clenching at the youthful face. Then he noticed the black leather boots that protruded from the hem of the shabby homespun cloak worn by the driver, boots far too fine for any simple peasant. The bandit drew away in alarm, eyes darting to either side of the road. Even as he did so, the whine of arrows slashing through the air sounded in Dogvael's ears. The brigand holding the bridle of the mule cried out as a shaft crunched into his breastbone. The stricken man fell to the muddy earth, the agitated mule adding to his misery as its hooves pulped his left knee and shattered both of his arms. A moment later Dogvael's other minion cried out, hands clutching impotently at the arrow sticking in his belly. The man pitched to the earth and rolled onto his side, body shuddering as it bled out into the mire of the pathway.

Dogvael turned to run, not knowing who had fired upon his men, nor caring to find out. Even as he turned, however, a third arrow flew from the shadows, striking him in the small of the back and spinning him back around so that he once more faced the cart that had lured him and his companions to their doom.

The owner of the cart was leaning forward, soothing the mule with soft words and a reassuring hand. The man looked up from his labour, staring at Dogvael, all trace of fear, real or exaggerated, now absent from the man's handsome, rakish face. He smiled at the injured bandit, dark eyes twinkling with a roguish mischief, then stood, casting the shabby cloak from his shoulders and displaying a lean, muscular frame encased in a black leather tunic and dark leather breeches. An expensive-looking belt trimmed in fur and edged in gold completed his outfit, save for the slender longsword hanging from said belt.

'I'm afraid that you were a bit... tardy,' the young rogue told Dogvael. He spread his arms in a lavish gesture to encompass the mule cart. 'You see, this cart has already run afoul of bandits.' The rogue smiled again, swinging down from the seat of the mule cart, his booted heels landing upon the now still form of the man who had taken hold of the mule's bridle. The grinning thief looked down at the corpse under his feet, then daintily hopped across the spreading pool of gore emanating from it.

'Rather sloppy operation, you know,' the rogue told Dogvael, stepping closer to give the wounded brigand a reassuring pat on the shoulder. 'I mean... you really should be using bows.' He turned his head, staring at each of Dogvael's dead companions. 'Probably get a few more men, too,' he advised the bandit in an almost conspiratorial whisper.

Men were now emerging from the woods behind the mule cart, advancing upon the violent scene. The rogue gave an airy flick of his hand to indicate the approaching men.

'I have five men in my little company,' he told Dogvael. 'With bows,' he added almost as an afterthought. 'We do quite well for ourselves.' A harsh, hostile note slipped into the rogue's voice. 'Which is why we did not take too kindly to finding out that a pack of sloppy amateurs had set up shop in our hunting grounds. The ducs aren't the only ones can't abide poaching, you know.'

The bowmen were striding forward now, inspecting the bodies of Dogvael's men, rolling them over with the toes of their fur boots, rummaging about their clothing for any scrap of loot.

The cart master watched as his companions went about their ghoulish work, giving another wink of conspiracy to the injured man sitting near him. 'They're quite thorough, you know. Clean those boys as nice as a pig with a soup bone.' One of the archers, a big brute with a full black beard and a filthy hauberk loped toward Dogvael, pushing the injured man onto his back with a sharp kick.

'I was conversing with that fellow,' the leather-clad rogue called out in mock outrage as the bearded man began to search Dogvael's person.

'You can play around on your own time, Gobineau,' snarled the bearded brigand as his massive hands ripped brass buttons from Dogvael's tunic and patted down his chest in search of any hidden pockets.

'Neither manners nor memory,' Gobineau chided the other bandit. 'Our friend there has a bit of a reputation. Don't you recognise him?'

'By the Lady?' gasped one of the other bowmen. 'That's Dogvael!' Gobineau spun about stabbing a triumphant finger at the man who had called out.

'Precisely! One of the Black Prince's old custom collectors,' Gobineau said. 'I'm sure everybody here hasn't forgotten paying their tithe to that old tyrant.'

'If Dogvael is here,' another of the brigands observed, 'then the rumours must be true. The Black Prince is dead!'

'That seems a distinct possibility when one of his old lieutenants starts playing at honest work again,' agreed Gobineau. He turned away from the discussion however as he saw the bearded archer remove something from Dog-vael's body. The bulky man gazed at it intently a moment, then made to stuff it within his tunic.

'Hello, Manfret,' Gobineau called out. 'What is it that you have there? Not holding back on your fellows, are you?' The tone of warning did not go unnoticed by the others, and fingers began to play with bowstrings and arrows.

'Bit of scrimshaw the pig had on him,' Manfret snarled. 'I took a fancy to it, is all.'

'Perhaps I should have a look at it,' Gobineau pressed. 'I've been known to fancy scrimshaw too.' He held one hand out toward the sullen Manfret, the other hand closed about the hilt of the sword sheathed at his side.

'Damn you!' snarled Manfret. 'I killed the pig, so I get first pick of whatever he's got on him!' The bandit's hand closed a bit more tightly about the object he had lifted from his victim. Gobineau could see that it appeared to be a cylinder, perhaps six inches in length, apparently crafted from bone, its surface elaborately carved.

'I thought that we agreed that all loot was to be divided evenly,' Gobineau said, more for the benefit of the other bandits than the defiant Manfret. He peered sternly into the bandit's eyes. 'I suppose you know exactly how much that bauble of yours is worth, and where you can sell it?'

'Go hang yourself!' roared Manfret. 'I've heard enough from that slippery tongue of yours, Gobineau! I killed him, so it's mine. You lot can split the rest of it!'

Gobineau shook his head, laughing with disdain. 'No, no, no. I don't think that would be very wise. That little bit you're holding might just be worth more than the rest of this garbage put together.' Gobineau's voice dropped lower, into a scandalised whisper. 'You wouldn't be trying to cheat your mates now, would you?'

With another low curse, Manfret drew his own sword, backing away from Gobineau. The other bandit sighed with disappointment and, with one swift move pulled his own sword from its sheath, darting forward with the quickness of a viper. Manfret's blade fell into the mud as Gobineau's sword slashed open his hand. Before the bearded brigand could finish his cry of pain, Gobineau struck again, this time thrusting the point of his weapon into the other man's throat. The stricken Manfret fell, joining his discarded blade in the muck, a sickening gurgle sounding from his punctured vocals. Gobineau casually wiped the blood from his sword and returned it to its sheath.

'Never could abide a man who would cheat his friends,' Gobineau commented, spitting on the dying Manfret. Reaching down, he removed the engraved cylinder from the dying man's hand. He was immediately struck by the craftsmanship of the object, the interlocking symbols that wound about its surface and the elaborate silver base that sealed one end of the cylinder. His earlier observation that it was bone proved false, for it was crafted from ivory, a substance he had only ever encountered before adorning the jewellery boxes of lonely countesses and duchesses in Bretonnia's great cities. Gobineau looked away from his study of the object as he heard the other members of his band approaching.

'A fine piece, lads,' he told them, holding the cylinder up so that all of them could see it. 'No wonder Manfret took a fancy to it!'

'I've taken a fancy to that silver on it!' cried out one of the brigands, bringing soft laughter from the others.

'Some good drinking money to be had when we chip that off and sell it!' commented another.

Gobineau turned an incredulous look on his companions. 'Chip it off? Can't you lads see the craftsmanship, the quality of this piece of art? Why the entire thing must be worth far more than the price of the silver on its base!'

'The silver will be good enough for me,' grunted a bald-
ing man with a lean, wolf-like face.

'That is why you are still a bandit,' Gobineau told the
man. 'You don't ever think things through, don't look to
see the grander scheme of things.'

'You're talking like some sort of boss-man now,' complained the wolf-faced man.

'We agreed that we wouldn't have no leader!' chimed in
one of the others. Gobineau spun about, pointing at the
second man who had spoken.

'That's right! We agreed to have no leader,' he said. 'So lis-
ten to me and do what I say. We can get a lot more for this
piece if we don't break it up and try to sell it whole.'

'And who would buy it?' groused wolf-face.

Gobineau smiled, holding up his hand like an instructor
who sees an opportunity to press home his point. 'Ah, first
we need to know exactly what it is, then we can find out how
much it is worth and who might want to buy it.' Gobineau
pointed at the symbols carved across the surface of the cylinder. 'These fancy letters my friends, were written by elves.'
The other bandits drew a step back as they heard Gobineau
mention the fearsome fey folk. 'Now we all know that elves
are rich in magic. So it follows that we should take this artefact to somebody who knows a thing or three about magic.'

'You know such a man?' asked one of the brigands.

'Indeed I do,' Gobineau replied with a look not unlike
that of a cat who has just swallowed a songbird. 'There's a
little town near here, Valbonnec, and in that town they
have a wizard, a conjurer they call Mad Rudol. We'll go and
see this wizard and see what he can tell us about this treasure we've come upon.' The other bandits nodded their
heads, seeing the sense in Gobineau's proposal. The outlaw
continued to smile, regarding the ivory cylinder one last
time before tucking it through his belt.

Perhaps it had been some badge of office given to Dogvael by the Black Prince. Perhaps it was some piece of the

Black Prince's own treasure that had been looted by Dog-vael when his employer had been slain. Or perhaps it was simply a piece of the bandit's own plunder, taken from some wandering knight returning from some quest to distant and exotic lands. Whatever the history behind it and how it had come to find its way into the dead man's possession, it was Gobineau's now, and he would see to it that he wrenched every last groat from it before he was through.

THE CHILL OF night tugged at the dying man as he dragged himself from the road. He did not accept the fact that he was dying, any more than he understood why it was so important to reach the shadows of the trees. There was little enough of reason left in his mind, fogged over by the pain wracking his frame and the indignity of how easily he had been brought down. Dogvael, once one of the Black Prince's trusted servants taken by a simple bandit's trick every brigand from Kislev to Araby learned before he was out of swaddling. The blow to his pride pained him even more than the hole in his back. He'd allowed himself to get sloppy, allowed his wit and cunning to be dulled by the miserable poverty to which he had been forced into after his lord's demise.

The sound of horse's hooves slowly clopping along the mud and dirt lent a new strength to Dogvael's fading vitality and like some grotesque turtle, he tried to scramble at speed toward the safety of the shadows. He heard the animal turn towards him, walking with slow and deliberate steps to place itself between the stricken bandit and the refuge he sought. Dogvael could see the coal-black socks of the animal looming before him, the horse's hair spattered grey with the muck of its travel. A black boot rested in the stirrup of the saddle and as Dogvael craned his head upward, he found himself staring into the cold steel mask of a Reiklander's sallet helm. The bandit gasped in fright, for that helm and the man who wore it were not unknown to him.

'I am looking for someone,' Brunner called down to the wounded brigand. 'From the looks of things, I think you may have run into him.'

Dogvael scrambled in the mud, turning his pained body and tried to scuttle away. With a slow and deliberate contempt, Brunner directed his steed to once more impose itself between the bandit and the refuge of the brush. Dogvael stared up once more into the cold, stern countenance of the bounty hunter and, with a sigh of resignation, slumped down into the muck.

'Who did this?' the bounty killer demanded, pointing the barrel of the pistol gripped in his hand at the arrow protruding from Dogvael's body. The bandit licked his lips, trying to force some moisture into his voice as he tried to answer.

'Gaw… Gaw…' the bandit tried to speak, trying to voice the name he had heard his killers use to address the smiling, mocking rogue who had been in the cart.

'Gobineau?' Brunner prodded. Dogvael nodded his head slightly. The bounty hunter leaned forward. 'Do you know where he went?'

Dogvael nodded his head again, gulping down a mouthful of air in hopes that it would help his words. 'Walbec… Valbec… Wiza…'

'Gone to Valbonnec to look for a wizard,' the bounty hunter mused aloud. 'Most interesting.' Brunner replaced his pistol in its holster and looked down at Dogvael, studying the wretch for a moment. 'You've been most helpful, Dogvael,' the bounty hunter's words were like frost clawing at glass. His gloved hand fell toward the huge knife hanging from his belt, a butcher's tool which he had morbidly termed 'the Headsman' long ago.

'Just one more thing you can help me with,' Brunner told the bandit as Dogvael tried once more to drag his paralysed body off the road. The giant knife with its serrated blade gleamed in the moonlight as Brunner gripped it in his gloved fist and dismounted. 'A little matter of fifty gold crowns,' the bounty hunter stated as he closed upon the squirming Dogvael.

CHAPTER TWO

THE ROOM WAS small and dark, stinking of mouldering weeds and rank liquids. Tangles of mangy animal pelts hung from hooks fixed to the walls and overhead beams, alongside the severed claws of birds and bundles of dried herbs. The few walls not given over to such macabre oddities were dominated by shelves alternately filled with clay jars and glass bottles, or else by bundles of parchment scrolls and leather bound books, their pages slowly conspiring to free themselves of their rotted bindings.

Illumination came from a bronze, bowl-like lamp resting upon the surface of a long table of unfinished timber. Men clustered about that lamp, disturbed by the weird décor of the magician's workshop, their eyes turning away from the reassuring flame to consider the wicker cages that formed a part of that décor and the small croaking things that scrabbled and clawed at their bars.

Two of the men, however, did not share in the discomfort of the others. One of these was the unacknowledged leader of the others, a tall rakish man in black armour. His eyes did not stray to the darkness, nor the weird and unnatural bric-a-brac of the room. His attention was focused solely upon the man seated at the table, inspecting the slender ivory artefact set before him. Gobineau was no less intimidated than his men by the aura of menace that pulsated from the walls of the wizard's study, that indeed seemed to be exuded by the very wizard himself. But he was too old a scoundrel, too veteran a thief, to allow his unease to disorder him. He'd taken many a pilfered necklace or stolen ring to fences in his time and knew that studying the face, trying to read the thoughts of the man who was appraising the goods was every bit as important as the theft itself. Instinct told him that in the present circumstances, there was no difference between this wizard and a fence, and that his hopes for a tidy profit might rest upon his observations.

The wizard in question was seated, his intense gaze fixated upon the strange object Gobineau had brought to him. At times, the wizard would turn his attention to one of several decrepit books he had set beside him at the table. Gobineau peered at one of the books, the one which the wizard consulted the most, seeing that it appeared to be written in two different scripts: the flowing, graceful symbols of the elves and the much more angular and harsh letters of Reikspiel. The wizard's long, spidery fingers slithered among the pages, rummaging among them as he inspected the carvings that covered the ivory cylinder and its silver base.

The wizard's name was Rudol, and like Gobineau, he was garbed in black, a long flowing robe of fine cloth that was wrapped about his lean frame as though woven from shadows and the darkest hours of the night. As the wizard had descended the stairs that led from the tower above into his workshop to receive his petitioners, it had seemed as though stars had twinkled from within the depths of his garment. A skull cap of dark blue cloth rested upon his head, bound about the brow by a circlet of silver adorned at the centre by a polished piece of moonstone. Upon the breast of his robe, the golden outline of a comet had been woven.

The man beneath the robe was thin, of no great stature or strength. Yet even so, Gobineau could recall few men who had presented so intimidating an impression. The wizard's skin was dark, betraying his foreign blood, carrying with it the swarthiness of the southern Empire and lands such as Averland and Wissenland. His hair was black, and despite the evident age in the wizard's face, it was as dark and lustrous as any Gobineau had ever seen, without even the faintest suggestion of grey and silver.

Rudol's features were hard, a thin cruel mouth that was locked in a perpetual smirk of sinister amusement, a narrow knife-like nose and two dark eyes that gleamed with all the feverish obsession of a weirdroot addict. Even the wizard's hands were unsettling, the fingers long and thin, like two pale spiders rather than human hands.

As the wizard continued his examination, he glanced up at Gobineau. The bandit licked his lips nervously as their eyes met and it seemed to him that the smirk became slightly greater as Rudol returned to his study.

RUDOL HAD BEEN a promising student of the Empire's colleges of magic, before impatience and ambition had earned him the distrust and enmity of his instructors. He'd been kicked out for his reckless refusals to accept the caution and restraint the elder wizards were forever trying to drive home to their students. It had been as good as a death sentence, for Rudol knew that those who were banished from the Colleges always attracted the dangerous attention of the witch hunters, who hunted down most zealously any who delved into the forbidden arts without official patronage. So it was that Rudol had been forced to flee his homeland, staying one step ahead of the witch hunters as he rode for lands beyond their reach, the green and pleasant realms of Bretonnia.

Of course he had not done so empty-handed. The better part of one of his instructor's personal libraries had found its way into Rudol's keeping. Some day, Rudol had promised himself, he would return to Altdorf and collect the rest of that library.

The green and pleasant realms of Bretonnia had not offered much to further such ambitions. True, he had eluded the witch hunters, who seldom ventured into the lands claimed by the King of Bretonnia, but he found himself a foreigner in a land where even its natives were gripped in a hideous and perpetual poverty. He could find employment with none of the noble lords he had offered his services to, dismissed alternatively as a beggar, a charlatan or worse, hounded across the countryside as an Imperial spy if the knights proved particularly paranoid and distrustful of outsiders. Denied the patronage of the nobility, Rudol had been forced to eke out a living off the peasants, people who had little enough for themselves, much less enough to pay for the services of a wizard.

For twenty years, Rudol had found himself crushed beneath the same system of poverty that kept the peasants of Bretonnia in a state often worse than the conditions in which they kept their cattle and swine. He found himself keeping frost from fields for nothing more than a few bowls of soup and a wedge of cheese, calling up rainstorms for a handful of copper coins and perhaps a live chicken or two. And yet, amidst the peasants, even so poor a wage made him wealthy, respected and feared. The small, two-storey stone tower in which he dwelled had been built on that fear, constructed by the villagers during the long hours of the night after they had returned from their herds and their fields, fearful that the wizard might place a curse upon them should they refuse his demands.

Rudol smiled as he remembered that event. He had felt a tiny taste of the power he desired that night. But it would be no peasant rabble who would cower before him. It would be his own peers, the wizards who had cast him out from the Celestial College in Altdorf. They would repay Rudol for the years of misery he had endured, the hardships he had been made to suffer. They would hail him as the greatest of their order and confess their jealousy and envy even as they grovelled in the dirt and pleaded for his forgiveness.

The wizard's eyes turned once more to the pages of the book laid out beside him. It was a translation of many of the characters used in the elven Elthárin language into the more readily understandable letters of the wizard's native Reikspiel. With every step in his translation of the story carved upon the piece of ivory, Rudol's pulse quickened and his breath sharpened, hardly daring to believe what he was reading. The artefact was ancient, predating the establishment of Bretonnia and even Sigmar himself, preserved from the ravages of time by the lingering magic of the elves with which they protected most of what they made. The carved characters told a story, an ancient moment from a vanished time. It was the tragic story of an elf prince who fell during the legendary war between the elves and dwarfs that had raged while the tribes of the Empire still wore the skins of beasts and hid inside caves. The prince had been a great warrior and leader among his people, and he had commanded the wyrms of the earth to serve him and carry him to victory in battle.

Rudol let a sharp gasp escape as he considered what the importance of that might mean. Could it be? Could it truly be? He had read legends, legends related by the elves of Marienburg, about a potent talisman used by the elves to summon dragons, to bind the mighty reptiles to their will. It had been called the Fell Fang, to give its closest Reikspiel translation, and legend said it had been lost when its princely owner had fallen in battle with the dwarfs. Could the lord spoken of on the ivory cylinder have been the wielder of the fabulous talisman? Another thrill swept up the wizard's spine as he considered another part of the old legend, that which referred to the size of the magical arte-fact. The object resting before him matched very closely the dimensions given in the elf legend.

There was only one problem, and the excitement bled out of Rudol as he considered it. The stories were adamant about the material from which the Fell Fang had been crafted. The talisman had been made from the tooth of a dragon. The object he had been studying was unquestion-ably whale ivory, the sort of scrimshaw often worked by the so-called sea elves on their long voyages. Rudol's brow knit-ted for a moment as he considered the quandary. He stared intently at the cylinder, bringing one of the strange crystal lenses he had liberated from the Celestial College to bear upon the object. The wizard studied every inch of the arte-fact once more, this time ignoring his translations of the engravings and concentrating upon the surface itself. He laughed with joy as his closer scrutiny revealed a minuscule gap between the ivory and the silver cap that formed its base.

'You have discovered something?' Gobineau inquired, reacting to the wizard's sudden excitement.

'It is hollow!' Rudol exclaimed. The words electrified the observing bandits, each of the brigands drawing still closer to the table, thoughts of hidden treasure vanquishing their uneasiness. Rudol ignored the eager anticipation of the men around him, seemingly oblivious to their presence, his long slender fingers slipping among the engravings, pressing upon them.

'I have seen this sort of thing before,' the wizard spoke, his words directed at no one. 'It is like a Cathayan puzzle box. The question is, how does it open?' The wizard's fin-gers continued to press and pry at the elaborate engravings upon the ivory cylinder and its silver cap. Gobineau watched every movement, eyes locked upon the mystic's crawling fingers. He heard the faintest click as Rudol's index finger stabbed at a small sickle-shaped symbol upon the silver ring. The wizard laughed again, tugging the ivory cylinder free.

Gobineau had never seen such a look of greedy rapture as the one that flashed across Rudol's face when the wizard laid eyes upon the thing which had been hidden within the cylinder. The artefact was like a reliquary, like the small silver boxes in which pious peasants might carry the finger bone of a saint, or a lock cut from the hair of one of the Lady's holy damsels. But the thing which had been hidden within the artefact had never come from any man, however holy or heroic. Nor had it been part of an elf, however ancient and fabulous. It was a six-inch curve of blackened bone, its tip sharp as a dagger even after so many centuries. The surface of the bone was pitted in places by deep holes, each of the holes ringed in some light, shiny metal that was unknown to Gobineau and his men. Just as the cylinder had been hollow, so too was the object it contained. An evil, sickly smell seemed to fill the room as Rudol exposed the thing, and Gobineau started to feel hot with excitement.

'Magnificent!' Rudol gasped. 'It is true!' The wizard's fingers caressed the blackened relic, as though exploring the soft skin of a beautiful woman.

'Then we have found a very valuable treasure?' Gobineau inquired, intruding upon the wizard's glee.

'Valuable?' Rudol scoffed, so lost in his discovery that his words came without thought. 'It is beyond value! A king's ransom would be but a trifle next to the value of this artefact! All the gold in the Grey Mountains would be but a pittance to the worth of this…' Rudol snapped out of his reverie, looking up at the hungry faces staring at him, noting the greedy gleam of the bandits' eyes.

'Of course I speak from the view of a scholar,' Rudol explained, his voice uneven. 'It would command no great price from someone who was not interested in such things,' the wizard elaborated weakly. He rose from the table, the artefact still gripped in his hand. Gobineau reached forward, grabbing hold of the relic before the wizard could remove it. For a moment, brigand and mystic stared at one another, each clutching the relic. At length, with an almost apologetic shrug, Rudol relented, allowing Gobineau to reclaim the ivory cylinder.

'Naturally, you should be paid something for your efforts,' Rudol explained as he walked towards a section of shelving that lined the wall behind him. 'For the value of the silver, if nothing else,' he continued. Gobineau watched the mage, the hair on the back of his neck starting to stand on end. He observed Rudol remove a leather bag from behind a brass astrolabe, the distinct and familiar chink of coins striking against one another sounding as the wizard lifted the pouch.

'Perhaps three gold crowns would serve as recompense?' Rudol asked. Alone among the bandits, Gobineau looked away from the moneybag Rudol held towards them, observing the wizard's other hand. The long, spidery fingers were twitching and clawing in an elaborate series of motions.

Gobineau cursed himself for a fool and threw himself to the floor. He'd let his greed get the better of him, allowed it to overcome his natural caution. He hadn't appreciated that Rudol might decide to keep the elven artefact for himself. And, most disastrous of all, he'd momentarily forgotten that the strange old man was much more than a strange old man. He'd failed to keep at the forefront of his mind that Rudol was a wizard!

THE BOUNTY HUNTER slowly slogged his way down the muddy lane that formed the main road of Valbonnec.

Peasants hurried from his path, seeking the safety of doorways from which to peer in surprise and dread at the armoured figure and his foreign garb. Simple, hard-working folk, most of them had never been more than a few miles from their village and the only warriors they had ever seen were the resplendent knights who were both their lords and protectors. The man now striding down the narrow strip of mire was something different, his garb dishevelled and without the flamboyant heraldry of a knight. His weapons were strange, devices that none of the onlookers could quite figure out, but which they decided were deadly all the same. The eyes that stared out from the visor of his plain, unadorned helm were like chips of ice, more like the eyes of a wolf than the eyes of a knight. There was an air of menace about the man, a smell of blood and death, more than enough to make the quiet folk of Valbonnec keep their distance.

Brunner paid little attention to the frightened faces of the villagers. Their fear would keep the peasants from getting in his way. He'd hate to accidentally kill someone he wasn't going to get paid for.

The bounty hunter paused as he saw the spire of a tower. It was only two floors and yet even so it was the tallest building in the village. The lower floor was built of stone, unworked blocks of granite crudely fitted together. The upper floor crouched above it like the cap of a toadstool and was built of timber. It was like a coarse parody of the sort of place a merchant of the Empire might make his home, an unrefined copy of the sort of tower in which a real wizard would lair.

Brunner glanced away from the tower, eyeing the pistol holstered across his belly, ensuring that the cap was still fitted to it, then the bounty hunter caressed the heavy wood and steel frame of his repeating crossbow. With any luck, he could disable most of Gobineau's friends before it came to swordplay. Of course, he'd have to spare the bandit leader the worst of his attentions; no bullet or crossbow bolt for him. The bounty on Gobineau, at least the largest one being offered, the only one that was of interest to Brunner, specified that there would be a deduction of five hundred gold crowns if the villain was brought in dead. The Reiklander had no intention of being wasteful.

As the bounty killer studied the small tower, examining it for alternate means of entry, by which his quarry might effect an escape, a sudden commotion sounded from within the structure. It had sounded like an explosion of some sort, punctuated by the cries and wails of several men. Brunner spat into the dust, running toward the tower at a brisk jog. Perhaps this Rudol was less charlatan and more genuine wizard than he had presumed. Perhaps the bounty hunter wasn't the only one interested in the price on Gobineau's head. Amidst such desperate poverty as he'd seen in Valbonnec, Brunner could see even a wizard lending his abilities to more mercenary purposes.

Not that it mattered. No one was going to get between Brunner and his quarry, not even a wizard.

THE ROOM WAS a shambles, scrolls fluttering across the floor, feathers spinning slowly after being ripped from the bizarre collection of croaking birds that nestled amongst the wizard's cages. Gobineau found himself lying upon his back, sprawled beneath a smelly old wolfskin that had been torn from where it had been nailed to an overhead beam. Blood drizzled from his nose, his cheek also lacerated by the heavy pewter cup that had crashed into his face. The brigand pulled a white cloth from his belt, trying to stem the flow of crimson before it had a chance to stain his garments. Moaning voices sounded from all around him, telling Gobineau that his men were likewise alive, if not unharmed.

Rudol stood behind the table, glaring at the men with an expression that was as much a thing of contempt as it was annoyance. The wizard held his hand extended before him, the fingers splayed so that they formed something that resembled the claw of a vulture. It had been from that hand that the *power* had struck. Gobineau had once numbered piracy amongst his catalogue of crimes, preying upon fat merchantmen as they tried to slip into the port city of Marienburg. What had exploded within the wizard's room had been every bit as fierce and terrible as any gale born over the Sea of Claws, a blast of howling wind and invisible might that had smashed everything and everyone before it. Then, as suddenly as it had struck, the burst of wind had ceased, only the destruction it had wrought giving evidence that it had indeed occurred. Gobineau fancied that he could see a weird light slowly fading from Rudol's eyes, a wan blue energy that chilled the bandit's thrice-cursed soul.

Rudol's lip curled into a sneer as he returned the brigand's gaze. 'You fools!' he snapped. 'You dare think you can cheat Rudol of what he desires!' The fingers of his outstretched hand closed into a white-knuckled fist which the wizard shook angrily at the stunned bandits. 'You have felt but the smallest measure of my power! Give me cause and I shall destroy each and every one of you!' The wizard snarled, turning his fist toward the door. He extended his index finger and by his command, the heavy wooden portal crashed inward, ripped open by unseen hands. 'Leave while I am of a mind to let you live,' Rudol ordered, the words brooking no defiance. Gobineau turned his head to see the least shaken of his men already on their feet and sprinting toward the door. He turned his head back toward Rudol as he heard the wizard laugh derisively and reach toward the artefact still lying upon the table.

The bandit cast aside his blood-soaked rag, ripping the sword from his belt as he leapt to his feet. Gobineau roared at his fleeing henchmen, putting all the command he could in his tones. 'Will you let this charlatan swine steal our fortune, lads?' The look the wizard turned upon him almost froze Gobineau's heart, yet the rogue continued to shout his defiance. 'He's no Wastes-spawned daemon! Prick his hide and he bleeds red like any other thief!'

What effect, if any, Gobineau's bold words might have had on his men was uncertain, and irrelevant. As the first of the brigands who had gained their feet reached the door, they found their path blocked by a grim figure in armour. The foremost of the men found his belly caving in under the short rabbit punch delivered by the armoured warrior's fist. The bandit crumpled to the ground, his last meal splashing on the wall. The man behind him hesitated, eyes wide with fright, hand fumbling for the blade thrust through his animal-gut belt. The sword was never drawn, however, for the warrior blocking the doorway lifted the heavy crossbow gripped in his right hand and sent a steel bolt crunching its way through the Bretonnian's skull.

'Ranald's grace!' Gobineau heard one of his henchmen cry out as he sighted the killing machine that now strode into Rudol's workshop. 'It's Brunner!'

If the Blood God himself had clawed his way into the room, Gobineau didn't think the other bandit's voice could have been more filled with terror. Observing the heavy crossbow the notorious bounty killer held in his hands, Gobineau dropped back onto the floor he had so recently risen from. He was not ignorant of the price offered for his head, even if he did treat it with a boastful contempt. For someone like Brunner to be in a hog-hole like Valbonnec, there could be only one reason, and Gobineau was not terribly pleased by the prospect.

Instead he shouted at the top of his voice: 'There's Rudol! He's the one you want!'

The words did nothing to distract the bounty killer, who was already singling out Gobineau from the other bandits that cringed behind the room's wrecked furniture. Gobineau hadn't expected it to. The wizard, however, was another matter. Rudol had heard the terror with which Gobineau's man had named the armoured newcomer. And Gobineau was willing to bet that a wizard from the Empire living in poverty and exile did not do so without a few skeletons in his past, skeletons that might have long memories and thick purses.

Rudol snarled, spitting a string of foul words that seemed to sear the air. His hand crackled with a wild ribbon of light, a rope of electricity that the wizard sent streaking toward the bounty hunter. Brunner reacted far more quickly than Rudol had anticipated, hitting the floor and rolling behind the central column that supported the floor above. The lightning bolt swerved as it snaked about the room, exploding against the column that was now between it and its intended victim. The stone sizzled and blackened under the impact, shrieking like a banshee. The bounty hunter was unfazed, however, darting from behind his cover to fire a bolt from his weapon in Rudol's direction. The missile missed the wizard's neck by a hair's breadth, chipping the stone wall behind Rudol as it impacted.

'You shall die for trifling with me!' Rudol shouted, his words almost unintelligible as his accent contorted them. One of Gobineau's men sprang from cover, hurling himself toward the door. The wizard reacted to the motion, sending another bolt of lightning from his clawed hand. The electrical discharge slammed into the fleeing bandit, his scream reaching such a pitch that Gobineau was certain the man's vocal cords must snap. The stench of ozone and seared flesh filled the room as a jagged black hole was bored through the bandit's torso. The man fell against the floor with a meaty impact, acrid smoke rising from his ghastly wound.

Once again, Brunner emerged from his cover to fire on the wizard, taking advantage of the distraction presented by the unfortunate brigand. The repeating crossbow sounded once more, the steel bolt hurtling toward Rudol's chest.

Once again, the missile missed its target by the merest fraction, burying itself in the splintered wood of the wizard's table. This time, Gobineau was certain of something he thought he had only imagined when the bounty hunter had missed his first shot. The pattern of stars on Rudol's cloak had shifted, moving across the black cloth. Gobineau's flesh crawled at this further manifestation of Rudol's black arts.

The wizard retaliated once more, a snake of lightning punching a hole through the rear wall of his workshop, narrowly missing the bounty hunter as he dove for the shelter of an upended barrel. Rudol snarled again, a thick Averland curse, and sent another streak of lightning blasting into the barrel, causing it to explode in a shower of splinters and melted iron. But Brunner was already rolling across the floor, taking shelter once more behind the sanctuary offered by the support column.

'Gobineau!' The rogue turned as he heard his name called out. He glanced over to where the last of his bandits had found cover. The man shouted to be heard above the sizzle of lightning as Rudol sent bolt after bolt slamming into the column. 'We've got to get out of here!' the bandit called. 'Now, while they are trying to kill each other!'

'A capital suggestion,' Gobineau remarked, amazed that someone thought it necessary to voice something so painfully obvious. 'Why don't you go first, Pigsticker!' the rogue called back. The other bandit muttered a short prayer to Ranald, then made the sign of the Lady for good measure and broke from his shelter, scrambling on his hands and knees until he was across the threshold and out in the street. Still frenziedly assaulting the stone column, Rudol paid the brigand's departure not even the slightest notice. Gobineau braced himself for a quick sprint for the door, chancing a last look back at the enraged wizard.

The brigand chief's eyes fell away from Rudol and the magic lightning crackling from his hand, drawn instead to the ivory cylinder lying upon the table. Gobineau smiled as a new idea fixed itself in his mind. 'No reason why I should leave empty handed,' the rogue observed. He crawled across the floor until his legs were beneath the timber table. He braced himself and with a double kick of both feet, upended the table, spilling it onto Rudol. Gobineau heard the mage cry out as the table struck him down, but the rogue did not linger to see what damage he'd done. His hand closed upon the ivory reliquary that had been sent skittering about the floor.

Laughing, Gobineau scrambled to his feet and sprinted for the door, back bent low so as to present the smallest possible target should the wizard have already recovered, and keeping one wary eye on the badly damaged support column. He might have incapacitated Rudol, but that would be small comfort should a crossbow bolt from the bounty hunter's weapon dig into his chest. The dreaded shot did not come, however. Instead, there was a loud explosion and a bright flash of blue light. Gobineau risked a look back and shuddered at what he saw.

Rudol had freed himself from the timber table, splinters of wood surrounded him, oily black smoke slowly spiralling from the debris. The wizard's black cloak fluttered about him, the cloth whipping about in an unnatural breeze. Crackling energy snaked about Rudol's body, filling the air with a smell of ozone. The mage's eyes had gone white, lost within the eerie power that now filled his frame. The exile's face was contorted into an embodiment of pitiless hate and rage. His clawed hands gestured, sending rapid blasts of lightning flickering in every direction, disintegrating wood and cracking stone.

'Thieves! Scum!' the maddened Rudol was shouting. 'The Fell Fang is mine!' As the wizard continued his merciless assault, heavy wooden beams groaned overhead and clouds of dust fell from the ceiling. Gobineau could see the badly damaged support column shudder and moan, the horrific sight snapping him from the fascinated paralysis that had gripped him. With a leap worthy of a mountain goat, Gobineau jumped through the doorway and out onto the street.

Behind him, Rudol looked upwards, the colour returning to his eyes as the energy drained from him. His pupils dilated in fear as the entire structure began to tremble. Hastily he started to shout out in a strange language, words that no human throat was ever meant to utter. Even as he raised his arms up to make arcane gestures, the ravaged support column, unable to bear the weight of the rooms above, cracked and flew apart, followed a second later by the entirety of the upper floor and the timbered roof.

GOBINEAU BURST UPON the street, a cloud of dust billowing out behind him as the wizard's tower collapsed in upon itself, the outer walls no longer able to stand without the bracing support of the floors within. The bandit scudded through the mire of the street, then turned to face the structure that had so very nearly become his tomb. He looked away from the pile of wreckage, considering his torn and stained clothing. 'Damn poor waste,' he muttered as he considered the long gash that had manifested in the sleeve of his tunic. Then he considered the ivory cylinder still clutched in his hand and laughed heartily. 'I can buy new clothes,' he concluded.

A sound from behind him made the rogue spin around in alarm, his free hand pulling out his sword. He chuckled again when he found that it was only the other remaining members of his gang.

'You got it,' commented Pigsticker. The greasy bandit's eyes were once again displaying the cold gleam of greed that had shone within them when the bandits had overheard Rudol's appraisal of the artefact. Gobineau shot an angry look at the man, but quickly let it slip into a friendly smile. Gobineau did not favour confrontations that were two to one, or even confrontations with more equitable odds, unless the other party involved had his back to him.

'We're rich, lads!' Gobineau exclaimed, casting another lingering look at the pile of rubble that had so lately been Rudol's tower. 'The world is now our oyster!' He nodded back toward the wreckage. 'But let's discuss our fortune a good distance from this place. I half expect that wizard bastard to dig his way out of there!'

'What about Brunner?' wheezed the third brigand, his breathing still short from the brutal blow the bounty killer had introduced to the man's stomach.

'I wouldn't put it past him to dig his way out of there either,' Gobineau agreed. 'More reason for us to get a long way from here.' He pointed a finger at the brigand. 'Dux, you go and get the horses from the stables. Pigsticker and I will meet you at the mill just outside the village.'

Gobineau watched as Dux hurried down the street, still clutching at his belly. When the bandit was out of earshot, he turned to his remaining confederate. 'There's a stable at the southern end of the village. I suggest we go and relieve him of his two fastest horses and make ourselves scarce.'

Gobineau did not wait for the other bandit to comment, but slipped into the alley that wormed its way between the mud-walled hovels. The other bandit hurried after him.

'Why are we going to steal more horses?' Pigsticker complained. 'We already have some!'

Gobineau smiled at the other thief's lack of foresight. 'Tell me, from everything you've heard about him, do you think Brunner would let himself get crushed beneath a wizard's disintegrating manse?' The other bandit paused, his bleary eyes deep in thought.

'You think he's alive?' Pigsticker asked. Gobineau shrugged his shoulders by way of reply, kicking at the foremost of a gaggle of geese that was blocking the path of the two thieves. The birds hissed angrily, but diverted their march.

'Who knows, but I'd rather err on the side of caution,' Gobineau told him. 'Something to do with the rather extreme value I place upon my own neck.' The rogue stopped, turning to look at his companion. 'You're a bounty hunter who has tracked down his prey. The only problem is that they just happen to be in the process of being cooked alive by a mad wizard. The smart man cuts his wager, slips away and hopes his mark makes it out in one piece so he can be caught later.' Gobineau smiled, an expression of calculating admiration. 'From what I hear, this Brunner is a very cagey sort. He'd probably figure that if any of us made it out of that carnage alive, we'd head for our horses, straight as an arrow.' Gobineau chuckled darkly. 'I'm betting he's waiting there right now.'

Pigsticker surged forward, his callused hand closing about the neck of Gobineau's tunic. The larger bandit slammed the rogue against the mud wall of the hovel they were standing beside. 'And you sent Dux there to get killed!' Pigsticker accused.

'Not at all,' Gobineau replied, his voice strained as he tried to suck in a full breath. 'I sent him there to buy us time. If Brunner is there, and he sees only Dux, he might figure Dux was the only one who made it out of there in one piece. Meanwhile, you and I are sneaking away in the other direction.'

The rogue's calculating words gave the other bandit pause. Pigsticker slowly released his hold on the dapper brigand. Gobineau tried to smooth out the wrinkles caused by the bandit's clutch.

'I know people in Mousillon who will pay quite nicely for what we have,' Gobineau told the other bandit. 'And I'd rather split the haul two ways than three.' Pigsticker smiled back at the rogue, nodding in agreement.

FIFTEEN MINUTES LATER, Pigsticker sat slumped on the ground, his head lolling against his breast, eyes locked on the dark liquid spilling from his belly. He looked up as he heard a horse trot close by. The dying bandit's face twisted with hate as he recognised the rider as Gobineau.

The rogue threw him a mocking salute. 'Many thanks for your help dealing with the farmer,' Gobineau called down to his former comrade. He slapped the flank of his new horse. 'They really do raise some fine animals in this area.' The rogue sighed deeply, turning the head of his animal so that the horse began to trot away.

'It's a pity you can't come with me,' Gobineau called back. 'But sadly, I prefer not to split loot at all than split it two ways.'

The dying bandit watched his treacherous companion ride off, fury and rage suddenly overcoming even the cold chill of death pulling at his limbs. Pigsticker was unusual for a Bretonnian, he could read and write after a fashion, a skill he had learned during a brief legitimate phase as a warehouse warden in L'Anguille. Now he put that half-remembered skill to use, dipping his fingers into the pool of bubbling crimson that covered him. Pigsticker stabbed his fingers into the dirt beside him, slowly, one-by-one, drawing the letters that would betray his betrayer.

IT WAS NEARLY sunset when the bounty hunter found the body of Pigsticker, on the outskirts of the village. Brunner's scrutinising gaze took in the gruesome scene, reading at once the story it told. The bandit had been stabbed at close quarters and from the front, the wound too small for that of a sword, more likely the work of a knife or dagger. The bandit's own weapons remained in their sheaths. Quite clearly, the blow had been unexpected, unexpected because it had come from a man the bandit had thought to be his friend. A belly wound such as that would give the dying bandit a long time to consider the treachery of his murderer. It was with a smile of triumph that Brunner read the words the dying brigand had painted into the dirt with his own blood. It was the name of a place, the place to which, undoubtedly, his killer was heading.

Brunner had already gone through much trouble to find his prey. The battle with the wizard had been one the bounty hunter had been utterly unprepared for. Had it not been for Gobineau's timely distraction, Brunner might not have had the opportunity to escape, diving through a hole blown into the rear wall of the tower by one of the wizard's lightning bolts. The bounty hunter had then hastened to the stables, to await the arrival of any survivors from the bandit gang as they tried to reclaim their animals. There had been only one, and not the man he was after. But the bandit had confirmed that Gobineau had escaped from the wizard, and that the rogue was to meet him at the old mill. When Gobineau had not been where the bandit said he would be, Brunner had guessed at the rogue's cunning and duplicity, quickly riding a circuit around the village in the hopes of catching Gobineau's trail. That had led him to Pig-sticker, and the simple message the man had left behind.

The bounty hunter considered again the name and the place it represented. There were few places that Brunner hesitated to go, however, it seemed that his prey was making for one of them, the haunted, decaying city of Mousillon. Brunner let his gloved hand slip to the hilt of the Headsman. Gobineau was clever, in his way, but if he thought a little thing like hiding in the most reviled place in all Bretonnia was going to help him, then the rogue was going to quickly discover that his cleverness had run its course.

THE WIND WAILED and moaned through the tiny copse of trees, causing the scattered leaves to crackle and spin. Had anyone been there to observe it, they might have marvelled at the strange motion of air, a spiral of force that was contrary to the light breeze that moved the tops of the trees. The weird motion of air began to intensify, stripping loose bark from the trunks of the poplars, uprooting grass from the fragile soil. As the spirals of force became still more intense, it seemed they became visible, glowing with a pale blue light. The spectral display intensified until its brilliance seemed to rival the sun.

Then it was gone – force and wind and glow. In its place, amid the stripped bark and uprooted vegetation, there stood a figure garbed in black. The wizard turned his body, staring with eyes that were pools of fury at the distant cluster of poverty that was Valbonnec. Rudol's lip twisted in a spiteful sneer and his long-fingered hand spread into a claw, then snapped close into a clenched fist, as though crushing the village within his grip.

They had called him too emotional for proper mastery of the arts of wizardry and magic, too given to excess and the free rein of his emotions. The masters of the Celestial College spoke of restraint, of carefully measuring the power a wizard called into himself, of letting that power be used with care and caution lest it run wild and beyond the magic wielder's control. It galled Rudol to no end that they were right, he was given to excess, given to allowing his emotions to overwhelm him, letting his anger rather than his intellect direct the power he took from the winds of magic. In his tower, he'd allowed the celestial energies to almost overwhelm him, allowed them to destroy indiscriminately, allowed the power to build to such a level that it might have consumed him. Rudol had seen what could happen if a wizard allowed too much magic to gather in his blood. The lucky ones would die, exploding in a brilliant blaze of light or simply dropping as though pole-axed by an ogre. There were others who survived such things, their bodies consumed and degenerated by the awesome energies that had run rampant through their systems. Spawn they called them, living manifestations of the dread force that was father to all magic: Chaos.

Rudol's limbs trembled, unsteady and weak from the energies that had crackled about them. With a fumbling hand, the wizard opened a pouch on his belt, removing a small clay phial of filthy, tar-like liquid. The substance's narcotic smell steadied Rudol's hand and the wizard lifted the tiny bottle to his lips, letting his tongue lap some of the syrupy liquid from its container. At once, the calming effect of the drug surged through the wizard's wasted veins, calming twitching muscles and throbbing nerves. Essence of weirdroot was not easy to come by, especially in Bretonnia where the knights were quick to punish those reckless enough to grow the forbidden herb, punishment that as often as not meant quartering for the criminal. Yet it was a vital substance, an essential tool to maintaining Rudol's prowess with the black arts, keeping the wizard from reducing himself to a seizure-ridden cripple after one of his zealous magical outbursts.

The spell he had used, one that allowed the caster to vanish from one place and translocate himself to another, was a dangerous one, which called upon different winds of magic. To draw upon more than one of the colours of sorcery increased the risk of allowing too much Chaotic power to build within the wizard's body. Even a reckless man of Rudol's temperament hesitated to risk such things, yet there had been no other way to escape his crumbling abode save to embrace that risk and employ the Grey magic he had learned so long ago.

The wizard turned his gaze toward the south. He could sense it, the Fell Fang, being carried away by the filthy bandit scum who had brought it to him. The thief no doubt was unaware of the glamour Rudol had placed upon the artefact when he had guessed what it was. So long as the spell was maintained, Rudol would know exactly where the coveted relic was. It would not be long before he tracked down that snickering brigand.

Rudol considered his options. He could, of course, try and kill the bandit and whatever confederates he had with him when the time came, but if he did that he ran the risk of allowing the power to run away with him again. The Fell Fang was much too important to risk losing forever due to an excess of magic and his own impatience. No, he would be better served by securing swordsmen of his own, blades to cut down Gobineau and his trash while Rudol relieved the scum of their treasure. He would need an ally, a patron in this matter.

The wizard's sinister laughter cackled into the night. He had a good idea where to find such a patron, a man ruthless enough to support the wizard's schemes, so long as Rudol led him to believe that he too would profit by them. He looked south again, imagining the fleeing Gobineau, scuttling back into whatever spider hole he called his home. He hoped that the smiling rogue made good use of the days left to him, for they were most certainly numbered.

CHAPTER THREE

THE SMALL TOWN of Alelbec was little more than a hog wallow by the standards of the Empire, but for the sparsely populated countryside of Bretonnia it was a thriving centre of commerce and trade. It boasted not simply one but two taverns, each of which, it was said, put more ale than water in their drinks. It boasted an inn, an ironmonger, a couple of horse traders, and even a glass blower, though this artisan's wares mostly found their way into the cities of Gisoreux and Couronne. Indeed, the inn had the only glass windows and wood floors for a hundred miles. Such prosperity owed its existence to the location in which the town was situated, sprawling across the main roadway leading from Gisoreux to the royal court at Couronne, making the place a welcome stop for weary travellers, common and noble alike, to wash the dust from their mouths.

But by Imperial standards, it was still a slum and a pigsty, and Otto Kroenen would be quite happy to see the little dung heap retreating into the distance when he continued his journey. The toy maker despised his trips away from his native Reikland, most especially the ones that took him into Bretonnia. It never ceased to astound him the exceedingly low value the Bretonnians placed upon personal comfort. Quite the contrary, they seemed to take an almost sadistic pleasure in privation and hardship. Still, the lords of the kingdom took delight in Kroenen's clockwork mechanisms and never ceased to delight in watching his little tin knights unhorse one another. The lords of Bretonnia might not spend a groat to clothe their peasants, but they were certainly willing enough to trade gold for cunning mechanisms far beyond the ability of their own artisans to produce. In the Empire, there were many toysmiths with whom Kroenen had to compete, many of them, if he were honest, quite a bit more clever and inventive than himself. But in Bretonnia, Kroenen was almost unique.

Which still did not spare him the perpetual discomfort of sleeping under the draughty roofs of Bretonnian hostelries and drinking the thin, lacklustre brews that the peasants dared to call ale and wine.

Kroenen's mood turned even more sour as he sampled the amber liquid that festered within the wooden cup set before him on the counter. The only comforting thought was that his companion was enjoying himself even less. Kroenen turned a smug eye toward the small figure who brooded at the end of the long wooden bar. The short warrior's body was covered in a suit of chainmail augmented by sections of elaborately engraved steel plate. A helmet trimmed in gold shared the same theme as the plates, interconnecting spirals of runes that each seemed to be some sort of stylised axe-head. From belts affixed about the short warrior's broad shoulders and prodigious girth, a number of far less esoteric axes hung, keen edges gleaming from slits in the faces of their leather holsters. A far larger axe leaned against the counter beside the stout fighter, its shaft crafted from some exceedingly dark steel alloy, its double-bladed head gleaming with the keenness of a razor.

The warrior himself was grizzled, his skin dark and leathery. A flowing blond beard cascaded down his chest, the wiry hair obscuring almost his entire face saving the broad nose and narrow, surly eyes.

Kroenen considered himself rather fortunate to have engaged so capable a bodyguard as Ulgrin Baleaxe. Normally the services of a dwarf axeman would have been beyond the miserly inclinations of the toysmith, but Kroenen had happened upon the dwarf when his career had entered a decided slump. All the dwarf wanted now was a way to earn enough gold so he could return to the Empire without looking like a penniless mendicant.

It had been relatively easy for Kroenen to take advantage of the dwarf's misfortune. He suspected that Ulgrin was going to refuse his offer, the dwarf had certainly fingered his axe in a most unpleasant way when Kroenen had mentioned how much he was willing to pay, but he knew the dwarf was desperate. He couldn't return to the Empire without some coin to his name. He might be willing to have men see him as a near-beggar doing odd jobs for food and ale, but he'd certainly not suffer the eyes of his fellow dwarfs to see him in such a state. It was a part of the stubborn pride that had allowed men to advance their own engineering knowledge to a state where it was almost the equal to that of their ancient teachers, while the dwarfs themselves had scarcely advanced at all since the time of Sigmar.

Except in the arena of toy making... Kroenen made another sour face that had nothing to do with ale. He took a certain twisted joy in observing Ulgrin's discomfort, a vicarious revenge for all the times he'd been bested by dwarf toysmiths in the great houses of the Empire. Kroenen imagined that there would be another tense scene involving the dwarf's axe when the toysmith informed Ulgrin that the thin Bretonnian ale which the dwarf was imbibing by the gallon was being deducted from the warrior's fee.

Ulgrin slammed down another wooden cup. He raised a grizzled fist and motioned for the tavern keeper to bring him another. 'And see if you can't keep from washing your feet in it before you serve it,' the dwarf added. His harsh words were swiftly noted by a cluster of on-looking soldiers. Professional men-at-arms, they were part of the retinue of some petty lord who was journeying back to the royal court, and they had taken an instant dislike to the distinctive foreigner. Bretonnia did not enjoy the strong ties and shared history with the dwarfs in the way the Empire did, and it had been many centuries since more than a handful of the stout breed had travelled the green lands of the king.

The trio of soldiers rose from their table, an air of hostility preceding them as they strode toward the bar. Kroenen noted their advance, retreating deeper in the tavern to place a greater distance between himself and his bodyguard. After all, it was Ulgrin's job to attend to such difficulties, that was what he was being paid for. The dwarf, for his part, did not seem to pay the approaching ruffians the slightest notice, maintaining a glowering stare that focused entirely upon the upended wooden cups.

'Did it say something?' the foremost of the soldiers asked. He was a tall, lean figure, a rounded cap of steel encasing his skull, a bright tabard of red and yellow displayed over his suit of leather armour, both cloth and armour struggling to maintain the man's prodigious gut. Though he gripped a leather jack of ale in one hand, his other rested on the hilt of the sword swinging from his belt.

'I'm not sure. It mumbles so terribly,' a second, this one sporting a wide-brimmed steel hat on his head, commented.

'Maybe he is just too deep in his cups to speak,' the third, a large brute whose helm featured an immense steel nasal guard, said. 'After all, little men shouldn't drink so much.'

The dwarf did not turn to face the accosting soldiers, keeping his attention fixed upon the tavern keeper as he set a new cup before him. Ulgrin reached a gnarled hand forward, clenching his fist about the vessel and then made a point of draining its contents in one swallow.

'Is that supposed to impress us, little man?' sneered the first soldier.

This time Ulgrin did turn, staring up at the swaggering trooper. The dwarf's eyes were like tiny fires, just beginning to glow into flame.

'Not with this pigs'-piss!' the dwarf spat. 'Back in the High King's realm the babies are weaned on stuff stronger than this sewage. Fetch me a decent beer if you want a drinking bout, a contest with this mud would take a month.'

'I think I heard it insult our Bretonnian ale,' the brutish soldier grumbled. 'I think the little man is saying that our drink's not good enough for him,' he added with a note of menace.

'In the habit of thinking too much, or just too little?' Ulgrin shot back, his deep voice carrying with it the sharpness of a knife. At the far end of the tavern, Kroenen suddenly found a reason to be elsewhere, slipping out the door with a speed that did little to maintain his dignity.

'What a nasty little temper it has!' observed the fat soldier, chuckling with his domineering bravado. 'Short folk should be much more respectful,' he tutted, waving a warning finger.

'I think it is that ugly bird's nest of a beard hanging down his belly,' the soldier in the steel hat remarked. 'That must be what makes him so ill-tempered.'

'Maybe we should give him a shave then,' growled Brute. 'Improve his looks, if not his manners!'

Ulgrin rolled his eyes, one hand scratching at his beard. 'You grobi-fondlers do take a long time picking a fight,' he complained.

The dwarf's free hand came swinging around, hurling one of the wood cups from the counter behind him squarely in the face of Fatty. The soldier flung up both hands to protect himself as the cup bounced neatly off his forehead. The ale left in the cup was expelled as he threw up his hands, sending the amber liquid cascading into the face of Steel Hat, the alarmed soldier stumbling away from the unpleasant shower and tripping into Brute as the larger soldier began to draw his sword. The two men-at-arms crashed to the floor in a tangle of limbs.

'You should hire a few snotlings,' Ulgrin said, grabbing up his double-headed axe. 'Might improve your chances!' Fatty had drawn his sword and although one hand still clutched at the dent in his forehead, the soldier strode toward the dwarf to exact revenge.

Ulgrin smiled at the ungainly advance, firming his own double-handed grip on his axe. As Fatty leaned back to slash down at his antagonist, Ulgrin lunged forward, driving the heft on his axe into the man's groin. Instantly, the soldier's sword clattered to the floor, a dull groan of misery flying from his body as though to escape the pain that had given it birth. The man fell to his knees, eyes watering. Ulgrin smiled down at the obese soldier.

'A word to the wise: always buy a steel codpiece,' the dwarf told the stunned Bretonnian before bringing the blunt heft of the axe smashing up under his chin and breaking the soldier's jaw. Ulgrin turned away from the unconscious Fatty as the man's comrades untangled themselves and rose from the floor.

'He's mine!' snarled Steel Hat as the soldier considered the ruin Ulgrin had made of his friend.

The man-at-arms came lunging at the dwarf in a hate-ridden charge that was long on violence and short on grace. Ulgrin was reminded momentarily of the blood-mad rushes of orc warriors, but Steel Hat had neither the overwhelming bulk nor the unthinking ferocity to make such an attack problematic for the old dwarf veteran. Ulgrin brought his great axe upward, meeting the sweep of the soldier's sword. The Bretonnian steel shuddered as it impacted against the black steel of the axe. The runes upon the weapon seemed to glow for a moment, giving off a faint blue light. Undaunted, Steel Hat brought his blade slashing downward again. This time, the sword did not simply rebound from the cruel dwarf weapon, but snapped like a twig, the upper length of the sword skittering across the room. Steel Hat stared in horror and disbelief at his mangled weapon, then at the glowering dwarf. Ulgrin hefted his axe and took a menacing step forward.

'He's yours!' Steel Hat cried as he fled past the brutal-looking soldier, dropping the remains of his sword as he ran, struggling to push his way through the other patrons of the tavern who now choked the exit.

Brute snarled as he stalked forward, murderous eyes intent on the dwarf. 'You've made quick work of my friends, little man,' the thug growled. 'Now let's see how you do against me!'

The big soldier moved toward Ulgrin with more caution than Steel Hat had, clearly taking his enemy with a sobering degree of care. Ulgrin smiled beneath his beard. Sometimes too much caution was a bad thing.

The dwarf shifted his upper body, starting to bring the butt of his axe forward. Brute reacted by dropping his sword downward to intercept any crippling blow aimed at his vitals. But the dwarf had no intention of repeating his earlier attack on Fatty. In mid-motion, Ulgrin swept the upper part of his weapon around. Already leaning forward to protect himself, Brute's face was in easy reach of the double-headed weapon. The colour drained from his features as he saw the steel flash before his eyes. Something struck the floor with a loud thud. Brute cast his gaze downward, his flesh going even paler as he saw the severed nasal guard staring up at him.

Ulgrin leaned on his axe, glaring at the shocked Bretonnian. Brute looked away from the cleanly cut steel and it was with dread filling his gaze that he stared upon his adversary. Ulgrin's face split in a cruel smile of both mockery and challenge.

'You should probably go away now,' the dwarf told the Bretonnian. 'Before I take it into my head to give *you* a shave,' he threatened. 'With this,' he added, patting the shaft of his axe. Brute needed no further encouragement, slamming his weapon back into its sheath and running with all speed for the tavern's exit.

Ulgrin smiled coldly, turning around and beginning to make his way back to the bar. As he did so, the sound of two hands clapping together brought the dwarf to a stop. Firming his grip upon the axe, the dwarf peered into the shadowy recesses of the tavern. Ulgrin watched intently as his applauding spectator stepped out into the light. The dwarf was somehow not surprised that he recognised the man. The grip upon the axe became a bit tighter.

'Brunner,' the dwarf addressed the man from the shadows. 'Still slinking around like some damn tunnel goblin I see.'

The bounty hunter strode forward, one gloved hand dropping to rest on the butt of the pistol holstered across his belly.

'Still carrying around that monstrosity, Ulgrin?' Brunner asked. The bounty hunter let a faint laugh escape his lips. 'Of course, I suppose you'd no longer be called Baleaxe if you were to lose it.' Ulgrin stared back, clearly finding no humour in the bounty killer's jest.

'What brings you snooping around, Brunner?' the dwarf's voice was heavy with suspicion.

'Just heard that an old friend was in the area,' the bounty hunter replied, his voice level and even.

Ulgrin snorted with grim amusement. 'You don't have any friends, Brunner,' the dwarf stated. 'And if you did, I wouldn't be one of them.'

'Still angry about that?' the bounty hunter shook his head. 'I would have thought with that sharp dwarf memory of yours you'd be able to recall that I found him first. Besides, Judge Vaulkberg doesn't like dealing with dwarfs. He'd have dropped his price if you'd brought Selber in.'

'That's supposed to make me feel better?' the dwarf growled. 'Fifty or sixty gold in my hands is still better than none.' Ulgrin let his hands clench and unclench about the haft of his weapon, a silent display of his eagerness to use it.

'What if I told you I was looking for you?' Brunner told the dwarf.

It was true, after a fashion. The bounty hunter had known his old rival was in Bretonnia for some time now, he just hadn't seen any reason for their paths to cross before. Now the dwarf bounty killer could be of use to him. 'I need some help securing the mark I'm hunting. A good set of eyes to watch my back.'

Ulgrin laughed contemptuously. 'The great Brunner in need of help,' the dwarf jeered. 'Why do I find that story a bit hard to swallow?'

'The man's name is Gobineau. He's wanted for banditry, piracy, murder, arson and the deflowering of a small army of noblemen's wives and daughters.' Brunner paused, staring straight into the sullen eyes of Ulgrin Baleaxe. 'The reward being offered is two thousand gold crowns. If you help me, we split it right down the middle.'

The dwarf let his axe droop to the floor, shifting his grip so that one gnarled hand could scratch at his chin. Ulgrin's eyes gleamed with a new light, the glint of gold-lust. 'A thousand gold,' the dwarf muttered. 'More than enough to buy my way out of this wretched country and make my return in style.' Ulgrin turned his attention back to the bounty hunter. 'You have my interest, Brunner. Now let me see how the land lies. Why do you need my help?'

Brunner smiled at the other bounty hunter, considering his words carefully. 'You have heard of Mousillon?'

'The cursed city?' the dwarf said, his tone incredulous. 'They say that ghosts hold court in broken castles and toppled towers there, that ghouls prowl the streets and devour whatever flesh they find. It is said to be a haven of disease and plague, where madness is commonplace and children are born twisted and warped. They say...'

'...many things,' Brunner interrupted. 'Many of them are lies, but there is enough truth to the stories to make Mousillon a shunned and dangerous place.' The bounty hunter's tone became sombre as he continued. 'The man I am seeking has fled to Mousillon. That is why I need you.'

Ulgrin's gaze dropped, staring intently at the floor as the brain behind those eyes considered the bounty killer's offer. 'Two is safer than one, is that it?' the dwarf said at last. 'Sounds rather like how they hunt trolls in Karak Izor. They take a big old boar into the tunnels. The boar gets a sniff of the troll and takes off after it thinking it's going to find some nice tasty mushrooms. Of course, when it discovers a troll at the end of the trail, it starts squealing bloody murder, which gets the troll riled enough that its one thought is to smash the boar. That usually gives the troll hunters time to bring the thick-witted brute down before it can shift its attention over to them.' Ulgrin glared suspiciously at Brunner. 'I suspect you want me to be the boar,' he accused.

The bounty hunter's smile did not change. 'Let's just say that somebody with your flair for chopping heads first and taking names later might be a nice complement to my own methods.'

'Meaning I draw the enemies out while you pick them off from the shadows,' the dwarf sneered. He was quiet for a moment more, then gave voice to a boisterous laugh. 'For a thousand gold crowns, I can do that! You have yourself a partner, bounty killer.'

'You'll need a horse,' Brunner pointed out. 'It's a long walk to Mousillon.' The bounty hunter knew that dwarfs as a rule disliked riding, though he'd seen some manage well enough on mules and ponies. Ulgrin nodded his head.

'The slime I was working for, Otto Kroenen, gave me a mule so I could keep up with him on the road,' Ulgrin said. 'It's in the stable now. I'm sure he won't miss it.' The dwarf swung his massive axe, letting the blade rest against his shoulder. 'We'll just consider it my severance wage,' the dwarf laughed, following Brunner's lead toward the exit.

THE LONE TRAVELLER sat in a bleak, forsaken corner of the small inn. The little structure's floor was a morass of mud, planks of wood crudely thrown over the morass to provide relatively stable places upon which to walk and stand. A few ox-skins were stretched over the walls, a feeble and ultimately futile attempt to keep the all-intrusive chill at bay. Trickles of water dripped from the ceiling where the thatch had at last yielded to the harsh pounding it had taken since the rain had started some hours before. The villages that peppered the road leading toward the forsaken city of Mousillon were noteworthy for their poverty, even by the exceedingly low standards set by the peasantry of Bretonnia, and the shanty town that supported the desolate little inn was no exception to the rule.

The Griffon's Nest, the owner of the dive dared to call it. The Spider Hole might have been a more honest title to bestow upon the wretched hovel, at least in such a direction went Gobineau's thoughts. Still, the proprietor, a one-armed grey-head named Gaspard, did have a rather endearing quality. Maimed in his youth for the crime of poaching, Gaspard had little love for the knights who ruled Bretonnia and maintained the peace. The innkeeper was notorious for his lack of interest in those who chose to patronise his establishment, whatever their crimes or the prices on their heads. Or perhaps it was simply that only an outlaw would endure the slovenly standards of Gaspard's food and drink, and the positively hideous condition of the long straw-strewn stable where he allowed his patrons and their beasts to strive toward achieving some pale shadow of sleep and rest.

Gobineau shook his head in disgust as a cockroach large enough to give a housecat a decent fight sloshed its way through the mud and scurried under a gap in the nearest wall. A sigh worked its way from the rogue's chest as he considered the misery of his surroundings. Only two months ago he had been sleeping on sheets of Cathayan silk and dining upon roast pheasant and duck. Of course, his very eager and accommodating hostess did have that slight marital problem, as in the noble lord's five-month quest to root out a nest of beastmen in the Forest of Chalons had only taken three. Of course, the stunned look on the knight's face had almost been worth a cold flight through the nighted streets of Couronne, though Gobineau did regret leaving such a fine pair of boots behind.

Thoughts of finery caused the rogue to remove the ivory reliquary that he had tucked within his tunic. He studied the artefact that had so impressed the wizard, impressed him enough to try killing Gobineau and his entire bandit gang. With a twist of his wrist, Gobineau slid the upper portion away, exposing the item Rudol had called the Fell Fang, though Gobineau did not like to ponder the size of a creature that could have fitted something of such size within its jaws.

There was no mistaking the quality of the artefact, its graceful, peerless craftsmanship. And, if Rudol was to be believed, there was something magical about the device. That would make it especially valuable where he was going. Duc Marimund had been a sometime patron of Gobineau's when the rogue had operated in the southern half of the kingdom. Mousillon was a prime base of operations, if one had a constitution bold enough to resist the pestilent air that clung to the blighted city, and didn't mind leaving the hours of darkness to the unspeakable things that emptied from the city's graveyard at dusk. There were few knights in Bretonnia who would brave the cursed city, seeing it as a place of ill omen and sacrilege. That was very helpful when trying to escape a particularly determined baronet or marquis's warriors.

The duc was also obsessed with all things magic, hoping to achieve his mad dreams of restoring the glory days of his rotting city through sorcery and the black arts. He'd be quite interested in what Gobineau had to show him. And, of course, while Marimund was occupied with his new toy, his pretty young wife might be interested in a few hours' dalliance with her old paramour. Gobineau smiled again at that thought. His mind half-taken with amorous deeds, he eyed the fang once more, again noting the irregular holes that seemed to have been drilled into its surface. The rogue lifted the relic to his lips, blowing through the silver cap into the hollow fang, intending to evoke one of the many haunting melodies he had collected in his travels and which he employed to help melt even the coldest maiden's heart.

The rogue looked in annoyance at the fang when no sound issued from it. He drew a deeper breath, blowing into it once more, then chided himself for his foolishness. It was some hoary old elf sorcerer's talisman, not a minstrel's flute. Laughing at his flight of fancy, Gobineau slipped the curve of bone back into its ivory case, admiring the carvings once more before again concealing it within the folds of his tunic.

He'd need to set aside his thought of romantic trysts and glittering gold. It was more important that he watch himself on the road to the cursed city, especially now that he was only a day's journey from the safety of Mousillon's walls. He'd make an early start on the morrow, and be in Mousillon long before nightfall. It wouldn't pay for some knight to chance upon him now that he was so close.

Of course, there was another thought that lent speed to Gobineau's intentions. He'd ridden two horses into the ground, abandoning the dying steeds and stealing replacements, during his flight from Valbonnec, yet Gobineau was not so certain that he had eluded all pursuit. The bounty hunter Brunner was notorious for his tenacity, and infamous for his brutality when he brought his hunts to a close. The thought that the bounty killer, despite all of Gobineau's craft and care, might be close at hand chilled the rogue far more than the draught seeping in under the ox-skins.

The rogue lifted the watery mead that Gaspard had given him to chase down his dinner of lukewarm porridge. He'd be safe enough once he was in Mousillon, the rogue told himself as he tried to strengthen his nerves with what little fire was in his drink. Even a fanatic like Brunner wouldn't follow him there.

THE CASTLE'S GREAT hall was all but deserted, the sycophants of the court dismissed by a snarled command from their lord. A number of servants had remained, cringing in the background like badly whipped curs who knew not from which direction their master might kick them next. A second, even more murderous oath from the lord of the castle sent even these wretches scuttling off through the stone archways that opened into the hall. In their wake, the crackle of the fire was the only sound that intruded upon the silence.

In the centre of the chamber, where a vast array of benches and tables had been assembled for the recently interrupted feast, a high-backed throne stood, its occupant glowering at the two men standing before him. He was a cruel-featured man, his nose broad, his mouth a thick gash above his slight chin. His body was not one of height, but one of strength, limbs rippling with muscle, raw brute power visible even beneath the silky blue robes the nobleman wore. His neck was thick, like the stump of a tree, and about it hung a massive golden chain and pectoral. Upon the pectoral was a slavering wolf, the coat of arms of the Viscount de Chegney, a man as notorious for his tyranny as he was for his ruthlessness.

Augustine de Chegney leaned forward in his chair, fixing his intense, smouldering gaze upon his seneschal.

'Your story intrigues me, Pleasant,' the nobleman growled. 'Now that we are alone, I would hear more of the particulars.' There was an unspoken threat in the viscount's words, a promise that if the rest of the report was not as promising as the seneschal's intimations had been, then the viscount's underling would pay a stiff penalty for presuming upon his master's ambitions.

The man addressed was a tall, lean figure, wearing a long brown cloak over his red tunic and breeches. His features were sharp, almost bird-like, his head bald except for the fringe of white hair that persisted behind his ears and the faint wisp of moustache that hid beneath the shadow of his nose. Elodore Pleasant lifted a hand heavy with gold rings and pulled at his chin. He smiled nervously, then continued to make his report.

'This man,' Elodore pointed behind him at the dark-garbed stranger who had come to the chateau seeking an audience with the viscount, 'is the wizard of whom I spoke.'

'I have eyes, fool,' the viscount snarled, 'and the wit to use them.' De Chegney turned his attention away from his underling and stared at the man who had accompanied him. The wizard was not so thin and frail as the seneschal, though far from powerfully built. He wore a robe of black upon which tiny stars seemed to blink and flicker with the wizard's every movement. The fiery, intense eyes of the mage did not waver as the feral glare of the nobleman peered into them.

'This weapon you have told Pleasant about,' the viscount said. 'It will do what you have said it can do?'

'The true level of its power may be far beyond even what I have described,' Rudol boasted, his voice rippling with excitement. 'With such a weapon at your command, no enemy could hope to stand against you!'

'My enemies do not dare to stand against me now, conjurer,' de Chegney declared. 'I have the finest army in the Grey Mountains, and my enemies know it.'

'But if your enemies should band together...' Rudol explained. 'There is always that threat, is there not? That you might become problem enough that even the least amiable of your adversaries might find common cause in working your ruin?'

'And there is the simple truth that we cannot easily both defend ourselves and mount a decisive strike on le Gaires,' interjected Pleasant. 'The wizard's plan offers us a way to achieve both.' De Chegney waved a meaty hand indicating that his servant should curb his enthusiasm.

'This talisman you speak of,' the nobleman asked. 'It will truly enable you to control dragons?'

Rudol's eyes gleamed with an even more fanatic intensity as he responded to the viscount's question. 'It is a device worked by the elves long ago. Mortal wizards have never dared imagine such a device! With the Fell Fang, I can call the dragon which was bound to the talisman and bind him to my will! I can command him to destroy whomever you command. You can annihilate your enemies from afar, keeping your army intact and be ready to deal with anyone foolish enough to oppose you after you display your power!'

'What is in this for you?' de Chegney inquired, trying not to let himself become distracted by the fantastic prospect Rudol had laid before him.

'I am but a wizard,' the exile said, bowing humbly before the seated noble. 'I am no ruler, I can prosper only by serving a man who is firmly in command of the mundane matters of a mundane world, freeing me to pursue my researches into the mysteries of the arcane world. If I do this for you, I would expect your protection and patronage in exchange for my services.' A crafty quality entered Rudol's features and the smile he turned upon de Chegney was one of smugness. 'I should point out that it takes one well versed in the black arts to employ the Fell Fang, to rouse the dragon from its slumber. It is no dog whistle that any idiot can put to his lips!' The wizard nodded his head. 'We need each other, viscount. Neither of us can achieve his ambitions without the other.'

De Chegney leaned back in his chair. 'You have asked for protection as you secure this talisman from the man who has it.' The nobleman paused as he considered the request. 'I shall put twenty men at your disposal. One of my knights shall accompany them.' The viscount's tone became lower, more threatening. 'Sir Thierswind will be in command of the soldiers. You may voice suggestions to him, but make no mistake that he is in command of this little expedition.' The viscount lifted a warning finger. 'Be advised, Rudol, if Sir Thierswind once suspects that you intend to betray me, I have given him my blessing to remove your head from its shoulders and bring both it and the talisman back to me.' The viscount snorted with grim humour.

'After all,' he laughed, 'I can always find another wizard.'

LA ISLA DE Sangre was a barren scrap of volcanic rock jutting out of the ocean some two hundred miles off the coast of Estalia. It was an ill-regarded place, shunned by man and beast alike. The rocky slopes were devoid of all but the hardiest of mosses and weeds, their scraggly, skeletal stalks clothing the parched and stony earth. Except for the grotesque crabs that nightly crawled out of the muck and filth of the island's lagoon to prowl and hunt, the place was almost devoid of animal life. A few petrels and razorbills contested lordship of the island with the crabs, when the north was gripped by the frosty attentions of Ulric, Lord of Winter, their croaking cries audible for leagues out to sea.

Even pirates had forsaken La Isla de Sangre as a place from which to mount their raids and hide their treasure. Perhaps it was the blood-red sand of the beach, which had lent the island its name, that so disconcerted them. Perhaps it was the towering volcano that loomed above the island, an omnipresent spectre of impending doom as it smoked and rumbled. Or perhaps it was legend, the old stories that said the island had once been a lush paradise, home to a great and noble race of people. The tales went that the island had been turned into a barren wilderness after a single night of destruction and carnage, when a horrific force had descended upon the island and consumed all upon it. The legends did not agree upon what shape the destroyer had taken; some spoke of an angry god that dwelt within the mountain, others of a towering daemon who wore a crown of flame, still others of a rain of firebolts that had showered down from the sky to burn the island clean of life.

In primitive times, the crude ancestors of the Estalians had paddled their rafts to the island once a year to leave an offering upon its shore, hoping to placate the angry god of the mountain with their sacrifice. Even in more recent times, Estalian sailors would throw a small animal overboard when they passed within sight of the island. It was never wise to tempt daemons from their slumber.

Within the sulphurous depths of the gigantic network of lava tubes that snaked their way through the mountain, a vast form stirred upon its bed of glittering metal. Claws of polished black scratched at the golden coins that supported them, causing them to slide in an avalanche of wealth. A long tail lashed against the wall, knocking stones from the ceiling overhead. The rocks crumbled and broke upon the massive armoured back beneath them. Leathery lids rolled back to expose cold amber eyes, their slit-like pupil narrowing and widening as it roused itself from centuries of slumber.

A low hiss, like the sizzle of a thousand forges, rasped from the creature's immense form. Fully emerged from its interrupted slumber, the reptile's mind at once focused upon what had disturbed it. An ancient insult had been repeated, the stabbing, probing pain had lanced once more through its mind. The cold mind of the reptile suddenly blazed with a rage as fiery as the molten rock that surged in the caldera that warmed its lair.

Powerful limbs clawed at the heaped treasure that formed the wyrm's nest, pulling the mammoth shape through the lava tubes. A low rumble pounded from the reptile's body as its breathing increased, as strength began to surge once more through its gargantuan frame. A long, purplish tongue shot out from the colossal jaws that fronted the monster's wedge-like head, flickering as it tasted the air. The monster hissed again, crawling toward the faint suggestion of fresh air it had detected. The wyrm's colossal bulk widened the narrow lava tubes, grinding stone from the smooth walls with its passing. At last, it neared its goal. The tremendous speed of the reptile lessened as it neared the fresh air, and it was with a suggestion of caution that the monster approached the mouth of the tunnel.

Like a gigantic serpent, the dragon crawled from the mouth of the lava tube, sending a rockslide tumbling down the mountain as he wriggled his body to widen the hole. The enormous horned head looked skyward, staring with cool alien interest at the stars he had not seen for five hundred years and more. The weird light of the twin moons lent a colder hue to the reptile's crimson scales and black talons, but did nothing to ease the wrath boiling within the creature. The dragon freed his shoulders, twisting his body and sinking his halberd-like claws into the side of the volcano. With a speed that seemed beyond something of such a mammoth construction, the dragon crawled from the mouth of his lava tunnel up the sheer face of the mountain, stopping only when he reached the truncated peak of the volcano.

The dragon stared down at his desolate island, his predatory gaze considering the jagged rocks and scarlet sands. The dragon's eyes dismissed the scuttling shapes of the crabs, lifting to watch the placid surface of the wide ocean. There would be porpoises and whales there, meat enough to fill even the fiery belly of the ancient wyrm. A trickle of sizzling drool fell from the dragon's mouth as he contemplated such a feast. Then the monster's eyes narrowed as his mind returned to that which had disturbed him. As intense as the hunger chewing at his innards was, there was a still greater force motivating the mammoth reptile.

Leathery wings slowly folded open from above the dragon's shoulders. The pinions, as black as night and larger than a galleon's mainsail, fluttered up and down as the dragon tested them in the warm wind rising from the volcano. With a snap, the wings opened fully and the dragon let a mighty roar rasp from his powerful lungs, golden flames billowing from his jaws. Without further preamble, the two hundred foot-long monster launched himself from the side of the mountain, powerful wings keeping the giant reptile aloft.

Malok circled the island twice, then banked, speeding away in a new direction. What he wanted to find was not on La Isla de Sangre. No, it would be found somewhere else, somewhere in the north. Malok did not know where he might find it now, but he knew where it had been.

For now, that would be enough. If it was not there, then the dragon would simply extend his hunt. When enough of the land was cinder and ash, there would be no place for the little vermin to hide.

CHAPTER FOUR

IT LAY STREWN upon the banks of the River Grismerie like
the festering carcass of some colossal sea beast dredged up
from the pits of the ocean to die upon the shore. The once
gleaming walls of the city were now broken, charred black
in places by fires that had raged unchecked, or had toppled
when the foundations had been devoured by the boggy
landscape. Smaller structures lay crushed beneath those
tumbled-down walls, the immense stone blocks driving the
shops and hovels that had clustered in their shadow deep
into the mire so that only the occasional wooden strut or
shingle protruded from the quagmire. The rotting remains
of towers could be seen beyond the wall, the forlorn remnants of once proud castles from which the descendants of
Lord Landuin had once ruled. To the north and the west of
the city, great cemeteries sprawled, vast mausoleums and
tombs meant to endure through the ages, now crumbled
and cracked by the twin evils of flood and earthquake, and
by the neglect that had afflicted all of Mousillon.

Beyond the walls of the dead city, all was foul stinking marshland, a filthy bog of mud and mire formed by the river's frequent floods. The giant shantytown that had sprung up around the walls of Mousillon during the Dark Age of Bretonnia was now half sunk into the mire, second storey floors now level with the mud as the swamp consumed the floors beneath. Roofs peaked out from the morass, black croaking crows and grunting grey gulls making their nests in the ruins of chimneys and gable windows. Near the river, the last remains of quays and docks could be seen, half sunk into the mud banks that had built around them, the waters of the river many yards from the ends of the piers. Boats and ships of all shape and size were likewise trapped in the mud, their broken hulls displaying jagged gashes and splintered wood. The shore of a siren's island could have been of no greater grimness than the decaying port of Mousillon.

From the quays, a great stretch of crumbling warehouses and workshops sprawled, reaching back towards the city walls before completely slipping back into the mire that had devoured the shantytown. Here, a number of crude grauben hauses had been built, a structure employed by only the most backward and poverty stricken within the Empire. Little more than tents crafted from swamp reeds and driftwood, the tiny plumes of smoke rising from the structures suggested that they were not without their denizens, lairing within the mud like river vermin.

The two bounty hunters stared down on the miserable city from a small hillock. They were on foot now, their horses and mule left with a farmer some distance from the city, one whom the promise of gold and the threat of retribution had made certain to take good care of the animals. Ulgrin had grumbled about the tactic, but Brunner had informed his companion that it was unwise to bring the animals too near the blighted city. In a place as poor and desperate as Mousillon, horseflesh was as prized as Moot-land steak.

'Filthy looking place,' Ulgrin commented, rolling his shoulders to ease the weight of his axe. 'I've burned down goblin villages that were more pleasant to look upon.' Brunner turned and stared down at the dwarf.

'This place is more dangerous than any goblin hole,' he told Ulgrin. 'Keep your eyes and ears open. The people who live here are desperate, miserable and without conscience. They'd kill a stranger simply to boil the leather in his shoes.' Brunner caressed the grip of his pistol. 'Make no mistake, friend Baleaxe, you're going to earn your thousand gold.'

'You speak with the voice of experience,' the dwarf observed, a tone of suspicion in his voice.

'I do,' Brunner returned, marching down toward the river-bank. 'I have been here once before, though It was a long time ago.'

Ulgrin hurried after his companion, knowing that he would get no more from the close-mouthed killer. The dwarf was somewhat cheered by the notion that Brunner had risked the dread city once before and emerged alive. Then the relief drained from his heart as the dwarf wondered whether the bounty hunter had brought someone with him on that occasion as well, and whether his companion on that venture had likewise escaped the city.

A DIRTY, FOUL-VISAGED fisherman had ferried the pair of hunters across the wide expanse of the Grismerie, poling his flat-bottom skiff across mudflats where barely a foot of water covered the filth. For his services, the gap-toothed old wretch had been paid a pair of brass coins by the stern-faced Brunner, a pitiable sum back in the Empire, but something approaching a fortune for the dejected humans who cringed in the shadow of the cursed city. The fisherman had instantly thrust the coins into his mangy cloak, then shook his head as his passengers disembarked, hopping from the skiff to the rotten remains of a pier that lay close by. In his many years wrenching a living from the filthy waters of the bog, the old man had escorted only a few travellers into the city. He'd yet to see any of them leave. But, with the pragmatic survivor's instinct that had kept the fisherman alive in so blighted an environment, he decided that the wanderings of fools were no concern of his. Without a backward glance, he poled his skiff back into the morass and toward the deeper, cleaner waters of the Grismerie's far bank.

Brunner led the way, carefully negotiating the treacherous ruin of the old pier. Beneath the bounty hunter's tread, the rotted boards groaned and bent, reaching down toward the bottomless muck beneath them. Once, pressing his weight upon a seemingly sound plank, the bounty hunter had been startled by a sharp crack. Instinct caused him to press backward, restoring his weight to his opposite foot. The board upon which he had pressed snapped as neatly as a dry twig, the jagged ends slipping down into the grey mud. Within a few seconds, the broken plank sank completely into the morass and was lost to sight.

Behind him, Ulgrin Baleaxe whistled appreciatively. 'Wheew, now that's some nasty stuff!' the dwarf exclaimed. 'Even the tar pits below Karak Kadrin don't work that fast.' Ulgrin leaned forward, spitting into the greedy slime.

'Maybe you'd prefer to go first,' Brunner commented, extending his hand to indicate the dozens of yards of treacherous walkway yet to be traversed. 'I've always heard that dwarfs have a keen sense about unsafe paths.'

Ulgrin stepped back, setting the head of his axe against the pier, crossing his arms and resting them on the weapon's butt. 'That's true enough down in a decent mine or tunnel. We can feel the changes in the rock and the air that let us know when something's wrong. But with this,' Ulgrin gestured with his bearded chin to indicate the bog all around them. 'This isn't so much earth as water masquerading as ground. Only men would be foolish enough to build in such a place, so I'll be quite content to let a man risk his fool-all neck figuring out what can be walked on and what can't.'

Brunner turned away, stretching his leg to test the plank to the other side of the recently created gap. Finding it firm, he stepped across and proceeded to progress along the dilapidated pier. 'At some point Ulgrin, you do intend on earning your half of the bounty, or would that be an unwise assumption?' the bounty hunter called back. Ulgrin bristled under the comment, slinging his great axe back over his shoulder and following after Brunner with awkward hops and leaps.

'No dwarf ever accepted charity from anyone!' Ulgrin snapped, fighting to maintain his balance as he jumped across another gap left by a rotten board. The dwarf stared at the hungry mud below him for a tense moment before regaining his footing. 'And no dwarf ever took payment unless he earned it fairly,' Ulgrin added, his voice somewhat uneven as he considered how quickly the plank had been devoured.

'Don't concern yourself on that count,' Brunner stated. 'Unless Mousillon has changed a great deal since I was last here, these mud flats are the least of what this city will throw at us.' The bounty hunter pressed on, a series of jumps placing him several yards ahead of his diminutive companion.

'Now there's a pleasant thought,' Ulgrin grumbled to himself. He stared back at the grey mire. 'If that bastard had mentioned this gobbling muck, I'd have told him to go hang himself!'

A QUARTER OF an hour later, the end of the pier was within a dozen feet. Several times the bounty hunters had suffered a close call, treacherous planks shifting or breaking beneath their weight. Twice, Brunner had had to lift Ulgrin from the filth, the dwarf's desperate cries alerting the bounty hunter to his companion's distress. Only the timely speed with which Ulgrin had planted the head of his great axe into a support had prevented the dwarf from slipping entirely beneath the muck. It was with visible relief that Ulgrin beheld the relatively solid ground that rose beyond the end of the pier.

'Tell me that we have to cross that filth on the way back, and I'll cut your throat here and now,' Ulgrin snarled, wringing yet another clump of mud from his beard. 'If I never see this devil's porridge again, that will be soon enough!'

Brunner ignored Ulgrin's mutterings, his icy eyes instead watching the crumbling warehouses and dilapidated shops that crouched and slumped near what had been Mousillon's waterfront. The killer smiled grimly as he spied a shadow move within the darkness of one of the doorways. 'In a few minutes, you may be only too happy to see this sludge again. At least with it, you know where the danger lies.'

Ulgrin scratched at his unkempt beard, ignoring the other bounty hunter's cheerless comment. As he pawed at the matted, muddy mess, his eyes fixed upon a small shape scrabbling across the mud flats. He pointed a stubby hand at the tiny apparition.

'Looks like we should have engaged that cat as a guide,' the dwarf laughed. 'He seems to know the safe places.'

'He's not heavy enough to sink,' Brunner replied, only shifting his gaze for a second to observe the small animal. 'If he stops for a second, the mud will slurp him down just as hungrily as it tried to get you.' The bounty hunter kept his voice even, his stare steady and regular. The last thing he needed was to let the three or four shapes he'd seen moving inside the wasted innards of a wine shop know they'd been seen. 'Besides, he's got problems enough of his own.'

Even as Brunner spoke, the dwarf watched in astonishment as a dark, loathsome creature wriggled its way across the muck. It was not entirely unlike the cave eels he'd seen beneath the World's Edge Mountains, but it was much larger and its scales much darker, its back sporting a fringe of spike-like spines. The ugly thing moved with a strange sideways undulation that kept only the smallest portion of its body in contact with the mud, lending it a speed that the bedraggled cat could not hope to match. The dark furred feline howled in fright as the grotesque snake-fish reached it, the creature's long jaws snapping close about the animal's scrawny neck.

'Hashut's bald beard!' the dwarf swore. 'What madness is this, where fish hunt cats?'

'Better have that axe of yours ready,' Brunner said, his eyes still studying the rotting structures of the waterfront. 'We could be next on the menu.'

Ulgrin cast a curious eye on the bounty hunter, but did as he had been told, releasing the snaps that held his throwing axes in their holsters, firming his grip on his trusty great axe.

'How many?' the dwarf whispered.

'We won't know that until they attack,' Brunner replied, taking the first step from the pier. His boot squelched into the muddy ground, but the earth was firm enough beneath his tread to walk upon. 'Might be a dozen, might be a hundred.'

Damnit, Brunner!' the dwarf hissed. 'You've a bad idea of fair odds! I've met slayers who wouldn't look for fights that uneven!'

Brunner lifted his repeating crossbow from its sheath across his back, ensuring that the weapon was loaded and ready. The smile on the bounty hunter's face seemed only half-joking when he addressed Ulgrin's concerns. 'If things get too bad, we can always run. Then they might only get the slowest one.'

* * *

FOR LONG, TENSE minutes, the two warriors negotiated the winding, devastated streets of the waterfront. Everywhere the crumbling, decaying wretchedness closed in upon them, filling their lungs with the rank stench of rotten fish and human sewage. Vacant-eyed warehouses considered them like hungry giants, the broken boards of their walls grinning at them like jagged teeth. Workshops and what might once have been the homes of merchants and ship captains sagged and slouched at awkward, impossible angles, unimagined even by the eccentric architects of Miragliano's famed leaning towers. A filthy thing Ulgrin took to be a scrawny dog scurried down an alleyway, the bony remnants of a fish gripped in its mouth, but when it turned back, the dwarf shuddered to see a child's face, though he would still swear the limbs the creature loped away upon were not those of a man.

Furtive sounds, like the scrabbling claws of rats, followed the two hunters, dogging their steps like an audible shadow. Soon, Brunner and his dwarf comrade were catching glimpses of things regarding them from the narrow necks of alleys and the dark recesses of rotted doorways. They wore the most wretched of rags, mismatched scraps of cloth, fur and leather wrapped about scrawny limbs and twisted backs. Many faces were hidden beneath sackcloth hoods and thick scarves, others displayed their pock-marked, rash-ridden faces openly. The two bounty killers watched the ruins pressing in on them, having no idea how many miserable scavengers lay hidden within.

Brunner paused as they neared what had once been a cobbled market square. The stones were obscured now by the thick layer of semi-dried mud that coated them, the fountain at its centre long ago broken apart by the probing roots of weeds. A scraggly-looking man stood near the fountain, a long bill-hook clutched in his mitten-covered hands. The wretch turned his thin, boil-ridden face toward the two strangers. The eyes were as pale as boiled eggs, yet there was a cold, loathsome vision within them. The two bounty hunters simultaneously gestured at the dreg with their weapons, Brunner aiming his crossbow for the greasy forehead, Ulgrin hefting his massive great axe in a motion that promised a swift and messy demise.

The old wretch seemed unconcerned by the display, standing his ground with a deliberate calmness. As the two killers strode closer, they could smell the rotting odour crawling from the man's diseased skin, see the watery filth oozing from his sores. The apparition did not seem to mind their scrutiny, favouring the two with a gap-toothed idiot's grin. Brunner noted that the man's eyes were focused intently upon himself, their bleary gaze matching his own icy stare. Then, for the briefest of instants, the eyes flickered, looking away from the bounty hunter, gazing instead on the ramshackle guildhall that fronted upon the square.

In an instant, Brunner spun, firing his crossbow as the first of the lurking ambushers leapt from the building. The target of his first bolt was garbed from head to toe in slimy rags and as the bolt smashed into its chest, the cry that sounded from the creature was more like the chirp of a frog than the scream of a man. A second bolt ripped through the throat of the wretch immediately behind the slimy frog-man, pitching him to the ground to gargle upon his own fluids.

Beside the bounty hunter, Ulgrin leapt into action, charging into the sudden surge of ragged attackers that swarmed up the narrow street they had so recently travelled. A ropy limb holding a fish-bone knife flew off into the mob, even as its former owner howled in agony. The frenzied mob pressed forward, heedless of the dwarf's brutal axe, stabbing at him with crude spears and such base weapons as bits of jagged glass and sharpened stone. Ulgrin sent a leprous woman's head flying from its shoulders, only to have a spear-wielding hunchback push the still trembling body aside to stab at his prey. A twisted man with eyes on the sides of his head followed close on the hunchback, slashing at Ulgrin with a morning star fashioned from a belaying pin and a number of nails.

Brunner sent the remaining bolts from his weapon into the dregs swarming from the guildhall, dropping one with every shot. With the weapon spent, and no time to reload, he let it fall to the ground and drew his pistol from its holster, calmly exploding the head of a screaming wretch who hoped to cave in the bounty hunter's skull with a stone hammer. With even this weapon expended, Brunner pulled Drakesmalice from its sheath, the sword slashing outward the instant it was drawn, spilling the guts of an axe-armed attacker.

A snarl that might have come from some feral beast, were it not for the few syllables of the Bretonnian tongue mixed into it, caused the bounty killer to twist his head around. The wretch that had awaited the two men in the square was now entering the fray, spinning the bill-hook with an elaborate, yet murderous, skill. Brunner watched the madman advance with misgiving. The bill-hook was effectively a polearm, giving the villain a much longer reach than the bounty hunter's sword. And with a pack of howling peasants closing upon him, Brunner did not have the time to spend warding off the wretch's attacks until he could move in for the kill. Snarling an oath of his own, the bounty killer palmed the small pouch of salt hidden within his glove. Puncturing the fragile bag, Brunner cast the grainy mineral into the face of his approaching enemy.

Brunner's enemy gave voice to an undulating cry of such agony and mortal terror that even the two bounty hunters were momentarily stunned. The attacking mob fell away, creeping back from the ghastly tableau. As the wretch's bloodied hands fell away from his face, Brunner could see the steaming muck that dribbled from his now empty eye sockets. Whatever mutating taint had afflicted the dreg's eyes, it had reacted most spectacularly to the touch of clean salt. The screaming man crumpled to his knees, grinding his face into the muck in a vain, desperate effort to soothe his horrible injury.

The two bounty hunters used the momentary respite to retreat deeper into the square. Standing back to back, the two killers watched as their malformed attackers began to regroup. The mob spread out into the square, chittering and cackling with voices both mad and inhuman.

'I thought you said you were going to make a break for it?' Ulgrin mumbled to the other bounty hunter as the disfigured mob began to encircle them.

'I reasoned that a braggart like yourself wouldn't keep them occupied long enough to do me any good,' Brunner responded.

A huge, lanky brute with something crawling inside his mouth that was too thick to be a tongue, was eyeing the bounty killer, a curved, scimitar-like blade fashioned from a piece of anchor gripped in his meaty paws. The dreg opened his mouth to shout some battle cry, or else to simply howl in animalistic fury, when a black-feathered arrow suddenly sprouted from his forehead. The big brute fell instantly, crushing a smaller wretch who failed to leap away from the toppling corpse.

The mob set up a loud cry of terror and fear, racing back into rotted buildings and down narrow alleys, many of them dropping their makeshift weapons in their disorderly rout. Ulgrin set up a loud laugh, chiding the retreating murderers for their cowardice. Brunner paid more attention to the small company of armed men who had appeared on the other side of the square.

There were seven in all. Six of the men were on foot, garbed in suits of rusted chainmail over which they wore tattered black and gold mantles. Half of the force bore Bretonnian longbows, quivers of black-fletched arrows hanging from their belts, the other three carried antique halberds that looked to have seen a few too many wars in their centuries of use. The seventh man was mounted, his steed a midnight black that reminded Brunner of his own warhorse, Fiend. The plate armour that clothed the mounted knight was likewise black, and the tabard and caparison of man and horse, though in better repair than the liveries of the men-at-arms, was black and gold.

The knight gestured with a gauntleted hand, causing the archer who had fired to return to his position among the other soldiers. Then the mounted warrior fixed his attention upon the two bounty hunters.

'It is seldom we receive visitors to our humble city,' the knight spoke his Bretonnian with a lilted, antiquated quality. 'I fear that the prejudices and superstitions of the peasant rabble are not very accepting of strangers,' the knight continued.

'Empty bellies and starving children have a habit of doing that,' Brunner retorted. The knight chose not to take offence to the surly remark, shaking his helmeted head sadly.

'It is true,' the knight admitted. 'Our fair city is far from its glory days and the minds of the common folk are plagued with doubts and petty fears.' The knight straightened in his saddle. 'Still, I apologise that you should be met with such discourtesy.'

'We accept your apology,' Brunner agreed, turning to recover his weapons.

'Though it might ring a bit more sincere if laced with a touch of gold,' Ulgrin informed the knight.

Brunner froze in place, looking closely at the mounted warrior. The knight's face was hidden behind the steel of his great helm, betraying nothing of the emotion that might be playing across his features. The knights of Bretonnia were quick to take offence to any attack upon their honour, and Brunner had begun to suspect that this strange black knight was more than a trifle mad. The bounty hunter braced himself for the explosion of indignation and outrage he was certain would soon issue from the knight.

Instead, the helmeted head regarded Brunner exclusively, ignoring Ulgrin entirely. 'If you are seeking employment, you may find the situation in Mousillon slightly less than vibrant,' the knight informed him. 'Still, for a man of such skill with the blade and such ruthless determination, I might have a position available.' The knight chuckled inside his helmet, a sound that reminded Brunner of the sickening, insane giggle of the jester Corvino who had summoned the daemonic Mardagg to wreak havoc upon the city of Remas. 'You see, we had a very nice view of the whole thing. You impressed me, and I couldn't very well let the scum butcher your bones. Not when you might serve a nobler cause.'

'You saw the whole thing and did nothing to stop it?' snarled Ulgrin, fingering his axe. The men-at-arms tensed, the archers nocking arrows to their bows.

The knight waved a dismissive hand. 'What is past is past,' he proclaimed. 'I had to make certain of the quality of my hirelings before discussing such complexities as payment.' The mention of payment stilled any further protest on the part of Ulgrin.

Brunner nodded his head in agreement that the issue was settled. He could even appreciate, in a way, the twisted efficiency of such an exploitation of the murderous wretches. Still, it sickened him to have slain men whose bellies had growled even as they shrieked their half-hearted war cries. It sickened him more to see such suicidal desperation so ruthlessly utilised.

'What is your proposition?' the bounty hunter asked, keeping his distaste to himself.

The knight looked askance at the crumbling buildings all around them, peering into the shadows. 'This is no place to talk. Every mouse has ears, after all. You will follow me to a place where we may speak more freely and more openly.'

* * *

THE PLACE TO which the black knight led the bounty hunters was just within the massive stone wall that had once surrounded the city. Here the ground was more solid, scraggly bushes occasionally poking through the sickly soil. The buildings were less dilapidated than those beyond the wall, though they were still a far cry from being well-maintained. Holes in the plaster and wood walls were haphazardly patched with dried mud and straw, gaps in tile roofs were stuffed with bundles of thatch. The few denizens of this inner district that the men encountered were still miserable to gaze upon, but their limbs seemed to match and what covered their backs bore a passing resemblance to clothing. The stamp of desperate poverty was still omnipresent, however. One old woman, upon sighting the approaching warriors, fished her meal from the boiling pot resting on the ground before her, cradling the half-cooked rat to her chest with a scalded hand.

At length, amidst the misery, the knight stopped before what must once have been a prosperous eatery and inn. The black-clad figure dismounted his warhorse in a single fluid motion, then turned his obscured face back toward his guests. 'We can talk here,' the knight informed the two bounty hunters. 'The owner of this establishment can be trusted to keep his mouth shut.' Again the sinister chuckle echoed from within the knight's great helm. 'Not that a man without a tongue can do much talking anyway.'

As if dismissing whatever threat Brunner and Ulgrin might pose to him, the black knight ordered his soldiers to remain outside, to guard his horse and ensure that their meeting went undisturbed. Inside the inn, the men found a large common room, a gaggle of mismatched chairs and tables staggered about the floor. A large fireplace, from which many of the hearthstones and most of the iron work had been stripped, dominated one wall. A collection of mangy, lice-ridden animal heads adorned another. A faded painting, depicting some past lord of Mousillon riding out to war, rested behind the bar, green spider webs of mildew already picking at the pigment.

The knight sat down with a bold flourish at one of the tables, indicating with an armoured hand that his companions should take seats beside him. The warrior looked away, stabbing a finger at the little, gnome-like man who stood dejectedly behind the bar. The man hopped into action, snatching up a chipped crystal glass and a clay bottle, hurrying to place both before the knight. Brunner noted the extremely pale liquid that the knight poured into his glass, wondering for a moment just how much water had diluted the brew. He also noted that the knight made no motion to remove his helmet or lift his glass. And, of course, the fact that the innkeeper had brought only one glass was not lost on the two bounty hunters.

'You spoke of a position?' Brunner inquired after the uncomfortable silence had persisted for too long. The knight seemed to rouse himself from some inward contemplation, lifting his helmeted head to stare at the bounty killer. 'What is it that you need us to do?'

The knight leaned back in his chair, his armoured bulk causing the wood to groan in protest. 'That should be obvious,' he said. 'I need you to kill someone. Someone who has made the atmosphere within Mousillon quite unpleasant of late.'

'I wouldn't think it would be possible to make this place any less pleasant,' muttered Ulgrin, picking splinters from the tabletop. Again, the knight chose to ignore the flippant comment.

'There is a malcontent, you see,' the knight stated. 'One whose interests are at odds with those of the other noble houses yet left to Mousillon. Often violently so,' the knight left the vision of murder and battle hang in the air a moment before resuming his speech. 'As you may know, after the heresy of Duc Maldred, the realm of Mousillon was effectively destroyed and the position of duc abolished by the king. Our best farmlands were given over to Lyonesse and the rest left to rot and fester in whatever fashion the gods might deem fitting. Of course, those of us who were left, after Maldred's madness and after the red pox had run their course, tried our best to rebuild our land with what was left to us. It is more by sufferance and indifference on the part of the king and our neighbours that we are allowed to do so. If any of them felt that our humble city was again becoming a threat, it is not impossible that the king might declare a new Errantry War to dispose of us for once and all.'

'All very interesting, I am sure,' Brunner interrupted. 'But how does all of this concern me?'

'I was just coming to that,' the knight responded, a faint suggestion of annoyance in his lilting voice. 'This miscreant I have mentioned, one Marquis Marimund, has made himself a threat to the other noble houses of Mousillon, and indeed to the city itself. Like a bloated leech, he preys upon this city, sucking the life from it, scavenging every last scrap of power and control he can seize. From his castle in the north-east quarter, Marimund's ruffians have made themselves the horror of the peasants, exacting a gruelling tribute from them, leaving nothing for the rightful rulers of the other districts to collect and claim. His thugs do battle with our soldiers in the streets, dozens of bodies are dumped into the bog each day, with no end to the strife in sight. But worse than all of this, Marimund has started to call himself Duc Marimund, and begun to cast his eyes beyond the walls of this city. That would bring down the wrath of the king upon us, and we cannot defend ourselves against his ire.'

'Why not attend to this Marimund yourself?' Brunner asked.

'We have tried,' the knight stated frankly. 'He does not fight his own battles but leaves them to his champion, an honourless brute named Corbus, who has yet to even be scratched by our best knights. His blade is swift and his strength is that of a titan. The heads of a score of heroes who fell before Corbus now grace the gates of Marimund's castle. And then there is his enchantress, a dire witch who now serves the Duc Marimund and his twisted ambitions. Her spells warn him of any ambush we ready to capture him. Between Corbus and the witch, Marimund has managed to keep himself beyond our reach.'

'It sounds like a challenging prospect,' Brunner said. He lifted himself from the table. 'But I am no assassin. I have come here looking for a man, a stranger to Mousillon like myself. I have no time to intrude upon local politics.'

The black knight's mailed fist came crashing down with such force upon the table that the rotten wood crumbled beneath it. 'Damn your insolence, sell-sword! You will do whatever I tell you to do!' The fiery words seemed to explode from within the great helm, echoing like the roar of a troll. Brunner's hand closed about the hilt of Drakesmalice, drawing it several inches before he was even aware of the motion. Ulgrin had fallen from his chair, startled by the violent outburst, yet was quick to regain his footing, and his axe.

Yet the tirade was over as soon as it had begun. With elaborate calmness, the black knight began plucking wooden splinters from between the steel plates of his gauntlet. 'For this service, I shall pay you the princely sum of one hundred golden crowns,' the knight spoke as though Brunner had never taken issue with the offer. 'As for this man you are looking for, I can tell you that yourself and your little friend are the first strangers who have found sanctuary with any of the nobles of Mousillon. Perhaps the man you are looking for has found shelter within Marimund's household. Otherwise, you should look to the graveyards and the bellies of the ghouls for this man you are seeking.'

'It is a simple plan, really,' the knight informed the two bounty hunters. 'Sadly, we need an unknown quantity such as yourselves for it to work properly. I had a very promising Norscan who happened into our city to serve the role I would hire you to play, but sadly the fellow simply could not heed my advice to stay off the streets at night. The ghouls, you understand.' Brunner had the impression that the face behind the helm was favouring them with a mocking smile. 'Luckily, everything is still in place, just waiting for a man of your particular skills. Tomorrow, in the old hay market, I have arranged for one of my squires, a man named Feder, to be collecting tribute from the corn farmers. Of course, Marimund will get word of this and send his champion and a gang of his animals to secure that tribute for himself. I'm afraid that quite a fight will unfold when Corbus discovers that the information regarding how many men-at-arms are with Feder is a bit, shall we say, on the conservative side. That is where you come in. You will intervene in the fight on the side of Corbus. Impress him enough and he is certain to offer you a position with Marimund's guard.' A chortle of anticipation bubbled from behind the helm. 'That will get you inside the castle, and get you close to Marimund. The rest, I leave to you.' The knight waved his gauntlet in a dismissive manner. 'Bring me the scoundrel's head when you are finished and you shall have your payment.'

Brunner glared at the arrogant armoured warrior for a moment, then thought better of pursuing any confrontation with him. The bounty hunter simply nodded his head, turning on his heel and marching for the door. Ulgrin hesitated a moment, then hurried after his comrade. When the two stood once more upon the desolate street, it was the dwarf who spoke first.

'Surely you don't mean to accept that braggart's offer?' Ulgrin inquired. 'One hundred gold crowns!' he scoffed. 'That might be pretty money, but not to someone searching for two thousand!'

'He might be right, if he's telling the truth,' Brunner observed as he began to lead the dwarf away from the inn.

A pair of the black-and-gold garbed soldiers followed them at a discreet distance. 'Gobineau had a definite purpose in mind when he rode for this place. If he's not taken up with any of our patron's friends, then perhaps he has sought shelter with Marimund.'

'What if that other possibility is what happened?' growled Ulgrin. 'What if the fool got himself killed or eaten by the scum that infests this dung-heap?'

Brunner smiled down at the surly dwarf. 'In that case, we're wasting our time.'

'Ah well,' Ulgrin sighed. 'I suppose splitting a hundred is better than splitting nothing at all.'

'Oh, he won't pay us,' Brunner told the dwarf, speaking from the corner of his mouth. 'He can't afford to. Even if we do all that he hopes, even if we kill Marimund, Corbus and the witch, our friend back there won't pay. They have peculiar notions about honour and nobility in Bretonnia. A knight may kill another knight, but for some untitled commoner to strike down even the most hated nobleman is a great affront, something that simply cannot be tolerated.' Brunner shook his head. 'No, if we were to kill Marimund, we'd be putting a death mark on our own heads. Besides,' the bounty hunter continued, 'I don't like being hired like some gutter-crawling assassin. There are certain lines that even I won't cross.'

'So what do you propose that we do?' Ulgrin demanded.

'I'll go ahead with our friend's plan,' Brunner informed him. 'It's far too good an opportunity to gain entry to Marimund's castle to pass up and it will convince our friend back there that I'm following his plan.'

'I couldn't help notice that you were referring only to yourself,' Ulgrin pointed out, his face contorted into a scowl beneath his dishevelled beard. 'What about me?'

'You, my friend, will need to find another way into Marimund's castle,' Brunner said. 'After all, we might not be able to get out the same way I got in. I'd prefer to have another route open to me.'

'And why does the dwarf get to find this magic entryway?' Ulgrin grumbled, kicking a loose corner of paving stone down the narrow street.

'I've been here before,' the bounty hunter reminded him. 'The castles of Mousillon all share one common feature, something of a rarity in Bretonnia. They were built with a drainage system, a network of underground culverts that empties into the Grismerie. Who better to send sniffing around for a tunnel than a dwarf?'

Ulgrin Baleaxe nodded his head as he considered the wisdom behind Brunner's plan. 'You always were a cautious character,' the dwarf declared. 'But I see the sense in these schemes of yours. When do I go looking for this secret slop chute?'

'When it's dark, naturally,' Brunner returned, looking past the dwarf to stare at the two soldiers trailing after them. 'Better chance of losing any unwanted hangers on that way.'

'One way, or another,' Ulgrin replied, his fists clenching about the heft of his axe.

'Just make certain you don't get yourself killed,' Brunner warned the dwarf. 'At least not until after we've found Gobineau if he's there and found a way out of the castle.'

Night had fallen upon the cursed city, casting its darkness upon the rotted ruins and festering slums like some dour priest drawing a shroud over the face of a corpse. Screams and laugher sang out from the desolation, insane sounds that seemed loudest where the light and life were least. The broken, burned-out ruin of one castle, which Brunner had been told once belonged to Duc Malford, glowed with an unearthly shine. From its darkened halls, the faint strains of a waltz seemed to issue, the ghosts of the perpetrator of the infamous False Grail and his court of the damned forever cursed to haunt the mouldering passages and corridors.

Ulgrin Baleaxe crept through the blighted streets, cursing once again the folly that had made him set aside the past and join forces with Brunner. The bounty hunter's plan had sounded feasible enough in the light of day, but now, with the desolate city seeming to crawl with unnatural, unholy energies, the dwarf was regretting ever agreeing to Brunner's plan. It was not the dark that so disquieted Ulgrin, indeed, he had spent most of his life in tunnels and mines far less illuminated. It was the wispy shapes he'd seen dancing about the collapsed balconies of castle towers, the disembodied merriment that rang out from the most dilapidated and abandoned buildings. The dwarfs were a people who venerated and worshipped their ancestors, to them, the thought of dead spirits walking the earth in perpetual madness and misery was an obscenity beyond sacrilege, a horror that plucked at the very soul.

The dwarf shuddered as furtive noises issued from an alleyway to his left. Ulgrin thought of the grotesquely oversized rats he'd seen beneath Zhufbar, their fur matted with filth, their chisel-like teeth gleaming with the fresh blood of their prey. The warrior shuddered, bringing his great axe down from his shoulder so that he gripped it across his chest. He'd already seen the loathsome, sub-human corpse-eaters once this night. A pack of the ghastly scavengers had erupted out of a similar darkened alley, swarming about the dwarf, clawing at him with their long black claws, snapping at him with their fanged mouths. Ulgrin had stood his ground before the ghouls, removing the arm from the boldest of the pack, and taking the head from one of its friends. That had taken the fight out of the others. They had sullenly withdrawn, retrieving the corpses of their former comrades. Ulgrin guessed that burial was far from their intentions.

A scream had sounded from the street behind him. Turning, Ulgrin had found that the soldier detailed to follow him had maintained his vigil, even after the dark had settled upon Mousillon. The poor wretch had fallen prey to a second pack of ravenous ghouls, the scrawny, leather-skinned monsters pressing upon the man-at-arms from every quarter, bearing him down with sheer weight of numbers. Briefly, the dwarf considered intervening in the fight, he doubted if he'd leave even an elf to such a fate. But the soldier's screams had suddenly died into a liquid gargle and as one of the ghouls turned its rat-like face toward Ulgrin, the gory object hanging from its jaws had told him that it was much too late to help the man.

Ulgrin listened as the scuffling noise faded away. Ghoul or phantom, whatever had made the sound was moving away from him, heading back toward the graveyard. The dwarf continued on his way, seeing the black bulk of Duc Marimund's castle looming up out of the darkness ahead. Torches flickered on the battlements and the dwarf could make out the sentries, high above. The sentries seemed competent enough, being careful to match their movements so that no quarter might remain unseen. The dwarf snarled a colourful oath under his breath. He had hoped things might get easy for him at some point during the night.

Even as he cursed his luck, the gods seemed to answer Ulgrin's complaint. A foul, raw smell wafted past the dwarf's nose, the stink of sewage and stagnant water. The dwarf turned from his contemplation of the castle's battlements and followed his nose. He had followed the rank stench for some time, allowing it to lead him down narrow alleys and across crumbling lanes, before he saw it, a slick of black sludge oozing from beneath the street. The dwarf hurried forward, scraping away at the muck and mud until he exposed the stonework beneath. There could be no mistake, the slime was indeed issuing from between two of the stones. Pressing his head against the ground, Ulgrin could hear the trickle of water flowing below. Surely the underground culvert Brunner had spoken of.

The dwarf lifted his axe above his head, driving it downward with all of his tremendous strength. The blade of the weapon sank into the join between the two stones. With an exclamation of victory, Ulgrin lent his entire weight into sliding the blade back and forth between the rocks. As he worried at the gap between them, the stones began to shift, crumbling apart where moss and mould had already weakened them. Before long there was a mighty crack and one of the rocks crumpled in upon itself, slipping into the darkness it had contained. A fountain of filth vomited from the opening, a black tar-like sludge that engulfed Ulgrin from head to toe. The dwarf retreated from the deluge, vainly trying to wipe the crud from his face and beard. After several minutes, the bubbling filth subsided, whatever blockage had caused it dislodged by the change in pressure.

'Damn you, Brunner,' Ulgrin swore, slapping a cake of filth from his helmet onto the ground. 'We're going to have another discussion about the split after this!' the dwarf decided. He sloshed his way through the abominable stream and gazed down into the culvert. It was a small tunnel, crude in the way that any man-built tunnel was bound to be. It was just wide enough for Ulgrin to fit into however, and high enough that the dwarf could walk through if he bent his body at the waist. An unpleasant prospect, but far more pleasant than crawling through the filthy tar that coated the bottom of the tunnel. Biting down his disgust, the dwarf dropped down into the culvert.

The dwarf's eyes, hardened by the perpetual murk of the mines and caverns his people called home, adjusted almost instantly to the blackness about him. Realising that his great axe was far too large to manage within the narrow confines of the sewer, Ulgrin strapped the weapon to his back, opting instead for a throwing axe gripped in each of his hands.

Ulgrin stopped for a moment to imagine Brunner, safe and warm within the black knight's inn, far from corpse-eating ghouls, laughing ghosts and tunnels reeking of excrement. The dwarf snarled a colourful curse on the bounty hunter's parents before beginning his trek into the darkness. He had not gone far, however, before a sound ahead of him made him stop in his tracks. It was a strange, moaning whine, somehow familiar yet magnified in such a fashion as to be unsettling and horrible. The dwarf's keen ears could detect the sound of something sloshing through the muck ahead, the sounds pausing every time the strange wail-chirp filled the tunnel, then resuming with a wet, slimy flopping noise.

The dwarf's sharp eyes could dimly see something moving in the tunnel, closing upon him with a strange, irregular undulating motion. Ulgrin fished a match from his belt, striking it upon the cold steel of his throwing axe. The light flared up, bringing a shudder of protest from the thing before him. The dwarf could only stare on in shock. In size it was no larger than a goat, but its shape was that of some gigantic frog. Webbed paws waved before its slimy green body, trying to ward off the light while mammoth black eyes blinked shut.

Ulgrin had only a moment to take in the shape of the tunnel monster, for the huge mouth that sprawled beneath its head snapped open and something wet and leathery wrapped itself about his hand, extinguishing the match. The dwarf struggled to maintain his footing as the loathsome frog began to retract its tongue, pulling the bounty killer towards its cavernous mouth. The slime coating the floor gave poor purchase for his feet and it was with a cry of frustration that Ulgrin slammed down onto his side. From his prone position, the dwarf slashed upward at the amphibian's ensnaring tongue, striking it a glancing blow with his first attack. Instantly the dwarf felt his hand released as the injured tongue snapped back into the frog's mouth. The dwarf could hear the *flop-splash* of the giant frog as it retreated back up the tunnel, no doubt to find prey that didn't bite back.

The dwarf lifted himself from the slime, recovering the hand axe he had lost during the brief combat when the frog's tongue had wrapped itself about his hand. 'Oh yes,' the dwarf grumbled. 'We are most definitely going to discuss the split.'

The now dreaded *wail-chirp* resumed, this time sounding from the darkness behind the dwarf. With an air of weary disgust, Ulgrin turned to face the approaching monster. The *wail-chirp* of the second giant frog was soon joined by others singing out from the gloom beyond it.

'Damn you, Brunner!' Ulgrin snarled as he prepared to meet the attack.

THE ROOM IN which Gobineau awoke was cold and dark and had the distinctive smell of an old latrine. The rogue groaned as his senses returned to him and the pounding inside his skull began anew. He tried to move a hand to press down on his throbbing head, but found that they were held, bound to the stone wall behind him by thick iron chains. The bandit licked his swollen lips. Obviously Marimund was taking no chances with him.

Things had seemed to be going so very well. He'd gotten into Mousillon without too much trouble, managing to avoid the more thickly populated slums and their perpetually hostile denizens. There were still enough men in the city that remembered him and had not become quite so desperate to murder indiscriminately. One of these old acquaintances had led Gobineau by the safest route to Marimund's castle on the edge of the city. The duc had permitted him entry into his castle without even any sort of haggling on Gobineau's part. It had truly seemed Marimund was pleased to see him after all these years.

Then things had gone wrong. It had started when the duc had personally offered Gobineau a cup of wine. Instead of placing it in the rogue's hand, the duc had smashed it against the side of his head, dropping Gobineau to the floor. Then the kicking had started and the duc was quickly joined by a dozen or so of his men. Somewhere along the way, he'd mercifully lost consciousness, to awaken within what must be Marimund's dungeons.

He'd have to talk to Tietza, try to get word to her of his predicament. Gobineau was certain that she'd be able to soothe her husband's temper and arrange to have him released from the dungeons.

'I would not entertain that particular hope,' a soft, melodious voice spoke from the shadows. Gobineau lifted his head, seeing a tall, slender figure illuminated by the light of a single candle standing in the doorway of his cell. As his eyes adjusted to the feeble light, Gobineau could see that it was a woman, garbed in a heavy cloak of red cloth fringed in fox fur. The woman's details were sharp and noble, and chilling in their impossible perfection of beauty. The long hair that hung about her shoulders caught the light like spun gold, and her eyes, impossibly, seemed of no less vibrant a hue. Gobineau had never seen one before, but he was certain that he looked upon the face of one of the fey folk, the mysterious elves of tale and legend.

'Why... why should I not have hope?' the rogue asked. 'Is that not the right of every prisoner?'

The impossibly perfect lips drew back in a soft smile. 'Yes, but your own hope is impossible,' the woman told him. 'Have you not wondered why Duc Marimund received you in such a manner?' As she voiced her question, the light from the candle narrowed, shining out like the beam of a lighthouse. The ray of light settled upon a skeleton shackled to the wall not three feet from where Gobineau was imprisoned. The necklace that hung about the skeleton's neck stirred memories.

'It seems the duc forgot to feed her,' Gobineau commented. 'I hope he doesn't have the same in mind for me. Starvation is a pretty unpleasant way to go.'

'I should not worry about it,' the elf told him. 'After learning of your tryst with his wife, the duc has had many years to reflect upon exactly what he will do with you. I am certain that it will make starving look rather appealing.'

Gobineau spent a moment imagining just what plans Duc Marimund might be considering, then decided that he certainly didn't want to be around for any of them. He tried to straighten himself as much as the shackles would allow, favouring the strange elf woman with his most ingratiating smile. He hoped that his face wasn't too badly bruised as to spoil the effect.

'You know, I am not an entirely impoverished man,' Gobineau told her. 'A bright, bold lass like yourself might make a good deal for herself if she were to help me.'

The elf's laughter was light, like the tinkling of tiny bells.

'You spoke much in your delirium,' she said. 'I'd sooner trust a serpent to watch over a songbird. Yet it is possible that you can help me. In your fever, you said that you were being hunted by someone. I would hear more about him.'

'And why should I tell you anything?' Gobineau demanded. The elf laughed again.

'Because as Duc Marimund's enchantress, the exact manner of your passing has been left to me to devise. How inventive your death will depend upon how much you tell me and whether your information pleases me.'

The elf witch's voice dropped into a low whisper that carried with it an overwhelming aura of command. 'Tell me what you know of the man they call Brunner.'

CHAPTER FIVE

SQUIRE FEDER WAS an unpleasant man to look upon. A quarter of his teeth were missing, victims of his violent temper and proclivity for engaging in fierce brawls when deep in his cups. His nose had been bent at an awkward angle by some bruiser's fist, spoiling the symmetry of his face. As though not already ugly enough to look upon, the squire's skin had contracted a livid red rash, some noxious yet non-lethal reminder of the dread red pox that had once decimated Mousillon. It was a commonly held superstition in the cursed city that the 'Blood Blight' only afflicted the cruellest and most wicked of the city's population, a curse visited upon evil souls by the Lady herself. Feder did little to discredit such superstitions.

The squire was seated behind a crude table formed by placing a rotting board atop a pair of barrels. A third barrel offered the thug a place to sit. His bleary gaze was only partially focused upon the set of iron scales that had been set upon the table. The corn farmers were obliged to provide a full measure every week during the harvest for their masters, a measure that had to match the one which balanced the scales. It was an unspoken understanding between squire and peasant that there was a lead bar hidden within the bundle of corn which the farmers had to balance. Feder felt the pretence of doing things honestly would be a waste of everyone's time.

Today, however, Feder had even less interest in the proceedings than usual. The squire looked around him, studying the narrow streets that opened into the old hay market. Soon, the dirty little square would be resounding to the sounds of battle, the screams of the dying, the pleas of the wounded. Feder smiled in anticipation. He appreciated combat, looked forward to it like a lover's embrace. The squire shifted his gaze to take in the four black-garbed men-at-arms who stood near his table, leaning on their spears with feigned boredom, but whose eyes were watching the streets every bit as keenly as the squire's.

Marimund's lackey, Sir Corbus, was expected to arrive before Feder had concluded his collection of tribute, at least so his master had told him. Feder dearly hoped that the brutal champion would show, because he had another twenty men hidden within the buildings that faced the square. Even Corbus would have trouble dealing with such odds. It was a pity that his master's orders did not allow for Feder to remove Marimund's champion once and for all, because the squire was certain that this time such a feat could be accomplished. Still, orders were orders, and Feder had seen far too often what became of those who displeased his master.

The frightened screams of peasants brought the squire out of his reverie. The smile grew broader on his ugly face, and he loosened his sword in its sheath. A trickle of peasants ran into the square, hastening toward the lanes that exited on the far side. Those farmers who had already begun to present their goods became panicked as well, joining the newcomers in their flight. Feder did not try to hinder them. They would only get in the way of what was coming, and besides that fact, few of the farmers had had the presence of mind to recover their crop before fleeing.

The source of the peasants' alarm was a group of armed men, only five in number. Sir Corbus had a very high opinion of his own abilities and would have deemed it beneath him to take any more soldiers along with him on his sordid little raid than he was expecting to face. The knight's arrogant contempt for his adversaries was one of the most predictable things about him. Feder smiled as he watched the minions of Duc Marimund stalk into the square, their steps sure and certain, as though they were within their own district, not deep within that of another of Mousillon's ruling nobles.

Marimund's soldiers were armed and equipped slightly better than Feder's. Each of the four halberdiers flanking Corbus wore a shirt of chainmail beneath his crimson and grey mantle and the kettle helms that shadowed their faces did not display the same signs of wear and rust that Feder might have expected to see. Sir Corbus himself was an imposing sight, fully a head taller than any of his men, his towering stature enhanced by the steel wings that formed the crest of his helmet. The knight wore a suit of armour that had been stained a dark crimson, every inch of the breastplate and greaves engraved so as to resemble the scaly hide of a serpent. The face that glared outward from the open face of the knight's helm was at once handsome and feral, like some great beast masquerading as a prince of men.

Sir Corbus lifted his sword, snarling an unintelligible command to his soldiers, pointing his sword at Feder. Despite the lurking troops awaiting only his word to spring the trap, the squire felt the colour drain from his face as the fiery eyes of Corbus burned into his own. Suddenly, he was not quite so eager to accept the imposing knight's challenge. Perhaps it would have been better to have brought thirty men, even forty?

Feder began to back away from his table, the sudden motion causing his chair to tumble onto its side and roll away. The squire's bodyguard watched their leader's nervous reaction, uncertainty written on their faces.

'Don't just stand there!' the squire hissed. 'Protect the tribute, you fools!' The four men-at-arms lifted their spears, shuffling forward to place themselves between Marimund's men and the sacks of corn that had already been collected.

Corbus paused in his steps to utter a laugh fairly dripping with contempt. He interposed his blade before the nearest of his own soldiers, motioning for his henchmen to hang back. Feder marvelled as he watched the crimson knight stride forward once the advance of his men had been halted. Surely even Corbus was not so arrogant as to face four spearmen by himself?

Corbus gestured with his blade once more, pointing it toward Feder. Despite the distance involved, the squire flinched. 'I allow you the honour of facing me,' the knight's voice bellowed like the roar of a lion. 'Impress me and I shall show mercy.'

Feder backed away from the imposing warrior, sweat trickling down his broken features. After a moment he composed himself, snapping his gaze from Sir Corbus to his own spearmen. 'What are you waiting for?' the squire cried. 'You are four to his one! Kill him!'

The spearmen cast worried looks at the glowering red knight, then slowly, almost reluctantly, began to approach him. As they did so, the soldiers spread out, seeking to enclose their adversary within a semi-circle of spear points. Corbus did not react to their approach beyond a twisting of his lip and a disappointed sigh. The knight kept his intense stare fixed upon Feder, who now had his back to the warped wooden wall of an old storehouse. His eyes still bore into the squire's when the first spearman attacked.

The soldier to the extreme left of Corbus thrust with his weapon for the comparatively weak join between the armour plates that enclosed the knight's front and those that guarded his back. It was one of the few places where a spear might be expected to penetrate the armour and injure the man within. The man-at-arms, however, did not anticipate the speed and agility of his enemy. With an almost inhuman snarl, Sir Corbus spun, lashing out with his sword, parrying the weapon with such force that the spearhead and nearly a foot of wooden shaft was severed from his attacker's weapon. Unbalanced, the soldier fell to the ground, staring with horror at his mutilated spear.

Hoping to capitalise upon the attack of his comrade, the spearman to Corbus's right thrust his own weapon at the knight's back as he spun. Yet even as the soldier struck, the knight was recovering from his own attack. Corbus bent at the knees, dropping into a crouch that let the spear stab harmlessly into empty air. As he bent, the knight also spun his body, bringing the murderous edge of his sword sweeping around. The sharp steel edge passed beneath the out-thrust spear, gnawing through the leg of the man who wielded it. The soldier spilled to the ground, shrieking, as he held the bleeding stump that had once been a knee.

The other spearmen hastily fell back to their original position, risking worried glances back toward their leader. The disarmed soldier scrambled up from the ground, hurrying to rejoin his companions. Corbus noted the sudden movement and with astonishing speed fell upon the fleeing man, his sword slashing downward and opening the soldier's back. The man pitched to the dirt in a bloodied heap that moaned and writhed in its death agonies.

From his position near the storehouse, Feder had watched the entire gruesome display. He closed his gaping mouth, snapping out of his horrified fascination. The squire drew his own weapon now, but made no move to draw any closer to the knight who had challenged him.

Instead, the squire gestured with the naked blade toward the buildings that opened onto the old hay market. His signal given, the lurking troops that had been hidden within burst forth, spears, swords and axes gripped in their sweaty fists.

'Now you'll see what happens to curs who nip at their masters' hands!' Feder shouted, emboldened by the now overwhelming numbers he commanded. Corbus reacted to the sudden appearance of twenty armed men in the colours of his enemy with little more concern than he had shown to Feder's spearmen. The red knight stalked back toward his own halberdiers, who were themselves slowly forming into a defensive circle. Still, Corbus fixed Feder with a look that was more murderous than any the squire had ever met. Feder reconsidered his original intention to join his men in the attack. He'd stay back and co-ordinate things from a position where he might better be able to judge the situation.

He watched as one of the men-at-arms took a swipe at Corbus with a long-handled axe. The knight's sword clove through the man's shoulder and his return stroke sent the soldier's screaming head bouncing across the square.

Yes, definitely better to keep himself in reserve, Feder concluded.

BRUNNER WATCHED FROM the shadow of an alley as Feder's men sprung the ambush. He had to admit that the trap was a convincing one. It spoke volumes about how desperate the aristocrats of Mousillon were to be rid of Marimund that they should invest so many resources and so much effort in what was little more than a diversion. As the bounty hunter watched the crimson-clad Sir Corbus hack a chunk of meat the size of a melon from the side of a swordsman who had foolishly pressed the assault, Brunner also came to appreciate just how little human life meant to those same aristocrats. They would expend the lives of their own men without compunction or care, seeing them as just another resource to be gambled and replaced. The bounty hunter shrugged. Dwelling in a disease-ridden pesthole like Mousillon, he could understand how the value of human life might become a bit skewed in the minds of the city's nobility.

Ironically enough, it looked as though Feder might actually stand a chance of succeeding with the ambush. Brunner could see two of the red- and grey-clad halberdiers lying on the ground, and one of those who yet remained was favouring his left leg and the ghastly slash that had been dealt to it by an opponent's spear. Of Feder's men, only four of the ambushers had been taken out of action, three of them the handiwork of Sir Corbus. Always a quick judge of the fighting prowess of prospective enemies, the bounty hunter was suitably impressed by the amazing speed and brutal strength the knight possessed. It was almost as if someone had stuffed an ogre into the suit of red plate mail and then given it a heavy dose of Crimson Shade. Brunner had seen orcs sometimes work the sort of maiming, mutilating force that was behind Corbus's sword, but orcs did so with much less skill and efficiency. Still, Brunner calculated that even a formidable foe like Sir Corbus must eventually acknowledge the simple weight of numbers arrayed against him. Feder still had eighteen men, pitted against Sir Corbus and his two surviving halberdiers.

It was time to shift the odds.

The bounty hunter emerged from the alleyway, his prized repeating crossbow clutched in his gloved hands. Without warning, or waiting for Feder's soldiers to notice him, Brunner fired into the black-mantled attackers. His first bolt tore through the back of an axeman harrying the injured halberdier, the force of the impact spinning the axeman and causing his body to roll as it struck the ground. The second shot exploded the shoulder of a swordsman who had hoped to exploit an opening in Sir Corbus's greatly beleaguered defences.

The man cried out, dropping the sword from his now useless arm. Alerted to the backstabber's presence, Corbus spun, his own blade neatly opening the injured man's windpipe.

Two spearmen were the objects of Brunner's remaining shots, both men lingering at the fringes of the body of attackers, awaiting an opening through which to thrust their weapons. One of the men screamed in agony as his knee was pulped by the powerful steel missile, falling to the dirt and clutching his wound. His comrade, turning to see what had happened to the other spearman was rewarded with the last bolt, the steel dart crunching into the man's lower jaw. He crumpled into a gargling mass of agony.

The swift, brutal attack had its desired effect. The men-at-arms became disordered, their slow methodical effort to whittle away the defences of Corbus and his men broken by Brunner's unexpected attack. The bounty hunter smiled beneath his helm as he saw several of the black and gold liveried soldiers turn towards him, obscene Bretonnian oaths spilling from their lips. He knew that Feder had been informed as to the true purpose of the ambush, but it would be just like the cold, calculating mind of the man's master to also withhold that information from the men who would be doing the actual fighting. After all, the ambush had to be realistic.

Brunner let his crossbow hang from the leather strap that was affixed to its stock and wrapped about his own shoulders. The bounty hunter replaced it with the cold steel of Drakesmalice and the gaping barrel of his pistol. He suspected that the men rushing toward him did so not merely from anger at the bounty hunter's intrusion into their trap, but from thoughts that Brunner would prove a much easier kill than Sir Corbus. The bounty hunter smiled grimly once more. That was an illusion he would very quickly dissuade them of.

The foremost of the men-at-arms was thrown back as Brunner's pistol sent a bullet slamming into the man's chest. The loud report of the firearm was amplified by the narrow square, causing weird echoes as the sound danced amid the broken walls and rotting shingles. The three men who had followed after him came to a stop as though they had struck an invisible wall. Gunpowder was a rare thing in Bretonnia, and seldom employed in weapons. To the men-at-arms, the sudden death of their companion seemed an act of sorcery, and it was with the awe and horror of such dark magics that they regarded the smoking ruin left at the centre of his torso.

Brunner did not allow the men time to snap out of their shock, lunging forward into their midst before they had begun to recover. The bounty hunter's longsword slashed down the shoulder and chest of one startled spearman, dropping him before he could even raise his weapon. The swordsman beside him was given a killing thrust to his stomach, Drakesmalice's keen edge tearing through the antique leather armour that enclosed the man's body as easily as parchment. The third attacker saw the bleeding bodies of his comrades and gave voice to a pathetic cry of terror, flinging his weapon from him and running with all speed for the nearest alleyway.

Brunner looked up from his handiwork, not surprised to see that the other remaining men-at-arms had fallen into a rout, scattering across the hay market like rats flying from a sinking ship. Three more of their number had been killed, the bodies bearing the butchering wounds of Sir Corbus's sword. The red knight was glowering at the fleeing men, clenching his mailed fists in silent frustration. Then his gaze turned toward the storehouse at the far end of the square. The knight stooped and lifted a halberd dropped by one of his slain soldiers. Corbus hefted the heavy weapon in his hand, as though judging its weight and balance. Before Brunner could grasp what the knight was doing, Corbus drew his body back and threw the heavy halberd across the square as effortlessly as though it were a javelin. The halberd crashed into the door of the storehouse with a meaty *thunk* and the shriek of splintered wood. The rotten wood of the door gave way as the dead weight behind it toppled forward, the blade of the halberd embedded in the dead man's chest. The bounty hunter decided that Feder should probably have found a better place to hide.

The red knight turned away from his amazing feat, a deep and satisfied smile on his face. He paused, staring intently at the bloody carnage all around him, then made his way toward the bounty hunter. He found Brunner recovering his crossbow bolt from the skull of a spearman. Corbus paused long enough to stamp the throat of the corpse's injured comrade beneath his armoured boot. The bounty hunter pretended to pay no attention to the knight's advance, discreetly sliding the hilt of Drakesmalice around so that it might be easily drawn.

'Your advent in this affair was opportune,' Corbus growled down to him. 'I find myself wondering why? You are not one of Duc Marimund's men, and any man who would strike his enemies from behind and at distance is hardly going to take offence at an uneven fight.' There was both challenge and suspicion in the knight's voice, and Brunner had the impression that it was but the tip of a vast iceberg of rage boiling within the knight.

'You are quite correct,' Brunner replied with an elaborate calm, stuffing the recovered bolt into a leather box fixed to his belt. 'I have no scruples when it comes to a fight. Results are what matter, not outmoded concepts of honour on the battlefield.' The handsome features of Sir Corbus contorted into a feral snarl as the bounty hunter voiced his disdain for all rules of combat. For a moment, Brunner froze, wondering if perhaps he had overplayed his hand, antagonised the knight beyond any traces of gratitude Corbus might be entertaining. The knight's hand closed about the grip of his sword, and did not move from there.

After a tense moment of silence, Brunner continued: 'I spent some time watching the fight before deciding which side to help,' he admitted at last, moving to recover the bolt that had exploded the other spearman's knee.

'Why then did you help me?' Corbus demanded.

The bounty hunter stared into the knight's burning eyes. 'I reasoned that your enemies had everything rather well in hand,' Brunner told him. 'Certainly they might lose a few more men to your admirable swordsmanship, but in the end, they would carry the day. And they would hardly be interested in hiring a passing mercenary who saw fit to invite himself to their ambush. You, on the other hand, looked as though an extra man might come in very handy. You might be interested in engaging the services of a warrior who helped pull your bacon from the fire.'

Corbus shook his head, snorting with contempt. 'They had no real hope of victory. No matter how many of them they sent, I would have killed them all. There is not a sword in Mousillon that has yet impressed me.' The knight's voice fairly dripped with scorn and frustration. Brunner realised that Corbus was not boasting when he said that he could have slain twenty foes on his own; the man truly believed it. Brunner wondered if there was a sane knight to be found in Mousillon.

The knight gestured at the bodies strewn about, several of them Brunner's handiwork. 'Your skill with the blade is not entirely beneath contempt,' Corbus admitted grudgingly. 'But your tactics display no discipline, no nobility.' The knight sneered at Brunner. 'Such a man is like a wolf, a savage beast unworthy of trust, unworthy of honour.'

'Perhaps your master will see things otherwise,' Brunner retorted. 'Especially as you've lost two men this day. Possibly three, if your master does not have a healer in his employ.'

Corbus turned to gaze at his remaining men. The unharmed halberdier was helping the wounded one limp his way across the square. After a pause, the knight nodded his head.

'What you say is true, sell-sword,' Corbus said. 'Duc Marimund's forces have been diminished as a result of this treacherous attack. He may indeed find a use even for an honourless dog such as yourself.' The knight paused again, displaying his gleaming teeth in a mirthless smile.

'At least until warriors of quality can be found.'

BRUNNER WAS LED away from the carnage of the hay market, back to the castle of Duc Marimund. Corbus was at the head of the little procession, the two halberdiers following in his wake with Brunner forming the rearguard. The red knight paused several times to flash a hostile glare back at the bounty hunter, seemingly annoyed to find that Brunner was still there.

The journey took rather longer than Brunner had expected, winding through the rotting, dilapidated husk of the old city. Corbus seemed utterly unconcerned that they might encounter any wandering patrols in the service of Marimund's enemies. The memory of Corbus's insane boast that he could have prevailed against twenty enemies did nothing to ease Brunner's concerns. However, as luck or fortune would have it, the only people they encountered in their trek were some scrawny peasants, who quickly took flight back into the shadows of their hovels. Finally, when the position of the now distant ruin of Duc Malford's castle told him that they were nearing the landward edge of the city, Brunner saw the black mass of Marimund's fortress rise from the squalor.

It must have started its existence as a gatehouse, the bounty hunter decided, that role no doubt voided as the swamp beyond the walls had continued to grow in its rapacity and the once vibrant port of Mousillon became

choked with mud, squalor and ill-favour. With its old role
voided, one of the aristocrats of the city had taken it upon
himself to expand the old fortification, adding a curtain
wall that formed a large courtyard. Towers had come later,
and then still another curtain wall. Brunner could imagine
all the homes and shops that had been levelled to make
room for the castle's expansion. The result was something
as defended from an attack originating within the city as
the unlikely event of an attack issuing from the depths of
the swamp.

A narrow trench surrounded the three sides of the castle
that were within the confines of the city's outer wall. The
depression had filled with seepage from the swamp, foul
stagnant water from which reeds and lily pads protruded.
Brunner stared at the moat as they made their way toward
the drawbridge that spanned it, surprised to find a reptilian
eye staring back at him from the scum that floated upon it.
Apparently swimming hole was not one of the moat's other
functions.

Sir Corbus dismissed the two halberdiers after the group
had passed over the drawbridge and beneath the steel
portcullis that loomed above the castle gate. The two men
hobbled away to find relief for the injured man's wounds.
Corbus paid them no further attention, instead focusing
his intense stare on Brunner, snarling for the bounty hunter
to follow him if he still intended to see Duc Marimund.

THE DUC'S THRONE room was not unlike every other great
hall Brunner had been conducted into within the realm of
Bretonnia. A good deal shabbier, to be certain, but much
the same. Trophies hung from the walls, mostly taking the
form of the heads of mighty beasts slain in single combat
by the valiant knights of the household, but scattered
amongst them were the odd banner of some invading army
and the helmet of a vanquished rival. The animal heads were
showing signs of mould and rot, the old helmets starting to

display the rust quietly gnawing at them. Brunner imagined that Duc Marimund did not spend a great deal of his wealth on servants. The great hall in particular displayed the marked lack of a woman's touch.

Marimund himself was seated in a high-backed chair of some dark wood that had been polished to a bright shine. Brunner guessed that it could even be crafted from mahogany, a rare wood originating in the stinking jungles south of Araby. If such were the case, it was a relic from the days of Mousillon's prosperity, and as such a valuable symbol for any man whose ambition was to restore that prosperity. Any noble brought before Marimund could not fail to note the antique, exotic chair, and recall the splendour that had once made such things commonplace in the halls of the aristocracy.

The duc was a less imposing sight: of no extraordinary stature or physical strength, he was fairly dwarfed by the hulking knight he had chosen to be his champion. Indeed, the features of Marimund's face were soft, though with a cunning quality about them.

The noble's dark eyes were studious, cold and had a calculating shine to them. The duc wore his black hair cropped short in the rounded fashion favoured by many Bretonnians. His clothes were simple, a red tunic upon which was worked a rampant wolf in silver thread. The duc's leggings were grey, his boots black leather polished to a shine that rivalled that of his throne. A silver belt, inlaid with gemstones, circled his waist, a small jewelled dagger hanging from it.

The duc's keen eyes studied Brunner for a moment. Marimund turned to mutter a command to the two soldiers who flanked his throne, then returned his attention to Corbus and his guest.

'News has already reached my ears,' Marimund stated, 'of the aid you provided my champion when he was attacked by the treacherous forces of the malcontents within my city.' The seated noble extended a hand that was heavy with jewelled rings to indicate the glowering red knight. 'It is seldom that Sir Corbus is in need of assistance. However, you have the gratitude of Mousillon's rightful liege lord.'

Brunner took a step forward, ignoring the surly snarl that hissed from Sir Corbus. 'I am but a humble warrior, my lord,' Brunner told the seated nobleman. 'If I have earned enough favour with your excellency that you may see fit to hire my sword, then such is reward enough.'

'Reward?' repeated Marimund, as though the word was strange to him. 'You would have me engage your services as a way of repaying the assistance you gave my champion?' A cruel smile spread across Marimund's features. 'Are you not content to serve a single master?' the duc asked, his voice maintaining its cool, unemotional tone. 'Do not think I am unaware of your identity, Brunner. Nor why you have come here, assassin!'

As Marimund spat the last word, the guards flanking his throne surged forward. The bounty hunter, his body already tense, coiled for the attack, was in motion even before Marimund's guards had started to move, drawing his sword and pistol. Brunner was not certain exactly what had gone wrong, but the bounty hunter vowed he would not go down without taking several of his enemies with him.

Quick as the bounty hunter was, he was not quick enough. With a speed that Brunner would have judged to be impossible, Sir Corbus lunged at him, the knight's armoured hands closing about Brunner's own. The bounty hunter struggled in the powerful grip, feeling the awesome strength of Corbus as the knight's gauntlets clenched tighter. Brunner cried out in pain, unable to maintain his grip on his pistol. The weapon clattered to the floor, quickly recovered by one of Marimund's guards.

Brunner fought against the incredible pressure, striving to maintain his grip on Drakesmalice. But it was like struggling against a bear; the bounty hunter's efforts seemed to go unnoticed by the red knight. Sir Corbus began to lift his arms, pulling Brunner upward so that only the tips of his boots maintained contact with the floor. Then the knight began to twist his grip, savaging Brunner's wrist until Drakesmalice began to slide free of the bounty hunter's wavering clutch.

Brunner snarled through the red tide of pain pulsing through his body. Leaning back as far as he could, he sent his head smashing forward, the black steel of his helmet crunching against the knight's exposed face. Corbus gave voice to his own snarl, tossing the bounty hunter across the room as though he weighed no more than a child. Brunner struck the marble floor on his side, skidding across the polished stone. The impact forced the air from his lungs and succeeded in tearing his sword free of his grip. The bounty hunter rolled onto his back, dazed by his fall.

Corbus glared at the prone bounty hunter with eyes that no longer resembled anything human but glowed red within the dim light of the great hall, like twin pools of blood. The greasy, translucent treacle that flowed from where Brunner's helmet had broken the knight's nose was no such thing as should flow through the veins of mortal men.

The knight stalked forward, not deigning to draw his blade. 'I generally do not lower myself to preying upon beasts,' Corbus hissed, his voice brimming with fury. 'But I find myself of a mind to make an exception.' The knight smiled again, this time displaying his powerful wolf-like canines. The enraged vampire reached down and gripped the front of Brunner's armour, lifting him from the floor with one hand while the other bent the bounty hunter's head back, exposing his neck.

'He is of no use to you dead,' a soft, melodious voice cautioned. During the combat, another figure had emerged from behind the duc's throne: a tall, slender woman garbed in a red flowing gown. She laid a delicate pale hand upon the armrest of Marimund's throne.

'Ah,' smirked the nobleman, 'but it is so rare that I am allowed to enjoy watching Corbus do what he does so very well.' Marimund seemed to revel in the momentary flicker of disgust that crossed the woman's sharp, striking features.

'It can be dangerous to indulge such distractions, my lord,' the woman told him. 'This man may know things that we do not. For instance, can you be certain that your enemies have repeated their past error and sent only a single assassin?' The enchantress hid the satisfaction she felt as she saw Marimund's eyes droop with a mixture of doubt and concern.

'You are quite right, as usual, my dear,' Marimund concurred. 'It might be rash to waste such an opportunity out of hand. Corbus!' The nobleman's shout froze the vampire. The undead knight turned to regard its lord. 'I want that man alive,' Marimund decreed. The vampire scowled as though it had eaten something rotten, but relinquished its grip upon the bounty hunter, letting his body fall none-too-gently onto the marble floor.

'A wise decision, my lord,' the elf maiden told Marimund. 'There are spells I can employ to pry information from this man, information that might be of benefit when dealing with the men who sent him here.'

'Your sorcery certainly does have its uses,' Marimund replied, his voice as cold as a serpent's. 'But I am afraid that I am still a bit old fashioned when it comes to matters of torture.' He redirected his attention to the still glowering Sir Corbus. 'Take that scum to the dungeons,' Marimund declared, punctuating his remark with an imperious wave of his hand. 'Make him regret the day he was ever born,' the nobleman added. 'Just see that he remains alive.'

Corbus grinned, reaching down and lifting the dazed bounty hunter once more. The huge knight waved aside the guards who came forward to help with its burden, striding toward the great hall's exit as though the man he carried weighed no more than a chicken. From beside the throne, the elf enchantress Ithilweil watched the vampire depart, a worried expression on her face.

'Do not fret so,' Marimund consoled her. 'If Corbus does not get the information we require from the assassin with his methods, then we can always try your sorcery later. It should not be of any great importance if your subject is a little worse for wear, or missing the odd finger or two.'

THE WIND HOWLED, gnawing at the fragile walls of the Griffon's Nest. It was a fell, stagnant zephyr, thick with the stink of smoke and death. Under its unseen assault, the thatch roofing began to be stripped away, disappearing from the ceiling in ragged clumps. The proprietor of the inn, old Gaspard, emerged from the heavy bundle of fur blankets that covered his sleeping form. He squinted into the tearing sting of the wind, watching as the furs and strips of cloth he used to cover the holes in his establishment's walls danced and writhed in the gale. The sound was like thunder, a deafening din that grew ever louder.

Gaspard rose to his feet, at once struck by the foul stink that filled the air, a sickly evil smell that caused the bile to rise in his throat. Some of the guests of his inn were already stricken by the loathsome stink, spilling their dinners into the muck that passed for the floor of the Griffon's Nest. Gaspard, through determination, kept his own dinner in its proper place, and staggered into the bar room. The old man's mind was at a loss to explain what was happening. Storms were common enough, and they had savaged his ramshackle dive more than once in the past. But this felt different somehow, this breeze was not cool, but hot, almost sweltering. Then there was the abominable stench. The innkeeper determined to look outside and discover if the smell had afflicted the rest of the village or simply his own establishment. Perhaps a lodger had died the past night and gone unnoticed.

As suddenly as it had begun, the gale abated. However, though no more thatch was stripped away and the fur wall

hangings ceased to dance and sway, the sound of the wind
had not abated. It was still as discernible as ever, rasping
like some mammoth bellows. And the sickly smell had
grown as well. Abruptly, the entire building shook, rocked
as though a giant had kicked the inn's foundations. Gaspard was thrown to the floor and it was only with some
difficulty that the one-armed man regained his feet. He
could hear curses of annoyance and fear sounding in the
darkness as his guests reacted to the sudden tremor.

What was going on, the innkeeper asked himself? Steel-
ing himself to find the answer, Gaspard reached out and
threw open the front door. A blast of withering heat caused
him to cover his face, the overwhelming concentration of
the evil stench making him stagger. As he blinked through
tearing eyes, he saw a shape beyond the doorway, but it was
only a small part of some far vaster whole. There was an
impression of powerful muscles, red scales and black claws.
A hissing shriek such as might herald the murder of the sun
shook the night. The innkeeper screamed as he clamped his
hand to his bleeding ears, the terrible roar having ruptured
them.

Then the ceiling crashed inward, brought to destruction
by the gigantic clawed foot that smashed down upon it
from above. The sight of the timber and thatch rushing
down upon him was the last to fill the horrified eyes of
Gaspard. He was already dead when the flames came, rushing through the Griffon's Nest, consuming wood and flesh
and stone with equal ferocity. And as the inn burned, there
sounded once more the hissing roar of something that was
already ancient when men were finding names for their
gods.

In the morning, only a stretch of blackened slag marked
the place where the Griffon's Nest and the village that had
surrounded it had once stood. The few survivors hid
beneath rocks deep within the surrounding woods, their

minds half-broken by the awesome force that had annihilated their homes and families. In frightened whispers, they
gave a name to the mighty destroyer, a name as ancient as
that of any god. The name of *dragon*.

CHAPTER SIX

THE BOUNTY HUNTER awoke to find himself in a place of pain
and darkness. Memory struggled to return to him even as the
chill of the damp stone floor bit into the bare flesh of his back
and legs. Brunner clenched his jaw against the sudden red hot
rush of agony that shot through him as he rolled onto his
side. The stirring memories told him that Corbus had done
this to him, lifting his body like a rag doll and dashing him
against the stone walls with the knight's inhuman strength.
Yes, Corbus and the torturers who had assisted the monster
had been very thorough, brutalising their captive for several
hours before tiring of their sport. If his cell was not absolutely
without light, Brunner imagined that his body would seem
like a single gigantic bruise.

More memories began to trickle in. The red-gowned witch
who had stood beside Duc Marimund in his throne room,
and who had later come to the torture chamber to remind Sir
Corbus that their mutual lord and master did not want the
prisoner killed. He remembered Corbus's snarled oath that

they were simply 'softening him up', that they wouldn't even start asking questions until the next day. The witch had grown angry at the knight's surly, unapologetic remark, but had held her tongue, her strange eyes narrowing with a mixture of caution and fear.

Brunner slid his battered body across the floor, biting down on another cry of pain as his scarred back met a cold stone wall. He turned his face in the direction in which memory told him the door of his cell lay. He knew that two men had been left to guard him, men who had seemed properly motivated when Corbus had informed them to keep a careful watch on the prisoner. Brunner strained his ears to detect any sign that the guards had heard him. He needed time to think, time to work out some plan of action and time to begin recovering from his injuries. The bounty hunter worried that if the guards knew he had awoken, they might fetch Sir Corbus, so the inhuman knight could again sate his wounded pride with another round of torture.

The sound of movement and the flicker of light in the hall outside his cell brought a curse rolling from Brunner. Since arriving in Mousillon, he'd had nothing but ill luck and misfortune. Perhaps that was the real reason the city was called cursed.

He'd wondered why his captors had not bothered to shackle him to the wall. Now he had his answer – because Corbus did not intend him to stay in the cell for very long. The bounty hunter groaned as he struggled to his feet, forcing his protesting body to obey. He folded his hands together, making a hammer from his locked fists. If they thought to drag him from his cell, they would not do so unopposed.

The light grew brighter behind the door, shining through the narrow barred window, illuminating for Brunner the small extent of the miserable hole in which Corbus had discarded him. The bounty hunter braced himself against the wall as he heard the sound of iron keys rattling. Slowly, the door began to inch open. Brunner did not wait a moment, lurching clumsily at the retreating portal and pushing it outward as fast and violently as he could. The bounty hunter knew the rushed attack was foolhardy, but had decided that even if his bravado were rewarded with a sword in his gut, it would still be a much quicker end than being left to the mercies of Corbus.

Brunner's lunge forced whoever had opened the door to retreat to the far wall of the corridor to avoid being struck by the hurtling portal. He stumbled after the retreating figure, bringing his locked fists over his head in order to drive them into the skull of his enemy with the maximum amount of force. Brunner paused in his attack, however, when he found that he faced not one of Marimund's guards, but the witch who had shown such marked interest in him since his arrival in the castle.

Now that he saw her up close, without Corbus's fist smashing into his face every few seconds, Brunner saw the source of the unsettling grace which had haunted the woman's movements, the strange beauty that had characterised his impression of her. Marimund's enchantress was an elf, something that did little to ease Brunner's mind regarding his chances of escape. Even when dealt with from a position of strength, elves were dangerous folk to trifle with. Their minds were far older than those of men, filled with secret knowledge even the wisest wizard would find difficult to comprehend, their bodies possessed of an agility and quickness that made a mockery of even the most skilled acrobats. Brunner saw that Marimund's witch had replaced her red robes with a tight-fitting leather tunic, breeches and knee-high boots. There was nothing about her lean, supple form to suggest the physical weakness and frailty of those human sorcerers Brunner had encountered in his travels.

'Stay your hand, Brunner,' the witch commanded, her piercing eyes fixed upon the bounty hunter's. 'I have come to help you,' she told him. 'My name is Ithilweil. I have put a powder in the guards' wine that will make them sleep for hours.'

'Why would you help me?' Brunner demanded, his voice filled with suspicion. He kept his locked fists raised, though with the element of surprise gone, he doubted if he would be able to so much as touch the wiry elf woman. 'You are Marimund's sorceress. You told him I was coming.'

'Yes,' Ithilweil admitted, nodding her head in apology. 'It was I who told the duc about your intentions.' The elf's face twisted into an embarrassed smile. 'I have my reasons for not wishing to see Marimund dead.' This last was spoken in such a manner that it was obvious to Brunner that there was no love lost between Marimund and his enchantress.

'You fear Corbus,' the bounty hunter observed. A faint trace of the fear he had seen there before briefly flickered in the elf's eyes.

'Corbus is a monster, a foul perversion of the blackest sorcery,' Ithilweil stated. 'Only men, with their short lives and shorter vision, could have imagined such a loathsome use for magic.' The elf shook her head, sickened by the mere contemplation of such things. 'Corbus is one of the undead, a vampire. He clings to the martial pride and chivalric honour that were his in life, using them to try to prevent being completely devoured by the terrible urges that torment him. He took service with Marimund shortly after arriving in Mousillon. It is that oath of service that gives Marimund control over his vampire.'

Brunner fought not to show the horror that gnawed at his gut. He'd had encounters with the undead before and had always found their chief weakness lay in their lack of skill as warriors. But he'd seen Corbus in action, seen him to be perhaps the finest swordsman the bounty hunter had ever encountered. To learn that the unholy powers of the vampire were behind that blade… Brunner decided that the greater the distance he put between himself and Sir Corbus the better.

'That explains why you didn't want me to kill Marimund,' Brunner said. 'But it does not answer my question. Why free me afterwards?'

Ithilweil took a step toward the bounty hunter, reaching forward with a slender hand, the pale flesh hovering inches from Brunner's discoloured chest. 'Because I need your help,' she confessed. 'I am as much a prisoner here as yourself. I was aboard one of my people's ships, a research expedition dispatched by the arch-mages of Saphery. We were to collect specimens of the strange plants that the mystics of Araby employ in their crude experiments. But there was a terrible storm, one even our magic had not foreseen. The storm blew our vessel north, at last driving the ship into the mud banks that surround Mousillon. Though the city had an ill air about it, we decided to seek the assistance of its denizens in repairing our ship. The first poor wretches we saw fled at our approach, taking us to be daemons. But it was not long before they returned, in huge, howling mobs. They blocked our escape back to the mud flats, filling the streets and alleys behind us with their numbers. It was with great reluctance that the warriors among us lashed out, so miserable and dejected were their foes, and it was that reluctance that doomed them. They waited too long, letting the mob draw too close. One by one they were dragged down and ripped apart by fishbone knives and driftwood spears. The rest of us fled the only way we could, retreating deeper into the city. But we found no refuge there.

'In the end, only I escaped. My flight had taken me to an old, decaying stone chapel. I had sensed the sleeping power of the place, the faint echo of a magic that was kindred to my own. There was a man in the chapel, an armoured knight. It was Marimund, and he at once demanded to know why I had disturbed his devotions. I explained as well as I could what had happened, thankful that this man, at least, seemed rational. Marimund was silent for a moment as he considered my story. When he spoke, it was to offer me protection if I would serve him. With the sound of the pursuing mob drawing close to the chapel, I had no choice but to accept his offer. In exchange for my magical talents, Marimund keeps me safe from the superstitious peasants and from the soldiers of the other nobles, who hate and fear me as the Red Enchantress.

'I must escape. Time for me is running out,' Ithilweil continued, her voice filled with dread. 'But I fear to do so on my own. I do not know my way through the city, Marimund has always been careful to keep me within the walls of his castle. And my skill lies not with the sword were I to encounter trouble. I need a strong, skilled warrior to take me from this accursed place.' Her eyes took on a crafty quality as they stared deep into Brunner's own. 'One who has just as pressing a need to be far from this place as I.' She reached into a pouch fitted to the belt that crossed her waist, her hand emerging with a lump of dun-coloured paste.

'This healing salve will restore your strength and ease your wounds,' she told the bounty hunter. 'Agree to help me and I shall administer it to you.'

Brunner was quiet for a moment. He was not certain just how much of the enchantress's tale he could trust. She had betrayed him to her master once before, and Brunner could tell that there was something she was not telling him. Perhaps his escape was nothing more than an elaborate hoax, a way for her to outshine Corbus in the esteem of their master? Brunner considered the possibility, then shrugged his shoulders, a motion that caused a fresh jolt of pain to surge through his body. He had nothing to lose by accepting Ithilweil's terms.

'I agree,' he told the elf.

Ithilweil smiled at him, her pale hand lighting upon his forearm, kneading the paste into his skin. Brunner could feel his flesh tingle as the paste did its work, numbing the pain.

'I have brought the uniform of one of the guards,' Ithilweil said, moving her ministrations to the bounty killer's scarred chest. Brunner winced as her fingers passed over a jagged slash that recalled to him the brutal strength of the orc warlord Gnashrak. The elf did not pause, knowing that the bounty hunter's discomfort had no connection to her salve.

'You are much more likely to pass unnoticed dressed as one of the guards,' Ithilweil continued, a slight flush coming to her graceful features, 'than you are clad in naught but a loin-cloth.'

Brunner nodded his head in agreement. 'So long as you brought along his sword as well,' the bounty hunter told her. 'I do not intend to be recaptured.'

SEVERAL MINUTES LATER, Brunner slid the mail coif over his head, completing his transformation from prisoner into guard. The bounty hunter tossed aside the heavy kettle helm, which had proven too large for him. Perhaps the guard to which it belonged suffered from a swelled head even when he wasn't drinking drugged wine. Brunner grinned as he gripped the longsword that went with the uniform, carefully studying its balance.

'Any idea where Marimund took my sword?' Brunner asked as he made a few practise swipes with his new weapon.

'He has taken your equipment to his own chambers,' Ithilweil told the bounty hunter. 'Marimund was impressed by the unique character and foreign cast of your arms and armour. He is obsessed with all things magical and no doubt intends to compare them with the enchanted devices illustrated in the many scrolls and books he has collected.'

Brunner stopped practising with the stolen sword. He fixed the elf woman with a demanding stare. 'How well guarded are the duc's chambers?'

'When Duc Marimund is within them, very well guarded,' Ithilweil told him. 'However, I have arranged for the duc to be occupied elsewhere in the castle, a minor enchantment I arranged that should keep him distracted for some time. With him gone, there should only be two guards.'

Brunner nodded his head. 'Two men should not prove an insurmountable challenge.' A sceptical smile broadened across the bounty hunter's face when he looked back at the enchantress. 'Why did you arrange the distraction? How did you know I would ask after my belongings and not simply drag you to the nearest exit? What is it that *you* are looking to steal from Marimund?'

Ithilweil took her time in answering, her eyes narrowing with annoyance that the bounty hunter continued to treat her with such suspicion, and annoyed that she now had to give voice to the fear that had been gnawing at her for days, the fear that had at last spurred her to action.

'Several days ago,' the elf said at last, 'Marimund captured another prisoner, a petty thief who led the duc's wife astray some years in the past. This thief had on him a device, a magical talisman crafted by my people.' The elf's features became stern, as unyielding as marble. 'I cannot leave here without it.'

The bounty hunter pondered Ithilweil's confession. 'It was from this thief that you learned of me? He told you that I was hunting him? That is how you knew my name?'

'Yes,' Ithilweil admitted. 'When I heard the story of how you helped Corbus, I knew that you had made a deal with the other aristocrats, and there are only three people in this castle they hate enough to see assassinated. I could not trust to luck that it was Corbus they wanted dead.'

Brunner waved aside Ithilweil's explanation. 'If this dog still lives, I want you to take me to him.' The bounty hunter clenched his fist in anticipation of the gold Gobineau would bring him when he got the rogue back to Couronne.

'He is not important,' the elf protested. 'Leave him to Marimund. It is more important that we get the Fell Fang and escape!'

'He's important to me,' Brunner countered. 'As for this artefact of yours, we'll still make a detour in our escape to collect it. If Marimund has promised Gobineau as pleasant a stay here as he did myself, we may even find him most eager to help us.' Ithilweil opened her mouth to argue, but the bounty hunter motioned her to silence, gesturing for her to lead the way.

* * *

GOBINEAU STIRRED WITHIN his cell, alarmed by the sounds emanating from the corridor outside. Had Marimund decided his fate already? The rogue ground his teeth together. He knew that he shouldn't have trusted the elf witch. With a fatalistic sigh, Gobineau watched as the faint gleam of torchlight began to grow in the window of his cell.

The door swung open, revealing the elf witch. Gobineau stared for a moment, drinking in the sight of her lithe body in its new covering of leather, much more appealing than the voluminous red gown she had worn on their first meeting. So enthralled was he by Ithilweil's slender figure that Gobineau did not notice the armed guard with her until the man made his way into the cell. The rogue quickly forgot about the elf's shapely body when he sighted the sword clutched in the soldier's fist. Gobineau flinched away from the bared weapon, squirming against the wall.

The guard fixed Gobineau with a stern gaze, his icy eyes boring into the bandit's own. Hastily concocted pleas and entreaties died on the tip of Gobineau's tongue. A man with such eyes as these was beyond calls for mercy and promises of gratitude. There was more chance in reasoning with a wolf.

The warrior spoke in a harsh, brutal tone. 'Do you want to live?' he demanded. For the first time, Gobineau noticed the set of iron keys gripped in the guard's other hand.

'After careful deliberation, I would have to answer yes,' the rogue told him. He did not have any idea what was going on, but anything that would see him unchained had to be an improvement.

The guard continued to glare at the prisoner, making no move to unlock his chains. 'If I free you, you will do as I say until we have made our escape? Upon whatever gods you honour?'

'You cannot trust him,' Ithilweil stated from the doorway. 'Time is short. Leave him.' Gobineau rolled his eyes toward the enchantress. Most certainly it was an unwise man who trusted any woman, even an elven one. He scowled at her, then returned his attention to the soldier.

'If it means seeing this castle at my back, you can tell me to walk on fire, and I would just start walking,' Gobineau declared. The guard considered him for a moment longer, then unlocked the manacles fixed to the rogue's wrists and the iron bindings that crossed his waist. Ithilweil uttered a sharp whistle of disapproval from the hallway.

'By the Lady,' Gobineau crowed, massaging his wrists, 'you'll not regret this! My gratitude and friendship are legendary across all of Bretonnia! I am in your debt and shall never be able to repay you, though I shall endeavour to do so until the crows come for my eyes and the worms nip at my feet.'

'You can make a start by shutting that flapping mouth of yours,' the guard growled, turning to leave the cell.

'One question,' Gobineau said, hurrying to keep pace with his rescuer. 'Why free me? Not that I am complaining,' he hastily added. The guard shot Ithilweil a warning look.

'Strength in numbers,' he told the rogue. 'The more people Marimund is looking for, the less likely he is to catch them.' The soldier tossed the key ring aside, the iron ring clattering down the corridor as it rattled its way into the darkness. 'Besides,' he added, 'I don't trust the elf.'

That, at least, Gobineau decided, sounded very close to the truth.

ITHILWEIL WALKED AT the rear of their small procession, her face contorted with misgiving. Perhaps she had made a mistake in pinning her hopes on the bounty hunter. Brunner seemed intent on only one thing – securing the gold he hoped to gain when he returned Gobineau to the royal court in Couronne. He was hardly the noble hero she desperately needed, nothing more than a mercenary parasite, a lone wolf intent only on filling his own belly.

Still, there was little chance that she would have another opportunity. There was small hope that one of her own people would miraculously appear in Mousillon – let alone survive the superstitious mob that had claimed her own shipmates. She might hope for one of the wandering knights of Bretonnia to arrive, but after seeing the examples of Bretonnia's knighthood that Mousillon had presented her, she could hardly take comfort in that possibility either. In any event, time was running much too short. She had to act now.

The Fell Fang. It was little more than a legend, a sorcerous device crafted long ago by disillusioned princes from the realm of Caledor. Caledor had once been the mightiest of the realms of Ulthuan, and the elf princes of that land had ridden to war upon the backs of their mighty allies, the dragons who dwelt in the mountains of Caledor.

But over the ages, the dragons had fallen into deep slumber so that fewer and fewer of them would answer the call to battle and war. Some among the nobility of Caledor had resented the waning might of their realm that resulted from the long slumber of their allies. A faction had set out to restore their prestige by crafting sorcerous talismans that bound the sleeping dragons to their will, enslaving them and forcing them to rouse when their masters called upon them. But such a reckless and greedy use of magic had been deemed not only cruel and dangerous by the other princes of Caledor and the arch-mages of Saphery, but also a despicable act of treachery upon creatures who had been and still were the friends and allies of the elves. The disillusioned princes had been exiled, branded as the Grey Lords, never to set eyes upon the shores of Ulthuan again.

Ithilweil had studied the great books of lore kept in the Tower of Hoeth in her native Ulthuan, and in one of those books she had learned of the Fell Fang. The thing that Gobineau had brought with him looked very much like it – too much so to be mere coincidence. One of the exiled Grey Lords must have made his home in the colonies that had once existed in the lands of Bretonnia, and he must also have continued his experiments with the dangerous sorcery he and his fellow renegades had proposed.

Now Marimund had in his possession a device of such awful potency that he could not begin to appreciate it even if he understood what it was. The Fell Fang had been intended to enslave the dragon to which it was bound, but even the strongest willed of the Grey Lords had found such control beyond them. They could rouse the wyrms from their slumber, this much they had achieved, and they could even manage to communicate with the reptiles, their minds touching upon those of the ancient creatures in a spectral communion. But true control was beyond them, and the ire of the dragons when forced from their sleep had been a thing to bring nightmares even when dulled by centuries of memory. How much worse should it be were an unthinking, unknowing man call upon such forces without the slightest idea of what he did? An entire nation might burn if the dragon bound to the Fell Fang were to stir.

There was another danger as well: Corbus, Marimund's pet vampire. The undead knight had once been a noble and heroic example of his kind, if the history she had heard the monster speak was more than simple lies. Corbus had taken up the quest, riding across the green lands of Bretonnia, answering the challenges of man and monster as he found them, hoping that he might prove worthy enough to find the sacred grail of his land's patron goddess, the Lady of the Lake. But in his quest, he had been brought low, his courage and valour proven to be wanting and unworthy. He had encountered a black-armoured knight in the shadows of a haunted forest. He had answered the rival knight's challenge, and had contested his foe in combat for nearly an hour before his rival had struck him down. But the blessing of an honourable death was not to be for Sir Corbus. The other knight had removed his helm, revealing the pale features and elongated fangs of a vampire. Corbus had impressed the vampire enough that it had decided that he must share in its curse.

Corbus had been inducted into the foul order of the Blood Dragons, a brotherhood of vampiric knights who existed by their own twisted code of honour, a perverse mockery of the chivalry and martial pride that had filled them in life. They existed only to find foes worthy enough to face them in combat, the search for ever greater challenges the only motivation in the dark and miserable midnight of their existence, despising and hating the loathsome, uncontrollable monsters they had become. Corbus had forsaken his quest, slinking to Mousillon, the city that had been cursed by Malford's false grail, the only place in Bretonnia vile enough to endure the beast he had become. The vampire knight had found service with Duc Marimund, desperately clinging to the oaths of service and loyalty he had sworn to the nobleman as if they were the final bridge between the monster he was and the man he had been.

But that would all change if Corbus were to find out what Marimund had. The vampire had not been there when Gobineau had told the duc what the artefact was and what it was reportedly able to do. Marimund himself had not believed the rogue's wagging tongue, but Corbus would have. The Blood Dragon would have seized upon it with the same desperation a drowning man would a floating piece of wood. For there was a tradition, a myth common to the accursed order of vampire knights. If ever one of them should taste the fiery blood that flowed through the veins of a dragon, then that vampire would never again be stricken by the red thirst, never again feel the need to slake his unholy hunger upon the blood of the living. To achieve such a thing, Ithilweil knew, the vampire would do anything. He would be beyond anyone's control, even the oaths he had sworn to Marimund would not restrain him if he thought that he might rid himself of his curse.

No, Corbus would seize the Fell Fang and use it the instant he learned of it. Ithilweil shuddered as she considered what that might mean. The vampire would call up a monster that would be beyond its control, beyond anyone's control, a monster that would seek out and destroy the fool that had called it, and anything else it found in the vicinity.

She would have to trust that it was not already too late, that Corbus had not somehow learned what his master possessed and that Marimund himself had not been toying with the dread artefact.

THE TRIO CONTINUED to make their way through the narrow maze of corridors that led upwards from Marimund's dungeons, past dingy cells and iron-doored storerooms and the faded tapestries that hung like mouldy cobwebs from the dank stone walls. Ithilweil had directed Brunner to the safest route, the one that held the least possibility of being patrolled at such a late hour. True to her word, the halls had been empty of life. Now if the path she had chosen to bring them to Marimund's chambers was as easily achieved, Brunner would be extremely content.

A sudden smell brought them to a stop. Ithilweil's face contorted as the full reek struck her more discerning senses. Gobineau fell back a step, trying to place both the guard and the witch between himself and the corridor ahead. Brunner firmed his grip upon his sword, shooting a warning look at Gobineau as he stalked forward, reminding the rogue that whatever else might occur, he was not going to be forgotten.

A short, dark shape shambled into view, the stink increasing as it did so. There was a gleam of steel in its hands, the razor-keen edge of a massive axe. Brunner shifted his stance so that he might be better able to address the difference in height should trouble occur.

'Hand over that scum!' the shape snarled. 'Or I'll see your heads lying on the floor!'

'You're late,' Brunner replied. The dark shadow crooked its head, staring at the man who had spoken. A grim chuckle rolled from the dwarf.

'I didn't recognise you, Brunner,' Ulgrin laughed. 'A good disguise.' The dwarf gestured with his axe at Gobineau. 'I see you've saved me the trouble of fetching him.'

The bounty hunter spun, kicking out with his leg as Gobineau braced himself to flee back down the hall. Brunner's foot struck the rogue's knee, spilling the prisoner to the floor amid a flurry of curses and snarls. He loomed over the prone man, the steel edge of his blade hovering near Gobineau's throat.

'He was playing nice until you gave the game away,' Brunner snarled at the dwarf. 'Now I'll have to watch him twice as carefully.' He leaned forward, letting the blade touch the soft skin of Gobineau's neck. 'Or we could just settle for the reward his head will bring.' The rogue went pale as he heard Brunner's words, balled fists opening into empty hands.

'You know this disgusting creature?' Ithilweil interrupted, her features trying to conceal the horror she felt as her senses were assailed by Ulgrin's smell and filth-crusted appearance.

'My partner,' Brunner informed her. 'Ulgrin Baleaxe, renowned dwarf huntsman and mercenary.' Ithilweil stared even more intently at the muck-crusted figure. She'd read many accounts of the terrible war between her people and the stubbornly vindictive and irrational dwarfs, but had never actually seen one before. She rubbed at her nose as Ulgrin's stink continued to assail her. She had never imagined them to be so disgusting, wallowing, it seemed, in their own filth. Suddenly, war between her people and these foul tunnel rats did not seem so tragic as inevitable. Indeed, she marvelled that there had ever been peace between her kind and such offences against nature.

'I don't suppose you could shoo him away?' Ithilweil asked, her voice distorted by the fingers pinching her nose close.

'Not after what I've gone through to get here!' Ulgrin cursed. The dwarf gestured again with his axe, this time at the other bounty hunter. A clump of filth tumbled from Ulgrin's arm. 'I've had to hide from ghouls, sneak past ghosts and hack apart a street just to get here! Then I get half-drowned by a geyser of filth before crawling through a muck-hole no wider than a cart wheel!' The dwarf patted at the blackened patch of mud that had once been his beard. 'And let's not even start talking about the frogs!' he snorted. 'Those damn things are going to cost you fifty gold each!'

Brunner's eyes narrowed, his mouth becoming a straight-edged line. 'We agreed on one thousand, and one thousand it stands,' he warned. Ulgrin took a threatening step forward. An expectant silence drifted between the two bounty hunters for a moment before the slender shape of Ithilweil interposed itself before them.

'You two can argue over gold later,' the elf said, her angry glare encompassing both man and dwarf, an aroused temper overwhelming even her offended senses. 'After we do what has to be done and escape this place.'

Brunner and Ulgrin slowly looked away from one another, each of them casting a surly look at the enchantress. At length, Ulgrin shrugged his shoulders, adopting a less com-bative stance.

'My ancestors would skin me for saying it,' the dwarf hissed, 'but tall-ears here is right. Best we settle this when the timing is better. But I can tell you right now, I'm not splitting my reward with an elf!' Ulgrin tipped his head, indicating the way he had come. 'I'll lead you to the tunnel, but if we run into any more frogs, you're the one who gets to play with them. I'm not touching another one unless we agree on how much they are worth first!' Ulgrin turned to begin to lead the way out.

'We're not leaving yet,' Brunner said. The statement brought looks of shock to the faces of Ulgrin and Gobineau.

'Not… not leaving,' the dwarf sputtered incredulously. 'Why not!' he demanded.

'If there is some sort of disagreement,' Gobineau said, ris-ing to his feet. 'Why don't I just go with the dwarf, and you can go off and do whatever you have to do here.' The rogue put on his most disarming smile. 'I can assure you, I'm as eager as anybody to get away from Marimund, even if it means a hanging in Couronne.'

Brunner turned to glower at his prisoner. 'I'd trust you out of my sight about as much as I'd trust a hungry halfling in a pantry.' The bounty hunter looked back toward Ulgrin. 'I'm not leaving here without my sword,' he told the dwarf. 'Ithilweil knows where Marimund put it. I'd rather have you with me on this than kill you over it.'

Ulgrin chuckled at the bounty hunter's words. 'Kill me? I think you've got a distorted opinion of how that particular fracas would resolve.' The dwarf smiled beneath the filth crusting his beard. 'But I might help with this foolishness you are set on... for another hundred gold added to my share. And another ten for any more frogs I have to kill.'

Brunner eyed the dwarf for a long moment, then nodded his head. 'Watch the thief,' he muttered as he pushed past Ulgrin, motioning for Ithilweil to again lead the way. Ulgrin laughed, slinging his axe so that it once again rested on his shoulder. The dwarf took up position at the rear of the odd procession.

'Ten gold for a frog,' Gobineau whistled as he walked in front of Ulgrin. 'That has to be an even bigger act of robbery than anything I ever tried.'

'You haven't seen the size of the frogs,' Ulgrin snarled back.

Gobineau stopped, favouring the dwarf with an embarrassed smile. 'I'm sorry, but do you mind switching places. I'm afraid you're standing upwind,' the rogue told him.

Ulgrin sighed deeply, taking a step forward before realising what he was doing. With another snarl, the dwarf pushed Gobineau forward.

'Well, it was worth a try,' Gobineau commented.

Sir Corbus descended the narrow stairs that led from Marimund's cellars to his dungeons. The vampire's mood was foul, the thirst burning in his veins. It had all been that miserable elf witch's doing. She'd placed some sort of enchantment upon one of the duc's cisterns, causing it to change water into wine. Marimund was entirely enthralled by the spectacle, ordering every cask and barrel in the castle brought down and filled. Corbus didn't trust the witch, and wondered what sort of trick she was playing at. Perhaps the enchantment would only last for a few hours, or perhaps the wine would all change back when dawn broke. There was some sort of mischief in her magic, of that he was certain. Her excuse that her efforts had worn her out and that she needed to sleep and restore herself had rung hollow in his ears as well. Still, Marimund had been too engaged to pay her departure any notice. That was just as well, she would not be there to mollify him when the magic at last failed, and then Corbus would have the pleasure of seeing her try to appease the duc's anger.

Such a sight would bring Corbus a great deal of pleasure, not the least reason being the way the sight of all the churning red liquid filling the cistern had awoken his own thirsts. Corbus existed precariously, striving to control and subjugate the unholy hunger that always threatened to consume him. It was an effort not to fall upon slain enemies like a feral beast, a torment not to rip open the throat of a peasant in the street and drain her of her life's blood. But Corbus did manage to exert some control, denying his hungers as long as he could, until at last they built up within him to such a degree that it seemed he must burst from the pent-up demand. Then he would indulge his abominable hunger, falling upon the wretched prisoners Marimund kept in the dungeons for just such a purpose.

The vampire stalked into the guardroom that opened into the lower dungeons, then stopped. His eyes blazed into crimson embers as he saw the two men-at-arms lying asleep on the floor. Striding forward, Corbus lifted both men from the ground, one in either hand, and shook them like rag dolls until they awakened. Their stupor vanished in an instant, their eyes growing wide with horror as the vampire's enraged countenance glared at them.

'You shall wish your mothers barren for this dereliction!' Corbus roared. He flung one of the soldiers from him, the man crashing against the table that stood at the centre of the room. 'Go and check on the prisoners!' Corbus snarled as the guard rolled out from the wreckage. The man-at-arms scrambled out of the door that connected with the cells. A few moments later he returned, his face paler even than Corbus's undead flesh.

'The… the assassin…' the soldier sputtered. 'And… the… the one… the one who…'

'Go and tell the duc about the escaped prisoners!' Corbus roared. As the vampire spoke, his powerful grip intensified, snapping the neck of the guard he still held. The soldier's body shuddered and twitched as life fluttered from it. The other guard needed no further encouragement, racing past Corbus and toward the cellars.

The vampire's fury blazed within his cold body. So, the elf bitch was feeling tired after her efforts? Corbus would make her suffer for betraying their master, the faithless witch! The undead knight sank his teeth into the neck of the still twitching body gripped in his hand. The dying man's warm blood coursed into the emptiness of the vampire's husk. Corbus did not intend to satiate his thirst, just sip enough to make his hunger more keen, to make his sense sharper. He would find the assassin and the adulterer and the elf witch. Between the three of them, the vampire intended to have a full belly indeed.

DUC MARIMUND'S PRIVATE chambers were opulent, by the impoverished standards of the aristocrats of Mousillon. The floors were covered in rugs of bearskin and shaggy windswept hide, and even included a few patterned carpets from distant Araby, quietly rotting relics from Mousillon's prosperous past. The furnishings were likewise relics, dark wood from

Estalia, the Drakwald and even more distant lands, carved by skilled artisans so that every inch of their surface was engraved. In one corner, a suit of armour worn by a distant ancestor of Marimund's stood in solemn silence, the grail standing out in bright gold upon the steel breastplate, testament to the heights of chivalry and virtue the dead worthy had achieved. A great marble fireplace stood against one wall, bronze lions flanking it, their forepaws raised in challenge. A mahogany bath stood in another corner, a patterned screen imported from Tilea standing beside it.

One large bookcase held a variety of curious objects – a small, rusty dagger, a wickedly grinning wooden fetish, a battered shield. These were the enchanted relics Marimund had acquired down through the years, items about which the aura of magic had gathered. Upon a large table were strewn the oddities the duc had collected more recently, those which he had yet to determine if they warranted a place in his collection, if they had indeed been imbued with a touch of sorcery. Here rested the arms and armour of the bounty hunter, a dragon-hilted sword, a dented steel helm, a breastplate of gromril. Beyond those things taken from the bounty hunter, there were only a few other curios. One of these rested near the edge of the table, a long cylinder of ivory, engraved with strange lettering and curious carvings. Marimund had discovered the secret of the cylinder, twisting it open to expose the strange relic that lay within – a darkened crescent of hollow bone. This sat beside its casing, forlorn and forgotten.

CHAPTER SEVEN

THE ROUTE ITHILWEIL had chosen was a rambling one, straying down side corridors and circumventing the main hallways, but Brunner was impressed by how alone their path had left them. Even in the desolate environs of Mousillon, Brunner knew that a nobleman of such station as Duc Marimund would have a host of servants seeing to the upkeep of his castle and the personal comfort of his household. Then, there were the duc's soldiers to consider. Given the hostile climate in which Marimund was surrounded, there would be quite a few men-at-arms residing within the walls of the castle as well. All things considered, the fact that they had not encountered a living soul was quite remarkable.

Gobineau had an answer for that. As they turned yet another corner only to find the hallway beyond vacant, the rogue cast an appraising look at Ulgrin. 'It must be the perfume you're wearing,' the man quipped.

Ulgrin's face contorted into a scowl beneath his beard and for a moment, it seemed he might allow Gobineau a much closer view of his axe. Then the glint of greed twinkled in the dwarf's eyes, draining the hostility from him as though he'd been drenched in ice-cold water.

'Five hundred gold if he dies,' Ulgrin muttered to himself, reciting it over and over again as though it were some holy mantra from far away Cathay.

After several more twists and turns, Ithilweil motioned for her companions to stop. She removed a large iron key from her belt, slipping across the hallway. Pressing her long, slender fingers to the stone wall, she slid one of the bricks upward, exposing a hidden keyhole. Ulgrin shuffled forward to get a better look at the cunning piece of engineering, wearing a look of interest that was no less appraising than that which Gobineau had favoured the dwarf with minutes earlier. The enchantress placed a pale hand to her face, recoiling from the dwarf's filth-caked figure. Ulgrin grunted angrily and stepped back once more. With the dwarf withdrawn to a less odorous distance, Ithilweil inserted the key, twisted it in the lock, then motioned for Brunner to assist her. The bounty hunter nodded, stepping forward to press his hands where the elf had indicated. Together, the two began to push the wall inward, exposing a hidden passage.

'This was used by the old lords of the castle, back when Mousillon was prosperous and the noble families more bound by the laws of honour and propriety,' Ithilweil told Brunner as they stepped into the passageway. Ulgrin, pushing Gobineau before him, stomped in after the pair. 'They found that such a hidden corridor allowed a certain discretion when seeking out dalliances that might have proved embarrassing were they to be known.'

'Where was this when I was dallying with Tietza?' Gobineau commented, eyes carefully studying the passageway. The passage was narrow, the monotony of its length broken every forty feet by a steel lever mounted beside a cogwheel. As Gobineau inspected the nearest of these devices, peering over the shoulders of an equally curious Ulgrin, the elf stepped to the device and released the lever. Instantly, the wall that had been pushed inward shot back into its former place, taking with it the light from the hallway.

'And how might an elf learn of such a hidden path?' Ulgrin asked, glaring even more suspiciously than usual at Ithilweil. 'A dwarf might spot a trick like that straight away, but how does some slinking tall-ear pick up something of that sort?'

Brunner ignored the dwarf's surly voice, removing a torch leaning outward from an iron sconce fitted to the wall and thrust it toward Ulgrin so that the dwarf might light it, illuminating the narrow passage for all with eyes less used to the dark than the cavern-bred dwarf. Ulgrin's annoyance hissed out from behind his beard, but he soon had a small tinderbox in his hand. A moment later, the torch blazed into fiery life. The first thing the bounty hunter saw was the icy smile that Ithilweil had forced onto her face. She bowed with strained, exaggerated courtesy toward the dwarf.

'I have been a prisoner within these walls for some time,' she spoke the words as though instructing a slow-witted child. 'I have had many lonely days to wander these halls, learning every crack in the stones. In time, even an elf might be expected to take notice of so elaborate an artifice.' She turned away from the glowering dwarf, facing Brunner once more. 'These halls are sealed, so that neither light nor draft might betray their existence. We can travel along the length to the far end of the corridor, which will place us just outside Marimund's private chambers.'

'You spoke of guards,' Brunner reminded her.

The elf nodded sadly. 'They will have to be dealt with,' she replied. 'If we are fortunate, there will only be two. They will be stationed outside the door.'

The bounty hunter nodded his head. 'If the wall retreats faster from the inside than it does from the outside, we can be on them before they know what is happening,' Brunner stated. 'That is, if there are only two.'

'If there are guards,' Ulgrin snorted, 'then they are your problem. I'm perfectly happy leaving this place right now.' He turned a menacing eye on Gobineau. 'I have what I came here to collect.'

'Gobineau stays with me,' Brunner warned, glaring down at the dwarf. 'If you want to hang back in this passage, do so. But the bandit goes where I go.' Ulgrin held the other bounty hunter's hostile gaze, then smiled beneath his beard.

'As you want, Brunner,' the dwarf agreed. 'I might even be persuaded to help you. Say for five gold pieces each guard.' Both of the bounty killers fingered their weapons, waiting for the other to make the first move. Gobineau appeared at Ulgrin's shoulder, waving his hands to gain the attention of his captors.

'If it is all the same,' he said, 'why don't I stay in the passage with the dwarf? You can do what you have to do and we'll still be here waiting when you get back.' The rogue clenched his fist, shaking it for emphasis. 'You have my solemn word of honour on the matter.' Both bounty hunters rolled their eyes.

'Just keep an eye on him,' Brunner snarled, pointing a finger at Gobineau. 'If there's any killing to be done, I'll do it.' The bounty hunter looked once more at Ithilweil. 'Lead the way, if you would.' The elf nodded her head, clearly eager to proceed. She had watched the haggling between man and dwarf with obvious impatience.

'This way,' she said. 'We must hurry. I do not know how long we may expect Marimund to be away.'

Brunner and Ithilweil started down the corridor. Ulgrin Baleaxe and Gobineau watched the two walk away. The dwarf's eyes began to narrow with suspicion. Brunner had agreed to allowing him to stand guard over their prisoner far too easily. Were the roles reversed, Ulgrin certainly

would not have trusted Brunner with a captive worth two
thousand pieces of gold. The dwarf rubbed at his beard as
he considered the problem. He groaned in disgust as he
reached the only possible conclusion.

'What... where are we going?' Gobineau demanded as
the dwarf pushed him down the corridor, urging the man
to hurry so they could catch up with Brunner and Ithilweil.
'Aren't we going to stay here?'

Ulgrin snarled at his prisoner to close his mouth and
keep quiet. Very cunning of Brunner, very cunning indeed.
There was only one reason the other bounty hunter would
have risked Ulgrin making off with Gobineau while he was
away. Retrieving his precious sword indeed! That elf witch
had told Brunner about some hidden treasure of this mad
duc, a treasure that would make the bounty on Gobineau's
head look like pig slop by comparison. So, Brunner
thought he could cheat Ulgrin of his share in such a find,
especially after all the hardships the dwarf had endured to
sneak his way into the cursed castle! Well, if he thought
dwarfs were such fools as that, then he'd been listening to
that elf wench far too long!

THE SENTRIES STANDING watch outside the chambers of their
lord, the Duc Marimund, leaned tiredly upon their spears.
Theirs was a dull, uneventful post. The possibility of any
intruder making his way into the castle was remote, some
might say impossible. None had done so for years, not since
one of the rival noblemen of Mousillon had employed an
Estalian assassin to attempt to remove their master's claim
over the city in a rather forceful fashion. So it was that the
two soldiers were less attentive and wary than they might
have been, their minds more focused upon the dice games
unfolding in the barracks during their absence then they
were upon the quiet, lonely stretch of corridor.

Abruptly, impossibly, the wall across the hallway disappeared, replaced by a patch of shadowy blackness. Even as

the two men-at-arms snapped out of their fatigue and stared in amazement at the strange sight, a figure rushed from the shadows. He was dressed in the same manner as the two sentries, and the minds of the two guards puzzled over this as much as the hidden passage from which the man had emerged. Was he some herald, some spy of the duc's carrying with him a vital message for their lord?

The confused guards hesitated, allowing the other soldier to close upon them before another fact registered in their minds – the man approaching them held a sword in his hands. Far too late, the two sentries began to raise their spears. Brunner's stolen sword split the belly of one before he had even begun to point his own weapon forward. The man shouted in agony, falling away to clutch at his mortal injury.

The other guard fared slightly better, stabbing at Brunner with his spear. But the guard's reflexes were still slow, his reactions dulled by the abrupt intrusion into his midnight snooze, and the thrust passed harmlessly to one side of the bounty hunter. Safely past the stabbing point of the man-at-arms's spear, Brunner lashed out with his blade, the sharp edge of the sword crunching down into the side of the soldier's neck. A gargling scream rasped from the maimed man, and he too fell to the floor beside his dying comrade.

Brunner studied his handiwork for a moment. Armed with his own equipment, he'd have been able to dispatch the two men-at-arms much more swiftly, sending a bolt into each of them before they'd even registered the opening of the secret passage. The bounty hunter did not avoid combat, but he preferred to save it for occasions when there was a price attached to his opponent. Men who had no value were better disposed of from a safe distance.

'Sloppy,' the gruff voice of Ulgrin grated upon Brunner's ears. The bounty hunter turned to observe his companions emerging from the hidden passage. Ithilweil looked upon the two dying soldiers, her strange eyes subdued by a covering of pity. She shook her head, then strode toward the doorway the two dying men had given their lives to protect.

Brunner watched with interest as the elf extended her hand, the delicate fingers lightly touching the cold bronze handle. Behind him, he could hear Ulgrin snort with contempt. 'If she thinks that door isn't locked, then she really is an idiot.' Ithilweil paid the dwarf's jibe no mind, concentrating upon the door. Faintly, Brunner could hear her speaking in a strange, somehow musical language. Though he could not understand the words, the bounty hunter knew that there was magic within them, drawing power into the elf maid's fingers. Soon, the sound of groaning metal could be heard above the whispered incantation of the enchantress. With no further warning, the heavy bronze handle, and the iron lock to which it was fixed, fell from the door, clattering upon the stone floor. Where they had been fitted to the door, Brunner could see that the wood was charred and blackened. A faint mist of steam rose from the swiftly cooling lock.

Ithilweil indulged in a smug smile, directing the expression back at Ulgrin before pushing the door inward. The dwarf grumbled into his beard, pushing Gobineau ahead of him as Brunner followed the elf into Marimund's chambers.

'Any damn fool can pick a lock with sorcery,' the dwarf spat under his breath, his hold upon his axe a trifle firmer than it had been before the elf witch had displayed her magic. The dwarf was even more sullen when he saw the nature of the duc's room. There was a modest degree of wealth displayed in the furnishings and appointments that graced the chamber, but hardly anything that would impress someone who had walked through the halls of dwarf kings. Since deciding that Brunner's true motivation in coming here was to loot Marimund's wealth, Ulgrin had built up an image in his mind that might have impoverished an Arabyan sultan.

The dwarf's eyes narrowed, however, as a new thought came to him. Perhaps Marimund didn't like to flaunt his wealth? Maybe he kept it hidden, a small chest filled with gold coins, or a jewellery box overflowing with diamonds... Ulgrin stabbed a finger at Gobineau.

'Stand right there!' the dwarf commanded Gobineau, pointing at a spot almost at the centre of the room. 'Move and I'll chop your legs off and feed them to you!' he added when the thief opened his mouth to protest.

Ulgrin saw Brunner and Ithilweil striding toward a large table set against the wall, their eyes focused upon the clutter of objects strewn upon it. The dwarf smiled. Even the most slovenly of noblemen was not going to leave valuables in such disarray. He left the bounty hunter and the elf to their foolishness, dropping into a crouch and peering under the duc's bed, hoping to discover a hidden strongbox.

Alone in the centre of the room, Gobineau's eyes strayed from one bounty hunter to the other, then gazed longingly at the door which connected to the hallway beyond. Now knowing about the hidden passage, the rogue was confident he'd be able to elude Marimund's guards were he to gain his liberty. The real problem lay in getting some distance between himself and the two bounty killers. The dwarf might be distracted with his hunt for hidden valuables, but the sour glances he directed at Gobineau told the outlaw that he was far from forgotten. He decided that he wouldn't forget about two thousand gold crowns either, no matter how high his hopes to better his fortune.

The rogue pursed his lips, watching and waiting. An opportunity might yet reveal itself if he was observant and patient. And perhaps a little lucky, Ranald willing.

BRUNNER FASTENED THE weapon belt about his waist, sliding the familiar length of Drakesmalice into its sheath. There were few things the bounty hunter placed any value upon, but the famous sword of the barons von Drakenburg was one of them. With the sword back in his possession, the gnawing sense of unease and loss that had afflicted him since Ithilweil had released him from the dungeons left him. He felt whole once more, complete. He began to wrap another weapon belt about his body, this one holding the array of knives he employed in his bloody vocation, the heavy weight of the Headsman, a massive butchering knife with a serrated edge, resting against his right hip. His prized repeating crossbow and blackpowder pistol were also among the objects scattered upon the table, and their recovery brought a grim smile to Brunner's harsh features. Marimund would regret not killing him when he had the chance. Brunner would make certain of that before he saw the last of Mousillon. His hands closed about the carved spike of wood he had purchased from an impoverished Sigmarite priest in the Tilean port city of Miragliano nearly a year past. Perhaps he'd attend to the vampire knight Corbus as well, if the opportunity presented itself.

While Brunner occupied himself reclaiming his weapons, Ithilweil lifted the Fell Fang from the table, feeling a great surge of relief well up within her. The dread artefact was safe now, out of the reach of fools who did not understand its power, and even greater fools who might be mad enough to use it. The elf took the carved ivory covering, slipping it back over the Fell Fang, concealing the ancient tooth once more. There would be much more to do now. The bounty hunter would need to get her out of the filthy human city. She was certain that she could prey upon the debt he owed her for his own release to at least get her that far.

After that, things were more nebulous. She would have to find a way to get back to her own people, for the Fell Fang's potential for destruction and ruin would only be fully averted once it was safely locked away within one of the vaults beneath the Tower of Sorcery in Ulthuan. There was a small colony of her people in the city of Marienburg, far to the north. She would have to try for that and wait for the next ship to return her to her native land. The bounty hunter might be less agreeable about accompanying her that far; she might very well need to engage others to protect her on the long road to Marienburg. That was a problem she would deal with when the time arrived. For now, she should allow herself to enjoy the successful acquisition of the Fell Fang before it was too late.

If it wasn't already too late. The thought sent a chill of dread coursing through the elf, purging her of the relief that had filled her only moments before. What if Marimund had been toying with the thing in his examination of it? The fool might have accidentally awakened powers he knew nothing about. If the dragon that had been bound to the Fell Fang were still alive, it would be ancient, older even than the vaunted Empire and the kingdom of Bretonnia and all the other realms which the humans pompously called 'the Old World'. Dragons were things that did not diminish with time, but continued to grow in might and power until death at last stilled their fiery hearts. The monster bound to the Fell Fang would be a thing of such power, more like a living storm than a mortal creature. And if that fool Marimund had been playing with the Fang, if he had awakened the beast, it might even now be flying for this castle. Even now, wings of doom might be descending from the night sky to crush the city into ash and cinder.

So lost in these morbid thoughts of dread was Ithilweil, that she did not notice the path her steps took her as she backed away from the table. Her slender shape strayed close to where Ulgrin had ordered Gobineau to stand. The rogue watched her approach with baited breath, seeing an opportunity about to present itself. The outlaw's eyes narrowed as he noticed the object the elf held in her hands, the same object he had come here to try and sell to Marimund. The Fell Fang. Perhaps there really was power within the object,

Gobineau decided, if both a crazed wizard and an elf witch coveted the thing with such recklessness as to risk their lives to gain it.

The rogue changed his plan even as he moved forward to implement it. After all, why should he escape without taking something with him to redress the trials he had been subjected to? Gobineau was certain now that there was a very real power encased within the ivory cylinder. He was not certain how, but he would use that power, use it to establish himself in the luxury that was his due, some place far from jealous husbands and bloodthirsty bounty killers.

Gobineau caught Ithilweil by the wrist, spinning her lithe body around so that his arm wrapped about her throat. The sudden movement caught the elf completely off guard, so absorbed was she by her own thoughts of dread. Her reaction, however, was far swifter than Gobineau had allowed for, a boot smashing into his calf with a strength the outlaw would never have imagined within so lightly built a person. The elf spun away from the clutching brigand as he crumpled painfully to one knee. But as she did so, Gobineau twisted the hand holding her wrist. Ithilweil grimaced in pain and the Fell Fang clattered to the floor. Before she could recover, the rogue had regained his prize.

Gobineau twisted the hidden catch, satisfying himself that the hidden relic was still safe within its vessel. Looking up, the bandit shuddered. His sudden assault on the elf had drawn quite a deal of attention. The looks in the eyes of Brunner and Ulgrin Baleaxe were as murderous as any the rogue had ever seen. He began to raise his hands in a gesture of submission, fearing that he was only a few seconds from having the unpleasant experience of either the dwarf's massive axe or Brunner's recently recovered sword bisecting his face.

'Stop him from using the Fang!' Ithilweil shouted, momentarily drawing the attention of the two bounty hunters.

Gobineau's thoughts raced. Use the Fang? And exactly how by all the Dark Gods was he supposed to do that? Still, there was no mistaking the terror in the elf witch's eyes. Gobineau noticed that he'd been lifting his hands when she had shouted and that the one holding the artefact was poised near his own face. A sudden thought occurred to the outlaw.

'That's right!' Gobineau called out in what he hoped was a threatening tone. 'Take one step toward me and we're all in trouble!' He set the hollowed out bone against his lower lip, bringing another gasp from Ithilweil. It seemed that his guess might have been right after all. He really must remember to tithe a bit of his next haul to Ranald to thank the mischievous god of thieves for the turn his luck had taken.

Unfortunately, Brunner and Ulgrin did not seem to be sharing the elf's fright. The two bounty hunters passed a look between them, then began to circle around their prey. Gobineau swallowed nervously. Hadn't Brunner said something about 'alive' not meaning 'unharmed'? The rogue inhaled sharply, the breath rasping against the surface of the Fang. Ithilweil winced in tandem to the bandit's breath.

'Don't antagonise him!' she cried. 'If he sounds the Fang, we will all die! He'll call up a monster that will bring this whole castle crashing down about our ears!' The already pale skin of the elf was now the pallor of alabaster as the warmth drained from her flesh, cringing within her fear.

'She's right! I'll do it!' Gobineau called out, trying to add as much support for whatever nonsense the elf was shrieking as he could. 'You two had better step back,' Gobineau warned when it became obvious that the bounty hunters weren't listening. Brunner's icy eyes glared into the rogue's own.

'Do as he says!' pleaded Ithilweil. To Gobineau's amazement, Brunner took a step backward. The outlaw felt a smile warming on his face.

'That's better,' he crowed. 'Now lower your weapons,' he added with a hopeful note. To his relief, Brunner slammed his sword back into its scabbard.

Ulgrin looked at his partner, the dwarf's eyes wide with disbelief. 'Since when do we take orders from some hussy tall-ear?' the dwarf demanded.

'We don't,' Brunner replied, removing his pistol from its holster. Ulgrin laughed grimly as the bounty hunter pointed the intimidating weapon at Gobineau. 'I just decided I didn't really feel like doing any more work today.'

'How do you know it's still loaded?' Gobineau protested feebly.

'How do you know it's not?' the bounty hunter retorted, his voice as cheerless as an open grave. The outlaw sighed loudly, glancing about the room around him, trying to find some way to salvage the situation. To his left, Ulgrin glared at him, the edge of his monstrous axe gleaming wickedly. To his right, a much more composed, though still visibly shaken, Ithilweil was beginning to step nearer.

Gobineau imagined she might be planning on replaying the little scene that had initiated the stand off, and he didn't think his chances of overcoming the elf were terribly good. Before him, the infamous Brunner had a pistol pointed at his face.

'Khaine's black blood,' Gobineau cursed as he exhaled into the Fell Fang. Whatever monster the magic artefact was going to conjure up, it couldn't be any worse than what he was already facing. The outlaw screwed his eyes shut, expecting a sound of thunder, an explosive display of sorcery as some daemonic horror manifested itself in answer to the Fang's summons. Instead there was only silence. Opening his eyes again, Gobineau saw the elf witch shaking, leaning against a chair to prevent herself from falling, such was the lack of strength in her limbs. Not exactly some hell-spawned abomination with claws and fangs, but he wasn't going to complain. Turning to regard the bounty hunters, however, Gobineau learned that his desperate gamble had not been universal in its effects.

'I don't think they'll mind if he's missing his hands when we turn him in,' Ulgrin growled, stepping forward. Once again, Gobineau found his eyes focusing on the wickedly sharp edge of the dwarf's gigantic axe.

No doubt about it. The next time he passed a shrine to Ranald, he was going to set fire to it.

EVEN AS THE two bounty hunters began to close on him, Gobineau's luck reasserted itself. Without warning, the door to Marimund's room exploded inward, propelled by some tremendous force. All eyes turned to the doorway to see the red-armoured figure of Sir Corbus standing in the corridor. The knight's face no longer resembled anything human, eyes blazing with wrath, gash-like mouth parted in a feral snarl, wolf-like fangs exposed. The knight held his sword in his hand, but it seemed to all observing him that he was more likely to rip them apart with his bare hands than remember to use his weapon.

'Traitor witch!' Corbus roared. 'Is this how you return the protection and support your lord has given you! Freeing his prisoners and robbing his rooms!' A trickle of bloody froth oozed from the corner of the knight's mouth as he spat his accusations at Ithilweil. 'I'll strip the skin from your flesh and toss the screaming carcass to the rats for your faithlessness, slattern!'

So intent was Corbus on the objects of his ire, the figures of Gobineau, Brunner and Ithilweil, that he had paid scant notice of the room's other occupant. Ulgrin listened to the vampire's hissed maledictions, his own anger boiling up within the dwarf.

With a savage cry, Ulgrin lunged at the red knight, swinging his axe in a gleaming arc of destruction.

'By the gods of my ancestors!' Ulgrin bellowed. 'I've had enough of this city!' The blade of the axe struck Corbus's breastplate with all the strength the dwarf's brawny frame could muster. The metal shrieked as it split under the cleaving edge and the axe chewed into the flesh beneath. 'You're not going to stop me from getting out of here!' Ulgrin ripped his axe free, leaving a great gash in Corbus's chest, torn flesh and fragments of bone clinging to the weapon as it was withdrawn. The vampire's face contorted in an expression of still greater fury, but before Corbus could react, the axe slammed into his body once more, knocking the knight to the floor. Ulgrin stood above the snarling creature, chopping into the prone vampire as though hacking at a log.

'Killer frogs!' Ulgrin cursed, chopping into the vampire's chest again. 'Cannibal madmen!' Again, the axe was ripped free. 'Acres of quicksand!' Once more the axe rent the knight's breastplate. Ulgrin leaned forward to howl into the vampire's face. 'I've done enough work to earn ten times what this scum is fetching and I'll be damned if I'll just hand him over to some preening, posturing manling knight!'

Ulgrin stared into the knight's eyes, waiting to see the life fade from them. With the carnage he had visited upon the warrior as the dwarf vented his frustrations, Ulgrin was certain that he would not have long to wait. Instead, the knight's eyes blazed into pools of crimson fire and his mouth opened in a grisly snarl. The knight's right hand came sweeping upward, striking the dwarf with a strength that would shame a full grown ox. Three hundred pounds of armoured dwarf sailed across the room, pulverising the glass curio cabinet as Ulgrin landed.

Sir Corbus rose to his feet, simply tilting his body upright rather than lifting himself from the floor. The knight's crimson armour was a ruin of twisted metal, deep and grisly wounds visible through the rents in the armoured plate. Any one of the wounds would have been fatal to any normal man, but Corbus seemed oblivious to them. He took a step forward, his mailed fist closing about the handle of the huge axe Ulgrin had left buried in his breastbone. With a single sharp tug, Corbus wrenched the axe free, dropping it to the floor with such casualness that it might have been no more than a splinter removed from a finger.

The vampire's face broadened into a predatory sneer, the face of a cat preparing to pounce.

'The little man has seen many of the ills of this abominable city,' the vampire hissed. 'Now I shall show you the true nature of horror!'

Brunner had watched the brief battle between Ulgrin and Corbus with a gnawing sense of doom. He knew what the knight was; he had seen similar creatures before and his experiences had told him that it took more than a strong arm and a sharp blade to destroy such a being. As Ulgrin had hacked away at the undead knight, Brunner had shifted his pistol into his off hand and once again removed Drakesmalice from its sheath. He had seen for himself that the enchanted blade could harm beings immune to natural steel. Had not the blade bitten deep into the daemonic flesh of the horrific Mardagg during the death elemental's rampage in the city of Remas? Perhaps it might prove no less effective in dealing with the spectral vitality of a vampire.

As Corbus stalked forward, Brunner noted that the elf Ithilweil had fallen behind the bounty hunter. He could hear the elf muttering in the same strangely musical voice she had used before destroying the lock. Brunner hoped that whatever magic she might be conjuring, it was quick and far more potent.

'You would cross swords with me?' the vampire sneered as he stopped an arm's span from Brunner. 'I've killed men whose boots you are not fit to lick with but three passes of my blade! Amuse me assassin, before I cut your filthy soul from your mangy carcass.'

Brunner dodged the first thrust made by Sir Corbus, exploiting the knight's attack to slash at him with the edge of Drakesmalice. But the bounty hunter had underestimated the unnatural speed of the vampire. With a blur of motion, Corbus recovered from his thrust, bringing his blade sweeping around in a parrying block. Such was the angle of the blow and the tremendous strength behind it that Drakesmalice was ripped from Brunner's gloved hand, the longsword bouncing from the far wall as it was flung away.

'Die like the vermin you are!' the vampire snarled, springing forward, his fangs bared. The bounty hunter retreated back a space, bringing up his other hand, slamming the barrel of his pistol under Corbus's chin.

'Take your own advice,' Brunner growled. The bounty hunter's finger pulled the trigger, the pistol roaring in response to the action. The violent explosion of flame and smoke set the vampire's flesh smouldering, the lead bullet smashing through the knight's face, breaking his jaw and cracking his cheek before bursting through the edge of his left eye. Shards of bone and black ichor sprayed from the monster's injury even as his strangled cry ripped across the chamber. Corbus toppled to the floor, armoured hands clutching at the smoking ruin of his face. Brunner glared down at the monster then kicked the vampire, waiting for any sort of response, but Corbus was as still as the grave he'd cheated. The bounty hunter nodded, then fingered the carved stake he had bought from an exiled Sigmarite priest months before in Miragliano. Maybe a vampire couldn't survive with half its face blown apart, but Brunner didn't like taking chances. Every tale he'd ever heard agreed that a vampire most certainly didn't survive a wooden stake stabbed through its heart.

'You can quit your spellcraft,' Brunner said, noticing that Ithilweil had not ceased her conjuring. 'He's as dead as he's going to get,' he elaborated, fingering the stake. 'Or at least he's about to be.' He glanced back at the elf, surprised by what he saw. The enchantress had ceased her conjuring, whatever spell she had worked upon Corbus now at its end. The bounty hunter had no way of knowing that it had been the elf's spells that had preserved him, that had slowed the Blood Dragon's unnatural reflexes to a point where a mere mortal might gain even the faintest hope of besting him. Now Ithilweil seemed oblivious to the vampire, oblivious to everything. Her eyes were focused upon the ceiling, darting back and forth as though she expected a horde of daemons to drop down upon her. The strange tongue she spoke seemed to be locked into a rhythm, repeating itself over and over. Her entire body was trembling, shaking like a river reed in a winter wind. Brunner took a step towards her, reaching out and carefully touching her shoulder. Ithilweil's head snapped around, her fear-filled eyes fixing upon the bounty hunter. The singsong rhyme died as reason reasserted itself within the enchantress's mind.

'The Fang!' she gasped. 'The fool used the Fang! He's called death down upon us all!'

The mention of 'the fool' caused Brunner to forget his interest in the elf woman. He spun back around, eyes scouring the room. He saw Ulgrin rising from the ruin of the curio cabinet, the dwarf's meaty hand rubbing at his bruised head. He saw Drakesmalice lying near the wall. But he saw no sign of Gobineau. The rogue had taken advantage of the vampire's attack to slip away once again. Brunner cursed under his breath. Forget taking the man's hands, when he caught up with the outlaw, he was going to take his legs to make sure the scum didn't run off again.

The bounty hunter shook his head. Ulgrin was right, catching this vermin was more work than it was worth. A cold smile flickered on Brunner's face. At least he'd be able to repay Corbus for the fun times he and the vampire had shared. But as Brunner turned back toward the vampire's body, he cursed again. The red armour was still there, but it was now empty. Looking past the spot, the bounty hunter saw a great black rat with a mangled face pause at the mouth of a crack in the wall to glare malevolently back at him. Brunner reached for a throwing knife, but as he started to move, the rat scuttled away down the hole.

'The Fang,' Ithilweil was beside him once more. 'We have to get it back! Before it's too late.' Brunner ignored her, walking to the wall and retrieving Drakesmalice. He looked back at Ulgrin, watching as the dwarf stumbled groggily away from the ruined cabinet. He'd be just as happy to leave the dwarf, but he needed to know where the tunnel entrance to Marimund's castle was.

The bounty hunter grabbed the dwarf, pushing him toward the door.

'I only care about catching that scum,' Brunner told the elf. 'That nick nack he stole from you is your concern.' The bounty hunter cast a worried look at the rat hole. 'You help us find Gobineau, you help yourself.' He did not wait for Ithilweil's reply, but strode out into the hallway, leaving her to make her own decision.

The elf hesitated a moment, then hurried after the departing bounty hunters. She'd made her play, now she had to see it through.

CHAPTER EIGHT

THE QUARTET OF men-at-arms standing watch in the guard-room behind the ponderous gates that fronted the massive keep of Duc Marimund's castle were more attentive than those who had been charged with guarding their master's private chambers. The threat of an intruder was not much greater, but the chance of a sudden inspection by one of Marimund's knights was, and not a man among them did not bear some scar to remind him that any deficiency in their duty would be harshly rewarded. So it was that the four men turned as one when they spied a ragged-looking figure race around the corner of the wide corridor that communicated between the gates and the keep's innards. The four men hurried into the hallway, spears at the ready, blocking the path of the runner, standing between him and the open gates.

'Hold,' the ranking soldier commanded, his hand lifted in an imperious gesture. The ragged man came to a skidding halt before the trooper and his comrades. He gazed at the menacing spear-points, then at the glowering, scarred countenances of the men who held them. A smile crawled onto the man's handsome features.

'Praise the Lady!' he cried, his voice carrying such relief and joy that it took the troopers by surprise. 'Then they've not gotten this far!'

'Who?' the leader asked, the tip of his spear lowering slightly as it responded to the soldier's distraction. 'Who's not gotten this far?'

'The prisoners,' the ragged man declared, a note of superiority and disbelief in his voice now, as though he could not believe his interrogator would need to voice such a question. 'There was a riot in the dungeons. Many of the prisoners have escaped and are running loose through the castle! His lordship is even now leading the hunt to track them down.' The man nodded his head once more in relief. 'But it seems none of them have made it past your vigilance.'

'No,' the leader said, his tone still displaying the confusion that filled his squinting gaze. 'You are the first person we've seen since two bells.'

'Excellent,' the stranger clapped his dirty hands together in pleasure. 'Then we may be certain that none of them have escaped this way.' He smiled again, stepping closer to the leading soldier. The other men-at-arms hesitated, uncertain whether they should continue to guard against the man's advance. 'I'll need to spread the alarm to the guards posted on the outer wall,' he told the sergeant. The leader cocked his head to one side, hostility dispelling the confusion in his eyes.

'Are you saying that me and my men can't keep a bunch of half-starved dungeon rats from taking this portal?' the soldier growled. He looked up and down his accuser, studying his grimy black leather garments and filthy skin. 'For that matter who, by all the Dark Gods, are you? I've never seen you before!'

'Nor have I,' chimed in one of the other soldiers, his spear poised for a quick thrust into the ragged man's kidneys.

Gobineau sighed, then met the suspicious stare of the commanding soldier. 'I am Percival, assistant torturer,' he announced with a note of pride. Around him, he heard the uneasy shifting of feet that his pronouncement caused. It would explain his dirty garments and unkempt appearance, and unless Marimund had changed vastly over the years, Gobineau knew that his men-at-arms were not exempt from being victims of his dungeons should they fail in their appointed tasks. The threat that they might one day be victims of the evil toys kept in Marimund's torture chamber tended to keep even the most sadistically curious of his soldiers far from the place. He doubted if more than a handful of men within the castle knew what Marimund's torture master looked like, or if the man had assistants. If Ranald were still being gracious, none of the soldiers he now faced would be one of them. He'd already been lucky in the fact that none of them had been involved in his capture in Marimund's throne room.

The leader looked somewhat taken aback by Gobineau's statement, but one of the other soldiers suddenly had a stroke of inspiration, probably the only idea that had entered the lout's head in a fortnight. 'How do we know that *you* ain't one of the prisoners?' the man-at-arms demanded. Gobineau maintained his smile, while inwardly cursing the god of thieves. Ranald certainly wasn't going to let him get out of this easily.

'If I was one of the prisoners, would I run up to a group of armed soldiers telling them there had been an escape from the dungeons?' Gobineau put a withering amount of arrogance and contempt in his tone. The accusing soldier could not maintain Gobineau's stare, glancing down at the floor.

Gobineau turned back toward the leader of the guards. 'Now, I must spread word to the outer guards. Not as any lack of faith in your ability to hold this portal, which I have the utmost confidence you shall do, but because there is always a chance in their desperation that these wretches might try to climb down the walls from one of the windows.'

The explanation satisfied the sergeant, who moved aside, allowing the outlaw to stride past him. Gobineau paused beneath the archway.

'Close these behind me, and be vigilant,' he told them, addressing the guards as though he were some mighty general and they a vast horde of local militia. 'The prisoners may have armed themselves, and they are quite desperate. Don't take any chances with them. His lordship will be just as pleased with them dead as alive.' A sudden thought occurred to Gobineau and he grinned. 'Beware of the elf witch,' he told the soldiers. 'She is the one who freed the prisoners. Don't give her a chance to place a spell on you! If you see her, cut her down as swiftly as you can!'

The outlaw turned to withdraw, but the sergeant rushed up beside him. Gobineau bit down on the sudden horror that seized him. Turning, he was surprised to see the soldier proffering him the sword that had formerly rested at the sergeant's side.

'You are unarmed and if, as you say, some of the prisoners have circumvented our post, you may have need of a weapon,' the sergeant told him. Gobineau accepted the weapon, bowing his head in gratitude.

'You are a quick thinker, sergeant,' the rogue told him. 'The duc could use more men of your penetrating intelligence and wisdom.' Gobineau allowed the man to bask in the compliment a moment before resuming his sprint across the courtyard. He heard the heavy doors of the keep slam shut behind him.

If the guards on the outer wall were as easily duped, he'd be quit of this place in only a few minutes. Of course, now he had something to fall back upon should his glib tongue not work its magic twice. Gobineau adjusted his grip on the guard's heavy broadsword. Truly, Ranald provided all things in his own devious way.

Even as he saw the outer gatehouse drawing closer, Gobineau turned his thoughts back to what must be unfolding within the castle. He'd studied the elf's secret passage mechanisms well enough during his brief travel through them to use them to effect his own escape – after some judicious tampering with the door mechanisms to ensure that the two bounty hunters would not be following him, even if they did survive their battle with the vampire. The rogue had almost been caught himself when he'd emerged from the passage, nearly running headfirst into a large group of men-at-arms and knights with a furious Marimund at their head, heading toward the room Gobineau had recently quit. Fortunately, they hadn't seen him. He imagined that even in the unlikely event that Brunner did best the vampiric Sir Corbus, the bounty hunter would hardly be able to fight his way through the force Marimund was bringing.

All things considered, Gobineau did not think he'd have to worry about Brunner following him around any more. The only thing that still puzzled him was the absolute terror the elf witch had shown of the musty old artefact. She had regarded it as though it were the knife of Khaine. Gobineau hadn't seen that it possessed any strange powers or the ability to work dark miracles, unless of course it had been responsible for Corbus's timely arrival.

Yet even as his thoughts turned in this direction, a strange sound impressed itself upon the outlaw, not unlike the soft roar of ocean waves washing upon a barren shore. The night seemed to have grown strangely warm as well, and Gobineau imagined that the air had gained a curious, acrid odour to it.

'WE'RE CLOSE NOW,' Ithilweil gasped as she led the way down yet another narrow corridor. Brunner turned his head in her direction for only a moment, then returned his attention to the hallway behind them, his crossbow held at the ready. The bounty hunters could hear their pursuers cautiously advancing to the last corner they had turned. With two of their number already having been rewarded for their zealous pursuit with one of Brunner's crossbow bolts sprouting from their chests, the remaining soldiers of Duc Marimund were playing things more carefully. Unfortunately, Brunner didn't think they'd stay careful for too long, and if the score or so men chasing them decided to rush them all at once, even if he brought down a man with every shot, it would hardly stem the charge.

'By Grimnir!' Ulgrin snarled from his position beside Brunner, a gleaming hand axe in each grubby fist. The dwarf's huge battle axe had been left behind in Marimund's private chambers, the dwarf having been too disoriented to think of recovering it until the duc himself and two dozen of his men stood between him and his beloved weapon. But if Ulgrin's spirits had been volatile, they were fanned into flames when Ithilweil announced that she knew where the old escape tunnel was located, making the route he had charted superfluous. 'What did I get myself covered in this filth for if we aren't even going to use the tunnel?' the dwarf spat.

'Maybe I just don't feel like paying you extra to kill more frogs,' Brunner directed the withering comment at the dwarf, keeping his eyes fixed on the hallway. An armoured head briefly darted around the corner, making certain that the persons they were hunting were still in sight. The observer lingered just a second too long and had his bravery answered by the steel bolt that punched into his forehead. Unseen hands dragged the body back behind the corner.

'Time to move,' Brunner told his companions. He gave Ithilweil a hard look. 'If this escape route of yours isn't close, we're dead. They won't let me pick them off one by one much longer. Pretty soon now, they are going to decide risking a massed charge gives them better odds.'

Ithilweil nodded her understanding. 'Only a few turns more and we will be there,' she replied. It would have been much easier on them if they'd been able to employ the secret passage again, but Ithilweil had been unable to reopen the hidden door, stating that someone had sabotaged the mechanism. Gobineau, without question, ensuring that he'd gain time on any pursuit the bounty hunters mounted. The real fiasco had been Ulgrin's insistence that he could get the door open again. A few moments of waiting for Ulgrin to manage this small miracle had seen Marimund and his soldiers storming down the corridor toward them. Even the stubborn Ulgrin had relented and abandoned his labour when he sighted the armed company racing toward them.

The elf witch led the pair around several more twists and turns in the corridor. As they passed a narrow flight of stairs that wound deep into the foundations of the castle, Ulgrin hesitated and pointed a stubby finger at the gloom below.

'That's the way we came up,' Ulgrin stated proudly. 'There's no tricking a dwarf when it comes to stonework.'

'That's nice,' Brunner told him. 'But we're going this way,' he added motioning for Ithilweil to lead on. Ulgrin spat a foul-sounding Khazalid curse into his beard, but hurried after his companions.

'Just around the next turn there is an old storeroom that is never used,' Ithilweil told Brunner as they paused before the mouth of a four-way intersection. 'The storeroom has a large cask inside it. But it is really a door that leads into the tunnel. I've followed it as far as its end, but it lets out in the very centre of the city. Not a very safe place for me to be.' Brunner imagined that the elf's pallid skin coloured slightly as she spoke. 'At least, not without an escort.'

'We'll get out of here,' the bounty hunter assured Ithilweil. 'Then we'll pick up that maggot's trail.' Brunner tried to give the elf a reassuring smile, but found that he was woefully out of practice. 'Gobineau won't stay free for long.'

But as he turned the corner, the sight that greeted the bounty hunter's words made him question the veracity of his last statement. The flickering light of torches cast eerie reflections in the polished steel armour of the half-dozen knights who filled the passageway, flanking the grinning, weasel-faced nobleman standing at their centre. Suddenly the seeming timidity of their pursuers was explained. They weren't supposed to catch the bounty hunters and the elf, but simply herd them into the trap, keep them looking behind instead of ahead. Brunner cursed his own lack of foresight. He should have expected Marimund to know every inch of his own castle, most especially something as vital as an escape route!

The duc's sneer was as vicious as the toothy grin of a goblin. Marimund considered each of the fugitives in turn, letting his keen, calculating eyes settle on each for a moment before looking to the next. His eyes blazed briefly with a restrained rage when he stared at Ithilweil.

'Most inconsiderate of you to return my hospitality with such,' Marimund hesitated, biting down whatever word he had intended to use, selecting a less vituperative replacement, 'malfeasance.' Brunner weighed his chances. He still had three bolts loaded in his crossbow. That would allow him to kill Marimund, maybe manage one of his knights before the others fell upon him. The bounty hunter discarded the idea. Marimund was the only chance of talking his way out of the standoff. The nobleman stared at the bounty hunter, as though reading his thoughts.

'You think you can kill me with that disgusting weapon of yours,' Marimund scoffed. 'The Lady protects her noble children. Have you never heard of the grace she bestows upon the valiant, turning aside the craven arrows of cowardly swine that they may be forced into honourable combat?' Marimund rapped a knuckle against his own chest. 'I am the legitimate ruler of the once proud realm of Mousillon! The blessing of the Lady flows through my veins! What need have I to fear your filthy arrows?'

'By Grimnir's axe!' Ulgrin hissed. 'Is every nobleman in this damn city insane?' The dwarf's outburst caused a flicker of discomfort to cross Marimund's face, then a cold fury to smoulder in his eyes.

'Kill them,' Marimund declared, waving a hand at the knights around him. The armoured warriors started to move forward. In that instant, Brunner acted, firing his crossbow at the only target that would possibly have any effect.

Marimund crumpled in a screaming heap, his sword fallen to the floor beside him as he clamped both hands at the steel bolt protruding from his knee. Several of the knights immediately turned away from Brunner and his companions, rushing back to aid their master. The bounty hunter turned and raced back the way they had come, the feet pounding to either side of him telling him that Ithilweil and Ulgrin had not hesitated in following his lead. Behind them, the clatter of armour told Brunner that some of Marimund's knights had ignored their lord's cries, intent on following his last command. Still, at least a few of them would be detained helping their injured master. With Marimund dead, they would have had all of the knights on their tail, focused on avenging their slain lord. This way, at least the odds were somewhat reduced.

Now if they could just reach Ulgrin's tunnel without running into the troops that had been herding them toward Marimund...

MARIMUND SNAPPED AT the men carrying him away from the scene of his wounding, lashing them with his tongue every time a fresh trickle of pain surged through his body. He'd have that filthy assassin's body carved into dog meat and his head would rot upon a pike until the flesh turned black beneath the sun. The audacity of the dog to strike him, *him*, with his filthy coward's weapon!

And the anguish he would visit upon the assassin's remains would be as nothing compared to what he was going to do to that traitorous elf witch. Marimund dearly hoped that she at least was taken alive. His knights were zealous in their work, and an elf witch, a single assassin, and some odd-looking shit-covered gnome were hardly going to give them a decent fight. But at least they would know it was by Marimund's command that they died, and that was just as good as the nobleman's own sword accomplishing the deed.

A foul, acrid stench impressed itself upon the duc, causing him to forget his pain for a moment, so strong and unsettling was the odour. Marimund wondered for a moment if something might not be burning in one of the rooms of the castle, perhaps some feeble attempt by Ithilweil to distract him and his men from their pursuit. But the duc did not have long to consider this thought, for he suddenly had much more important things to consider as the corridor around him shook and swayed as though he were within a ship at sea. The knights carrying him fell against the walls as the castle shuddered, dropping their noble burden to the floor. Marimund screamed anew as his maimed leg struck the hard flagstones.

Marimund began to lift himself from the floor when the castle shook again, knocking him flat once more. The impact was vastly more powerful this time, as though someone were hurling massive boulders into the side of the fortress. Marimund could hear the heavy stone blocks groaning and grinding against one another, thick trails of dust raining down from the ceiling overhead. He covered his head as the roof began to give way, rocks and heavy blocks of stone tumbling downward now. Again the castle shook as some incredible force shook it. The duc had seen mighty hurricanes sweep across Mousillon, and those relentless tempests had not even evoked a fraction of the force now assaulting his home.

The realisation of what must be happening dawned on Marimund just as the corridor shook again and the walls collapsed around him.

THE GUARDS IN the tower that rose from the north wall of Marimund's castle only just had time to scream before they died, as they witnessed the gigantic crimson shape that had fallen upon them from the night sky. Claws the size of ox carts had gripped the fortification, talons sinking into the stonework as though it were crafted from soft clay. Without losing any of its momentum, the swooping fiend had ripped the top of the tower free, spilling tiny figures from its battlements, and with a graceful motion had turned its sudden descent, ascending back into the firmament once more. But as it did so, the massive claws flung the broken tower at the brooding mass of the keep, lending it some of the ghastly power of the creature's momentum. The immense weight of the tower smacked into the side of Marimund's castle with the force of a dozen catapults, rupturing its northern face like the shell of an egg.

Then, as suddenly as it had come, the huge shape disappeared once more, vanishing from sight as it was consumed by the night. Behind it, it left a foul, mephitic smell, like the musk of serpents mixed with the stink of charcoal. The few soldiers standing gap-mouthed on the outer walls of the castle could not believe what they had seen, doubting their very sanity. All had happened so quickly, it was hard to believe it had happened at all.

It was a man-at-arms in the south tower who saw the first flicker of fire shine out from the blackness above. Soon, all eyes were watching as the flame hurtled downward, speeding toward the keep. There was no shout of alarm, no cry of horror. Somehow, the soldiers had a sense that what they were witnessing was too big for fear. They watched in an awed silence as the flame became more distinct in its descent, as it resolved itself into a fiery steam billowing out from the jaws of a gigantic visage. The hurtling leviathan crashed into the top of the keep and the awed silence was shattered by the shriek of wood and the rumble of stone. A vast cloud of grey dust blossomed about the immense creature, engulfing it for a moment like some grainy fog. Then the dust fell away and the watching soldiers were able to shout and scream, every voice crying the same word.

'A dragon!'

It was vast, gigantic. Two hundred feet from the tip of his snout to the pointed barb that terminated his immense tail. The dragon wore crimson scales upon his limbs and sides, fading into a thick armour of black bony plates upon his back. From these plates rose a rank of sharp spines, like a column of pikemen, their wicked points gleaming in the flickering glow of the dragon's exhalations. Each of the wyrm's legs was massive, thick as a tree trunk and bulging beneath its scaly covering with muscle and power. From the shoulders, colossal wings were stretched, great leathery pinions set in a framework of finger-like bones. The dragon's head leered before his body, supported upon a neck as thick as a river barge, long black horns stabbing back away from the face from just above the sunken sockets of his cold, yellow eyes. From the crater-like nostrils, an orange smoke wafted, illuminating the mighty beast and casting eerie shadows upon the enormous jaws beneath the dragon's head. Rank upon rank of jagged teeth, each longer than a man's arm, shone out from their setting of crimson scales.

The observers had one and all heard the legends of noble knights riding forth to slay marauding drakes, rescuing fair damsels and golden treasures from the caves of such scaly monsters. Such stories were common in the lore and legend of Bretonnia, and well known to even the poorest of its peasants. But none had ever seen the creatures spoken of in these tales, perhaps taking comfort in believing such beasts to be a part of the history of their land rather than something that might return in their own time. As terror overcame the awe that had gripped the hearts of the soldiers, the men-at-arms scrambled over one another in their haste to be quit of the battlements, to abandon the fortress to the legendary horror that had fallen upon it from the grim night sky.

Malok paid the fleeing soldiers little notice, intent upon pulverising the stone structure beneath him. The dragon's impact had shaken the very foundations of the keep, though the tough body of the wyrm had felt little of his violent collision with the unyielding fortification. Now he brought his heavy clawed legs smashing again and again into the cracked rubble that roofed the structure, causing the already weakened stonework to shudder and groan. Malok could feel the castle shifting beneath him as rooms and corridors collapsed below, shifting tons of stone to crush the little vermin within.

The dragon reared his head back, roaring into the night, a sound like the scream of hot steel thrust into icy snow magnified to such a degree that the eardrums of the human witnesses threatened to burst under such duress. Gouts of flame, like the expulsions of a blast furnace, flashed from Malok's jaws, staining the night sky a hellish hue. The dragon maintained his violent, boastful display of wrath and retribution for a lingering moment, letting his display of power build until he could feel the fiery heat swelling within him. Then the dragon turned his head downward, expelling a long stream of golden flame into the structure beneath his feet.

Wooden support beams exploded as the dragonfire consumed them, turning oak and pine into ash and steam. The already weakened pile caved in beneath the reptile as the supports were destroyed. Three floors of castle crumpled, crushing downward, pushing outward against the walls.

Malok beat his wings, lifting himself free as the castle disintegrated into a pile of rock and debris, smoke and dust billowing about him as the mighty wings caused the air to swirl and writhe.

The hovering dragon glared down at his handiwork, reptilian eyes narrowing into dagger-like slits as he contemplated the destruction. Deciding it was not enough, Malok drew in another breath, expelling a second stream of flame into the rubble, sending tons of stone exploding into the air as the fiery column struck.

The dragon snarled down at the rubble, a deep and satisfied hiss, then wheeled away, now intent on attending to all the tiny little men who had been running away from the curtain wall and guard towers. After all, any one of them might be the vermin who had driven the dragon to come here. And that was a summons Malok was not going to let pass unanswered.

'THIS SHOULD BE far enough,' Ulgrin announced, his eyes narrowing as he studied the black muck-encrusted brickwork overhead. 'We're past the keep now. Nothing to come down about our heads now. Except of course the courtyard,' the dwarf added with a morbid chuckle. Much to the annoyance of his companions, Ulgrin seemed to be almost enjoying himself as they crawled through the filthy, cramped confines of the tunnel. Brunner suspected the change in Ulgrin's attitude had much to do with the fact that his companions were so clearly discomfited by their circumstances. While the low ceiling of the tunnel made Ulgrin walk with a slight stoop, it forced the much taller Brunner and Ithilweil to creep along almost bent double, their hands groping into the muck coating the walls to maintain their balance. The dwarf's almost supernatural ability to sense the pressure of the stone above them had been the only real guide as to how far they had come, and how far they might yet have to go before reaching the exit.

They had reached the tunnel well ahead of the heavily armoured knights Marimund had sent after them, but they didn't have much of a lead over their pursuers. The knights of Bretonnia, for all their arrogance and pride, were some of the most dangerous warriors any land had to offer. In their armour plate, only the most powerful or expertly aimed blows had any hope of wounding the knight within, nor was the warrior likely to stand still while his enemy attempted such a strike. Their style was far more direct and brutal than the elaborate feint and deceive flourishes of Tilea's duellists, but the swordsmanship of a Bretonnian knight was no less intimidating, something Brunner felt better challenging from fifty paces away with a crossbow than in the cramped confines of a dungeon where room to manoeuvre was limited and every advantage lay with the knight.

The bounty hunters had decided that the only course of action, upon gaining the dank tunnel, was to wait out their pursuers and strike them down as they tried to follow, a tactic which Ithilweil opposed as being utterly base and cowardly. Neither Brunner or Ulgrin paid the slightest interest to her moral complaints. This was the real world, not some duel between princes in an elven court with all its rules of etiquette and tradition. There were trained, well-armed killers pursuing them, men who would strike them down without the slightest hesitation should they catch them. The bounty hunters were determined not to give them such an opportunity.

The first knight, almost crawling as he progressed through the narrow tunnel, his helmet removed in order that he might not be rendered completely blind, had found himself surprised by Ulgrin when the dwarf's axe bit cleanly through the warrior's mail coif and the neck beneath. The knight following the decapitated man rose in alarm, his mouth opening to give voice to a cry of warning. The sound was silenced when a bolt from Brunner's crossbow sank into the knight's forehead. After that, the pursuers had shown a bit more caution. They must have been joined by the larger company that had herded the bounty hunters toward Marimund, for the next men sent crawling through the dank tunnel were lightly armoured squires rather than bulky knights in plate mail. Brunner and Ulgrin waded further into the passage, weapons ready to repeat their grim labours. Then the walls shook.

The tremor was followed by others, far greater in strength and ferocity. All within the tunnel could hear the crash of stone and the screams of doomed men and women sounding from the castle. The groan and roar of toppling stone grew into a dull, almost organic thing, pounding against their ears with such violence that it seemed determined to deafen all who were victim of it. The squires who had been sent into the tunnel scrambled forward like panicked rats scurrying from a sinking ship. They had been closer to the mouth of Ulgrin's tunnel and had heard more distinctly the noise of their comrades being crushed beneath tons of stone.

In their heedless flight, the squires found themselves easy prey for the waiting blades of Brunner and Ulgrin. It was not a fight, it was a slaughter, but the bounty hunters had done far worse in their black careers than take advantage of disoriented foes; the slaying of the squires would be forgotten almost as soon as it was achieved.

Then another tremor shook the castle and the rumble of stone sounded from much nearer. The high-pitched death shriek of a squire cagey enough to linger back while his fellows met the blades of the two bounty killers told a terrifying story. The tunnel was collapsing behind them! The three fugitives began a mad scramble back down the dismal corridor, struggling to stay ahead of the roar behind them. Ulgrin, with a long history of mining and the cave-ins that are the constant worry of the miner, was better able to judge the nearness of the collapse. His words of gruff, oath-strewn encouragement lent a new speed to Brunner and Ithilweil's tired legs.

It was the elf who spoke now, wiping some of the muck from her soiled garments with as much dignity as the cramped confines of the tunnel would allow. 'It came,' she said, her voice heavy with resignation. 'The fool called it and it came.'

'What came?' Brunner asked, his voice low and cautious.

'The dragon that is bound to the Fell Fang,' Ithilweil responded. 'It must have been very near to have come so swiftly. And that fool called it, without any idea of what he summoned or how to control it!'

'Are you saying a dragon caused the cave-in?' Ulgrin demanded. Ithilweil nodded her head in response.

'By now, in its fury, it must have reduced Marimund's entire castle to a pile of rubble,' she stated. The two bounty hunters stared at Ithilweil, as though struggling to grasp the magnitude of the power her words bestowed upon this creature.

'Then that's the end of our hunt!' Ulgrin snarled, smacking a fist against the tunnel wall. 'Unless you have a few months to try and dig his bones out from under tons of rock.'

'Maybe,' Brunner told his partner. 'But maybe not. Don't forget, Gobineau was no friend of Marimund's either. He wasn't just trying to escape from us, but from the castle in general.' The bounty hunter paused, considering his own words. 'I think that with Marimund distracted by ourselves, our rather valuable friend might have gone a bit farther than we did.'

Ulgrin's eyes lit up as the possibility that Gobineau yet survived was presented to him. At the same time, Ithilweil's expression became one of dread.

'We must make certain,' she declared. 'We have to be sure he is dead.' She looked deeply into the eyes of first Brunner and then Ulgrin Baleaxe. 'Don't you understand? If

Gobineau is still alive, and he still has the Fell Fang, then this horror might occur again! Any time! Any place!' Noting the stone cold expressions of both killers, Ithilweil's voice became more imploring. 'It might be one of your own cities next time! Your own people crushed beneath its feet or incinerated by its breath!'

Brunner let the elf speak, then shook his head. 'We'll find Gobineau, dead or alive, but not for your reasons. This talisman that calls dragons is your concern, the price on Gobineau's head is ours. As I said before, so long as you don't get in the way, you're welcome to tag along.' The bounty hunter tossed aside the kettle helm that formed part of his guard's disguise and replaced his own steel sallet helm over his features. Without further word, Brunner began to make his way forward once more. Ulgrin paused to regard Ithilweil for a moment before hurrying after his partner.

'And don't get any funny ideas about sharing the bounty!' the dwarf growled. 'The shares aren't big enough the way things are, I'll be a grobbi's wet nurse if I'll let 'em shrink even more because of a tall-ear!'

Duc Marimund was dying. With each breath, a fresh bubble of gore dripped from his chin. He could feel the broken wreckage of his ribs, the cracked ruin that had once been his pelvis. Every inch of the would-be ruler of Mousillon was agony. Crushed beneath the walls of his own fortress, the nobleman's vision now swam, black and red dots flaring over the dust and rubble that reason told him he should see.

Marimund could not imagine what could have been responsible for the destruction of his inviolate fortress. It had withstood storm and earthquake and even siege, but now, in less time than he would have believed possible, the castle had been stamped into ruin and all his dreams of power crushed along with it. Was this the judgement of the gods? Had he, far from being chosen by the Lady, been cursed by her? Was he in reality the evil heretic Malford rather than the legendary hero Landuin?

Even as the mangled duc considered the renowned Landuin, first lord of Mousillon, his thoughts strayed to the mighty deeds the legendary knight had accomplished. And suddenly Marimund knew what force had destroyed him. Landuin had slain a dragon among the mighty feats of his long career. The adulterous wretch Gobineau had brought a strange old artefact with him, a device he claimed would call dragons to the one who wielded it. At once the nobleman recalled the horrific sound he had heard, or imagined that he had heard, a malefic roar bellowing behind the rumble of falling walls and collapsing floors. Marimund's lip twisted into a sneer. So, Gobineau's claim had been more than a frantic tall-tale to save his hide!

A shape slowly manifested itself before him. Marimund's vision flickered, but slowly he began to understand that the shape was that of a man, one of his knights. Sir Corbus was without his crimson armour now, clad only in a long wool shrift, his pale skin exposed. The knight's face was a grotesque ruin, one eye socket expanded in a ghastly and hideous manner, one jaw blasted and broken by some terrible force. Still, despite his horrible injuries, Marimund's most loyal follower had come for him. The nobleman tried to crawl toward his saviour but found that he could move only his left arm.

Corbus stopped very near the trapped Marimund, staring down at him with a single, baleful eye. The vampire's broken jaws worked to create a dry, hissing sort of speech.

'You were speaking,' the Blood Dragon said. Marimund closed his eyes, trying to remember. Had he been speaking? Was his delirium such that reason had flown from his tongue? The vampire leaned down, his hideously ruined face only inches from Marimund's own. 'Tell me more about this man who has the power to summon dragons.'

Marimund blinked. Why should Corbus concern himself with such things when his lord and master was dying at his very feet? The nobleman opened his mouth to remind the knight of his oaths and vows, but staring into the burning eye of Corbus, Marimund felt his soul shudder. For the first time, the would-be lord of Mousillon understood just how abominable a creature he had allowed to take service with him. Instead of calling for the vampire's help, the nobleman gasped out a name.

'Gobineau,' he said, bloody froth punctuating his words. Corbus smiled with what was left of his face. Gobineau. He had seen that wretch with the assassin and that traitor elf bitch in Marimund's chambers. So, it was Gobineau who had this power, this ability to summon the mighty dragons of earth and sky. The vampire let a low hiss of expectancy and depraved lust slither through the wound in his throat. Finding the thief would be the first step towards the only salvation left for one of his diseased kind, the only way of ending his disgusting curse and redeeming his lost honour. Corbus looked back at the trapped Marimund.

'Gobineau,' the vampire repeated. 'Thank you, Marimund,' Corbus continued, speaking his former master's name without hint of deference or respect. The vampire's eye fixed upon the froth bubbling from the nobleman's mouth. His long, wolf-like tongue flicked forth and licked his dagger-like fangs. 'There is just one more thing you can do for me,' Corbus whispered, leaning toward the trapped man so that he might feed.

FROM THE DARKNESS of his bolt hole, Gobineau cast his eyes skyward, trying to pierce the haze of smoke and darkness for another glimpse of the awesome form that had descended out of the night. His body still shivered as he remembered the sight: the huge reptile, clad in its armour of crimson scales, borne aloft by its midnight wings. No fresh young wyrm, this mighty destroyer that had answered the rogue's call, but a monster hoary with the crust of age and legend. Gobineau had been able to get a good look at the dragon as it rose from the rubble of Marimund's castle, soaring low above the castle grounds and the surrounding district. It was enormous, its scales scarred and dulled by the relentless march of time. The gigantic drake bore the marks of its long and terrible life – a great patch of blackened flesh marked its left shoulder and the side of its neck. Along its side ran a deep trench-like scar, as though some titan had raked the tip of his sword along the dragon's belly. Yet such old injuries did not seem to disturb or slow the malevolent creature as it rose into the night sky, its cruel yellow eyes scouring the landscape for the tiny fleeing figures that had scattered before its fury.

Gobineau clasped the talisman a bit more tightly in his trembling fist. He had been lucky to have escaped what had followed. The dragon, snarling like a starving panther, had circled above the outskirts of Mousillon, watching the fleeing guards. Then it had opened its jaws, and a great sheet of flame had fallen upon the running men. They were turned into living torches by the intense fire, screaming brands that shrieked and howled as they continued to run. The dragon had hovered in the air, turning its horned head with almost bird-like motions as it focused upon isolated groups of men before reducing them into charred piles of burned flesh. Nor did the wyrm seem inclined to distinguish between the guards flying from Marimund's fortress and the desolate peasants its rampage flushed from their hovels. Even a jaded villain of such experience as Gobineau had covered his ears against the screams and shrieks that sought to drown out the crackle and hiss of flame.

Then the dragon had turned its attention upon the miserable hovels themselves, raining its fiery exhalations upon them in a relentless fury. But in this, the dragon was somewhat thwarted, for the mouldering structures were damp with the rot carried to them from the swamp and they burned only with great reluctance. Only by concentrating its flame upon isolated structures could the dragon persuade them to collapse into heaps of cinder and ash, something the great wyrm quickly grew tired of. With a last malefic roar that rattled the teeth in Gobineau's mouth, and a sideways glance to ensure that no other scurrying figures remained in the streets below, the dragon had wheeled away, rising back into the smoke and the fiery night sky. In its wake, it left a hundred burning bodies lying upon the streets and a dozen fires smouldering in the blackened ruins that had once surrounded Marimund's fortress.

Gobineau again thanked Ranald the Trickster for bestowing such good fortune upon him. As near as he could tell, he alone had escaped Marimund's castle and the dragon's wrath. Ducking into a small outhouse, the rogue had eluded the dragon's keen eye, and so been spared the fiery death that had run rampant all around him.

Then the bandit considered the talisman clutched in his hand. Perhaps it was more than luck? Perhaps the talisman had not only called the dragon, but protected him from the monster as well? Gobineau had certainly been desirous of seeing everyone in the castle destroyed – perhaps through the Fell Fang the dragon had sensed his wishes and simply acted upon them? Marimund, Brunner, neither of them would be troubling Gobineau on this side of Morr's black kingdom, and Gobineau had the dragon to thank for such a boon.

The power to call such a creature and have it obey his wishes! No wonder mad Rudol had tried to kill him for the artefact.

Gobineau's face split in a sly smile. This was a power beyond his wildest imaginings. It would take some careful thought to decide how best to exploit it. But already several interesting possibilities were stirring in the outlaw's mind.

CHAPTER NINE

LEAVING THE CURSED city of Mousillon proved a much easier task than entering it had. No mobs of desperate, violent wretches roamed the haunted streets, no packs of hungry ghouls prowled the alleys. Even the armed patrols of Mousillon's decadent aristocrats seemed to be content to remain within the decaying castles of their masters. The city was as deserted as an open grave; only the croaking of vultures and the scuttling creep of rats disturbed the sepulchral silence that hung over the place.

The cause of such fear that even the degenerate inhabitants of a place like Mousillon hid behind locked doors was easily discovered when the bounty hunters and their elf companion emerged from the dank sewage tunnel Ulgrin Baleaxe had discovered. The castle of Duc Marimund was now just a pile of rubble, three of its outer walls collapsed entirely as though the fist of an angry god had smashed the fortress flat. The blighted districts of rotting houses and shops that had surrounded Marimund's stronghold were blackened and charred, scarred by a flame intense enough to prosper even in the mouldy swamp-tainted wood that prevailed in these environs. Dark silhouettes of bodies littered the cobbles of the streets, the only reminder left of men struck down by the all-consuming flames. The bounty hunters had resisted Ithilweil's desperate, terrified insistence that Gobineau had called down the wrath of some ancient monster with the artefact she had called the Fell Fang. Then, confronted by the evidence of their own eyes, they had had no choice but to believe her.

But there was little time to consider the desolation and the awesome power that had caused it. Every moment that passed put more distance between the hunters and their prey, if indeed Gobineau had been fortunate enough to escape the doom he had summoned. The assumption of his death, however, was not something Ithilweil was prepared to allow, nor one the bounty hunters preferred, for if the man was dead then he was either buried beneath the castle or one of the blackened lumps of slag sprawled upon the streets. In either case, there would be nothing to take back to Couronne for a reward.

Though unchallenged in their passage through the streets, the trio of hunters were not alone. On occasion a furtive shape might be seen picking through the ruins, desperate avarice overcoming the fear that gripped most of the city. Some of these fled at the approach of Brunner and his companions, others defiantly stood their ground, determined to protect whatever garbage they had discovered. The promise of a few copper coins or a glowering threat rumbling from Ulgrin's harsh mouth bought information from these wretches. Some had seen the fall of Marimund's fortress and described in exacting detail the horrific monster that had brought about such carnage. A few, at the prompting of Ithilweil, recalled the handsome rogue they had seen slinking away from the castle after the dragon had passed. They pointed with grimy fingers toward the south and the outer walls of the city. Brunner was not surprised. Freed from Marimund's dungeons, there was nothing to keep their quarry in Mousillon any longer.

Brunner insisted on checking every hovel and farmstead they came upon once they themselves were quit of the city. He knew that a man like Gobineau would not remain without a horse for long. Learning how near to the city he had been able to steal one would give them some idea as to how much of a lead the outlaw had on them. It was also of little surprise that the bandit had stolen the first animal he had come upon, a miserable old plow horse that represented the only possession of worth for its grey-headed owner. Reaching the farm where Brunner had stabled his own horses and the dappled mule Ulgrin rode, the bounty hunter paid a half dozen pieces of silver to secure a mare for Ithilweil, again earning a surly reminder from Ulgrin that the elf would not be taking any part of his own share in the reward.

It was not long before they were once again travelling the road leading south. Brunner was of the opinion that their nefarious quarry might be seeking refuge within one of the small pirate communities that could be found nuzzled amid the rocky shores of Aquitaine and Brionne.

But the keen eyes of Ithilweil caused Brunner to reconsider his thoughts when, on their first day out from Mousillon, the elf detected a black spiral of smoke rising in the east.

'It could be anything,' Ulgrin snarled. 'Some damn fool peasant setting fire to his hut, or maybe some nobleman removing an unsightly wood from his domain.'

'Or, more likely the beast is on the prowl,' Ithilweil replied, her tone sharp. The dwarf had baited her remorselessly throughout their journey and even her patience was coming to an end.

'You think our friend might be there?' Brunner asked. There was no question in his mind that Ithilweil had the right of it, that the smoke she saw was likely related to the dragon. The enchantress shook her head.

'Perhaps, if he is fool enough to use the Fell Fang again,' she replied. Brunner nodded, turning Fiend's head so that the horse began to head across a field that bordered the road. Ulgrin noted the action, sputtering a protest.

'You can't simply ride off on this tall-eared harpy's say-so!' the dwarf yelled. 'We don't know that the dragon caused that fire, or that Gobineau is idiot enough to go chasing after such a monster!'

'Please yourself,' Brunner called back to Ulgrin. 'But I think Ithilweil may be right. I think Gobineau did call that thing to Mousillon, and I'm betting two thousand in gold that where the brute is, Gobineau won't be far away.' Without any further word, the bounty hunter turned and continued to ride eastward, his packhorse trailing behind. Ithilweil indulged in a smug smile thrown in Ulgrin's direction before riding forward to join Brunner.

'Two thousand gold,' the dwarf grumbled. 'That bastard forgets a thousand of that is mine!' Ulgrin dug his heels into his mule, urging the animal to keep up with the others.

NIGHT FOUND THE hunters encamped within the ruins of an old farmhouse. It seemed that the caprices of storm and snow had doomed the structure rather than the ire of a giant fire-spewing reptile, and it had been many seasons since anything larger than a squirrel had called the roofless remains home. It made a decent enough shelter, providing defensible barriers should trouble present itself. The lands of Bretonnia were not without their predators. It was not unknown for wolves to become famished enough to try their paw at human prey and the grey wild cat of central Bretonnia, a beast almost as large as a small stag, was well known for a taste for horseflesh. And, of course, there was always the threat of human predators. The knights of Bretonnia were not so widespread and all powerful as to completely eradicate the bandits and highwaymen common to other, less chivalrous, lands.

Ithilweil turned away from her contemplation of the darkening landscape. To her elven eyes, the starlight served her almost as well as that of the sun, allowing her to watch the owl as it swooped down upon the field mouse, to observe the fox as it silently padded along a rocky outcrop. Only to the north-east was her vision obscured, denied by the thick blackness that told her they were nearing the carnage she had spotted many hours before. The warm breeze that picked at her garments and rustled through her hair carried with it the faint suggestion of the same acrid musk they had smelled about the ruins of Marimund's fortress: the sickly stink of dragon.

The elf shuddered. The beast was near, so very near that she could almost imagine its eyes watching her from the darkness, its ancient, evil soul contemplating her with a cold, unfathomable regard. She had listened well to those terrified wretches they had come upon during their exodus from Mousillon, and she had shared in that terror. They had good reason to know fear, for Ithilweil knew the name of the beast Gobineau had aroused, and knew its awful history.

Ithilweil turned back to the camp, stepping back toward the campfires Brunner and Ulgrin had set. The dwarf was crouched beside his flame, roasting a skinned squirrel. The dwarf had set his own camp at the far end of the ruin, as far from Brunner and Ithilweil as he could manage, even keeping his mule with him, as though it might become infected were it to linger near the elf's mare.

Ulgrin looked up from his cooking, a fell look in his eyes.

'Catch your own, tall-ear!' Ulgrin spat. 'This one is mine!'

'I had thought it little improvement on your looks after you cleaned yourself,' Ithilweil retorted. 'But at least you might have cleaned your mouth when you bathed everything else.' The elf's words brought a fresh stream of half-articulate invective from the dwarf. Ithilweil did not linger to wait for Ulgrin to run out of curses but strode instead toward the other campfire.

Brunner was seated before the fire, still garbed in his shabby brigandine armour. His helmet and weapons lay nearby, arranged about the makeshift bed of blankets and saddlebags the bounty hunter had created for himself. Only the slender length of his sword, Drakesmalice, was still with the warrior, resting across his knees as he stared into the fire. Ithilweil stopped, fascinated for a moment by the harsh shadows the flickering flames threw upon the killer's weathered features. There was something painful about that face, something that seemed to call out to her.

Such pain, such unspoken suffering. She could see it there, crushed beneath the scowling turn of his mouth, the jagged scars that creased his cheek and forehead. It was there in the eyes, frozen within the chill that had consumed the man's soul. Something terrible had happened to this one, something that had devoured his world, taken from him everything that had made his life worth living and in one final cruelty denied him the sanctity of a decent death, abandoning him to a ghostly existence among the shadows and the darkness. Perhaps only Ithilweil had ever seen such things in the cold eyes of the killer, the piteous tragedy that fed the ruthless hunter. For his were eyes not unlike those of her own people – a phantom race lingering among the forlorn remains of a once glorious civilisation whose hour of glory had passed.

'What do you see in the flames?' Ithilweil dared to ask. The bounty hunter did not look up at her as he replied.

'Things that never were,' Brunner told her. His eyes rose to meet her own, the tragedy subdued once more, overcome by the fire of hate. 'Things that will yet be.'

Ithilweil stepped closer, letting herself sink gracefully to the ground beside Brunner. 'There is a fable among my people that if one looks too long into a night fire, one sees one's own death in the flames,' she told him.

The bounty hunter shook head, a grim smile on his face. 'I see the death of other men, not my own,' Brunner stated. 'But death is too little to take from the man I see in the flames. He owes me much more.' The bounty hunter's hand clenched into a fist and his voice dropped into a low whisper. 'From him, I will take everything.'

'Those who give their lives to revenge are ultimately consumed by it,' the elf cautioned. 'I have seen what becomes of those who give themselves over to hatred. They are grim, wraith-like creatures, never knowing the solace of a soft touch or the warmth of a loving voice. You remind me of them, the lost people of Nagarythe.' Ithilweil shook her head sadly. 'We call them shadow warriors, but not because they dwell in the shadowy canyons of their broken homeland, nor because they strike their hated kinfolk from the cover of darkness. No, we call them shadows because that is all they are. They are not whole, for all the light and love has gone out of them, leaving behind only the hate, only the thirst for revenge.'

'Sometimes,' the bounty hunter cautioned, 'hate is all the gods care to leave us with.'

Man and elf were silent for a long time then, each staring into the flames, as though mesmerised by the dancing tongues of fire. It was Ithilweil who at last tired of the sight, turning her back to the fire with a shudder. The bounty hunter reached out to her, placing his hand on her shoulder.

'I know who he is,' Ithilweil spoke, her voice hollow, as though she were gripped by fatigue.

'Indeed,' Brunner said. 'Jean Pierre Gobineau, worth two thousand gold crowns, less five hundred crowns if he is brought back dead.'

'Not the rogue,' Ithilweil said, 'the dragon. The beast the grave robbers in Mousillon described, it is known to me.'

The elf saw that she now had Brunner's complete interest, the bounty hunter's eyes gleaming with curiosity. 'The blackened neck upon a body of crimson scales, the jagged scar running along its belly. Such were the marks spoken of long ago, by the refugees who left these lands when the eastern colonies were abandoned. They spoke of a great dragon, a horrible beast that brought fire and death upon those trying to make their way to the sea, hunting them as a wolf hunts a flock of sheep.'

Ithilweil paused, recalling the horrifying firsthand accounts she had read in the libraries of Saphery. 'I cannot doubt that this man's foolishness has brought the same beast back into the world, the one they named Malok – the destroyer!'

AFTER CENTURIES OF slumber within the fiery heart of La Isla de Sangre, the dragon Malok was two things: angry and hungry. The merciless destruction of the Duc Marimund's castle in Mousillon had temporarily sated the former of these two qualities, but the expenditure of energy and effort had fanned the fires of the second. The dull pang of appetite that had been clawing at the back of the dragon's mind had become a desperate need, pulling him away from the prospect of laying waste to the already desolate city in order to silence the protests of his belly.

In the predawn that glowed above Bretonnia, Malok's crimson scales seemed to catch flame, glowing like smouldering embers amid the ashes of an expired flame. The early-rising peasants, slinking through the waning darkness in order to tend their fields and herds, looked up in horror at the spectral visitation, their shrill cries of fright warning the countryside that a monster was abroad. For his part, the dragon paid the shouting, fleeing wretches little mind. He could crush them easily, but there was little meat on a man. Malok was interested in something that could satisfy his hunger, not simply tease it. The dragon had stirred often enough through the long centuries since the rise of the kingdoms of men to know that where men were to be found, so too would more satisfactory prey-animals.

After only a few moments since first sighting the fleeing peasants, Malok spied what he was looking for, his belly grumbling in anticipation. The dragon was not concerned that the large herd of cattle being led to pasture belonged to the Marquis Duvalier, nor that his herds produced the finest bulls in Bordeleaux and had done so for nearly a thousand years. He was not concerned with the men who tended the herds, loyal yeomen whose families had served that of the marquis for centuries and to whom the care of the prized herds was something dearer to them than their own households. All the dragon saw was meat, and that was enough.

Like a thunderbolt hurled by an angry storm god, Malok descended, jaws agape in a roar that could shake the roots of a mountain, fire and smoke flaring from his nostrils, black wings spread like the grim shroud of Morr himself. The terrified herdsmen stared at the mammoth shape of the dragon, faces turning pallid, mouths dropping open in horror. The herds around them began lowing in fright as soon as the acrid stink of the wyrm offended their noses, arousing ancient fears. To their credit, the herdsmen tried to contain the fright of the cattle even as they fought against the terror gnawing at their own hearts. But it was like trying to stand against a stormy tide. The huge herd of the Marquis Duvalier began to stampede, smashing the herdsmen beneath their hooves as they fled before the dragon.

Malok watched the herd stampede, swooping down low to intercept the cattle, to change their direction. Occasionally, the dragon would cast a quick gout of fire from his fanged jaws when the looming shadow of his form alone was not enough to turn the cattle, the fire repelling the bullocks instantly. There was a box canyon ahead, nestled between a cluster of small hills. The dragon was guiding his prey toward the natural, bowl-like depression. It would take more than a single bullock, more than any dozen, to fill the dragon's belly. The reptile intended to gorge himself on the entire herd.

The leading cattle encountered the stone wall of the canyon, slamming into it as the weight and momentum of those running behind bowled into them. Slavishly following the example of the animals before them, the stampede continued to pack itself into the canyon, filling the declivity with a solid mass of lowing, frightened beef. Even as the rearmost animals began to turn around, to escape the trap into which they had fled, the enormous shape of Malok dove upon the entrance of the canyon, like a lion pouncing upon a jackal. The dragon's gigantic bulk and evil scent turned the cattle yet again, crashing backwards into one another in their fruitless quest for another way out. Malok watched the animals for a moment, then drew his head back, allowing the fires within him to build and gather.

FOR SEVERAL DAYS now, the peasantry of Bordeleaux had been reporting that a dragon was despoiling the dukedom, slaughtering entire villages, and laying waste to crops and fields. Such reports had travelled far, taking on a life of their own, the awful aspect of the creature growing with each retelling, the record of atrocities laid at its feet increasing with every league the stories travelled. The lords of Bretonnia understood their humble people, knowing that they were a superstitious and simple folk, given to flights of fancy and populating their imaginings with all manner of dread beings. But they knew also that for such stories to have become so widespread that there must be some grain of truth behind them. Though no dragon worthy of the name had been seen in Bretonnia for centuries, such creatures had once been a common enough menace before their breed was all but exterminated by the valiant knights who bent their knee before king and Lady. Was it possible that one such monster had perhaps escaped the fate that had befallen all its kin? The very possibility ignited the ambitions of young knights wherever the stories spread. It was not long before isolated bands of bold knights errant eager to earn their name and stalwart knights of the realm intent on proving their mettle against a beast of legend found themselves on the ill-tended roads of Bordeleaux, journeying toward the lands from whence the tales had originated.

Among these knights was one who had taken up the quest, searching for the holy chalice of the Lady. When first he heard of the dragon, Sir Fulkric knew that this was the mighty quest the Lady had set him, the task he must undertake to prove himself worthy of drinking from the grail.

As Sir Fulkric rode southward, toward the region where it was said the dragon could be found, he encountered the small bands of knights who were likewise intent on smiting the wyrm. Once again, inspiration took its hold upon Sir Fulkric, and as he encountered these small bands of dragonslayers, he invited them to make their journey with him. Fulkric knew that it was just possible that he might prove unworthy, that it might be the beast and not himself to emerge triumphant in their contest. If such were to come to pass, it must fall to another to end the monster's rampage.

Many of the knights he encountered agreed with Fulkric's point of view, understanding that more than their own honour and prestige, the death of the dragon must be achieved for the good of the land. It was decided that they would take turns in attempting to smite the vile beast, the most valiant and noble of their company being allowed to make the first attack upon the monster. If that worthy should fall, then the next most heroic of their gathering should be allowed the chance of avenging his fallen companion and vanquishing the horrible monster.

Sir Fulkric's squire took down the names of each knight who joined the ever growing company, recording their deeds and honours and ranking them by these accomplishments, determining their place in the roster that would challenge what they had taken to calling the Beast of Bordeleaux. As a knight who had taken up the quest, and as the warrior who had organised the growing crusade, Sir Fulkric humbly allowed his own name to appear at the top of the list.

By the time the force of knights and their attendants reached the burned out cinders of a small village on the road to Mousillon, they numbered over a hundred men, including knights from as far away as Aquitaine and Lyonesse.

Early in the morning hours, as the knights began to stir from the tented pavilions their servants had erected some small distance from the ashes of the village, the sharp-eyed squire of a knight from Gisoreaux announced that there was smoke on the horizon. Thick and black, roiling like some sea-borne tempest, it was clear to every man in the company that what they saw was no simple peasant cookfire. The call to arms was shouted and squires hastened to help their masters into their gleaming suits of steel plate and colourful tabards. Warhorses were dressed and armoured, lances and swords sharpened in anticipation of the coming battle. It was little different from the eve of war, save that the light of ambition shone a bit more clearly in the eyes of each knight.

The armoured warriors spurred away from their camp at speed, leaving their retainers and many of the squires behind. The pillar of black smoke danced and writhed in the sky before them, as though calling out to them, beckoning them. At the fore of the knights, Sir Fulkric murmured a prayer to the Lady that his heart would hold true, that his courage would strengthen his arm, that his sword would strike cleanly. There was no question of the beast's doom, not with so great a company riding forth to smite him. Even if the dragon were able to slay some of them, each knight would take his toll on the monster.

Once, a visiting dignitary from Estalia had described the bullfights of his homeland, how the fighters would attack the bull in waves, each man not seeking to kill the powerful animal, only to injure it and draw off more of its strength, until the time came when the matador would step forward to finish the animal. The dragon could fare no better than the bull, not with so many knights opposing it.

For much of the morning they rode. Fulkric had to curb the eagerness that filled each knight's breast, that they might not fatigue their horses before they drew within sight of their quarry. It was nearing noon when the knights finally reached the source of the smoke. They reined in their horses at the base of a hill, beyond which the thick clouds boiled. Clearly the dragon had set fire to whatever lay beyond the hill, indulging its malevolent desire for wanton destruction and wickedness. The horses shied, clearly disliking the smell of the smoke, though the only odour the knights could detect was that of cooked beef. Fulkric, however, was inclined to trust the instincts of his charger. The smell of dragon was said to upset animals, and if that was the case, then the reptile might yet be near.

Sir Fulkric called out to his squire, who dutifully rode forward. The knight ordered his servant to read out the roster, that all in the company might know their position and take up his place should his turn arise. The squire had called out only a dozen names when the horses began to whinny in fright. Now there was no mistaking the thick, acrid stink, the reptilian musk of a great wyrm, overpowering even the reek of three hundred charred cattle. The knights, almost as a man, looked away from the squire's recitation, lifting their eyes to stare at the top of the hill.

A head slowly rose above the brambles and stones, an enormous wedge-shaped head, coated in scales of crimson. The knights stared in awe at the sight, for it was as large as a carriage, and the blackened object hanging from its jaws was, they realised, the entire carcass of a full grown bullock.

For a long moment, the dragon did not move, gazing off into the distance, its head framed by the black smoke billowing behind him. Then the monster's gaze shifted, its yellow, snake-like eyes transfixing the warriors arrayed at the base of the hill. The mammoth jaws opened, freeing the carcass to tumble down the face of the hill. A roar like the splitting of the earth itself bellowed from the dragon's maw, a shriek that rippled across the valley.

Sir Fulkric looked upon the awful sight, dumbfounded by the enormity of it. It was bigger than anything he'd ever seen, bigger than even the largest river barge or merchant ship he'd heard of, if the rest of the creature's titanic size matched that of its head. The idea of a single man trying his sword against such a beast seemed utter lunacy. He looked aside at the knights around him. He could almost feel their pride and courage withering beneath the dragon's gaze, and could almost see their noble hearts shuddering beneath their breastplates of steel. Nor was he alone in his imaginings. After its first wrathful stare, the dragon uttered a low snort of contempt, then the awful countenance withdrew behind the hill once more.

Fulkric fought to steady his steed as he drew his sword. If he did not act now, then the entire company might break apart, scattering as their fear devoured their honour. This, then, was why the Lady had led him here. Not to slay this terrible creature on his own, but to lead these worthy and valiant warriors in ridding the kingdom of this rampaging horror. This was his test, and Fulkric was determined that he would be worthy of it.

The knight raised his sword high above his head, lifting his voice in a great shout that drew the attention of his fellows, even those struggling to maintain control of their steeds. In a voice filled with the courage that had led him to victory in battle against the beastmen of Chalons and mercenary soldiers in the hinterlands of Couronne, Fulkric called upon the other knights not to allow their fear to unman them, not to cast aside their honour in the face of some malevolent beast. He extolled them to place their hearts and their faith in the Lady, to trust in her grace to see them through this mighty deed. Many of them might perish in the coming battle, but it was the manner of a knight's death that was the final testament to the worthiness of his name. And what more noble death could there be than sparing their beloved kingdom from the rapacious pillaging of this monster?

There was no cheer of approval, no mighty shout of support for Fulkric's impassioned words. But as the knight turned his horse about, facing the mouth of the little valley behind the hill, the little canyon that was now choked with a virtual wall of smoke, he found that he was not alone. To a man, the other knights reined their horses beside him, lances at the ready. There was no longer any thought of personal honour or prestige. This battle would be one they would share, one that would be fought for the glory of Bretonnia, not that of any one man. Fulkric held up his hand, and looked over at his waiting squire.

'Take the list back with you,' he told his servant. 'Let them know who it was that fought here this day. Let them know that in the hour of its need, the knights of Bretonnia did not abandon their people and their land!' Fulkric concluded his speech by dropping his hand, leading the charge into the thick black smoke.

His squire lingered until the last knight had disappeared into the valley, then turned away, riding with all haste back to their camp.

The squire's list would be used to inscribe the memorial that would stand for centuries at the mouth of the canyon. Beneath it, there was a grave, a single grave for Sir Fulkric and his knights, for the identities of the ash and heat-twisted suits of mail that were recovered from the valley could not be told. As one they had charged into the valley to face the dragon, as one they had died, and as one were they entombed. *In Pace Requiescat.*

FROM THE TOP of a small hillock, a group of men watched the smoke billowing in the distance. As they looked on, an enormous shape of crimson and black emerged from the smoke, its leathery wings beating the air with powerful strokes. Beneath the awful shape, a trio of mounted figures rode madly away from the mouth of a narrow canyon. Even from so great a distance, the shine of sunlight upon the armour that clothed the riders announced to the observers that the horsemen were knights.

The huge dragon circled above the racing steeds, then like some fiery comet, came hurtling down upon the earth. Like a hawk falling upon a hare, the immense reptile struck one of the riders, crushing both man and horse into the ground beneath its own tremendous bulk. The other riders did not spare a backward glance at their slain comrade, but spurred their own animals to greater effort. The dragon simply remained as it was, one claw poised above the mashed ruin of the rider it had struck down. It seemed the other knights had been granted a reprieve as the monster made no effort to lift itself back into the air. Then the dragon's head reared back like a coiling serpent. Flame and fire exploded from the dragon's jaws, engulfing the two riders as they tried to escape, igniting the hair, cloth and even skin of the stricken men and beasts. The knights fell from their chargers, boiled within their suits of steel plate. The chargers themselves continued to run – living torches that were soon lost behind a tangle of brush and trees.

Even from their vantage point miles in the distance, the watchers could hear the mighty roar of triumph the dragon sent lashing at the heavens. It was a sound to make even the most valiant of men shake and tremble. For the less stalwart hearts that had sworn their services to the Viscount Augustine de Chegney, the terror was even more profound.

Only one man among the small group of watchers seemed undisturbed by what they had seen. Indeed, upon the black-cloaked man's cruel face, an avaricious smile had formed and a greedy light had entered his eyes. Rudol, renegade wizard of the Celestial Order, pointed a claw-like hand to the spectacle unfolding in the distance.

'Look upon it, Thierswind! Look upon that magnificent brute!' Rudol cackled. 'What may stand before the might of such a monster!'

The man to whom the wizard spoke was a huge figure, easily towering above Rudol and the dozen men-at-arms who stood nearby. Sir Thierswind wore a suit of plate armour much like that favoured by the now vanquished men who had fallen prey to the dragon's ire. His helm, which he held beneath his arm, bore the likeness of a bull, great horns spreading out from either side. Normally, the dark coloured tabard of de Chegney would have been worn over his armour, but the viscount had called for discretion in this matter and anything that would boldly proclaim the identity of his servants was to be avoided. The knight had served his master long enough to know the danger of disobeying his wishes, even if they chafed at what remained of the knight's pride.

Thierswind's harsh, almost brutish, features did not display the same enthusiasm as the wizard, and it was with great unease that the warrior at last spoke. 'You told his lordship that you could control this monster,' the knight reminded Rudol. 'But how is any man able to do such a thing?' Once more, Thierswind's eyes strayed to the gigantic reptile, now picking bits of bone and flesh from between its talons.

Rudol laughed, a harsh and mocking sound. 'When I have the Fell Fang back in my possession,' the wizard proclaimed, 'even that fearsome beast will be nothing more than a slave, a faithful dog to obey my every command! Think of it Thierswind! That mighty beast descending from the midnight sky to burn down the homes of my enemies, to grind their bones into dust beneath his claws!'

'You mean his lordship's enemies,' Thierswind warned, reminding the wizard of his loyalty. The knight's hand was closed around the hilt of his sword. Rudol carefully considered the knight, and his blade, then nodded his head in apology.

'Of course, the wishes of the master come first,' Rudol said, his voice absent of the enthusiasm it had shown only a few minutes before. 'I fear that I let my excitement overcome me. Please, accept my humble apologies.'

Thierswind continued to regard the wizard dubiously, his hand still closed upon the hilt of his sword. He did not trust Rudol, nor did the viscount. The wizard needed their help, it seemed, in obtaining this artefact, but once it was secured, perhaps he would have no further need of the oath of service he had taken. De Chegney had warned his knight to take no chances with the dangerous sorcerer, to strike fast and true at the first sign of treachery. A master at betrayal and subterfuge himself, the viscount had an uncanny knack for sensing duplicity in others.

As if sensing the turn in Sir Thierswind's thoughts, Rudol's face darkened and his voice became stern. 'I would not use that sword, Thierswind,' he cautioned. 'Only I can sense the geas I placed upon the Fell Fang. Only I can lead you to it. Your master will not thank you for denying him such a weapon.' Rudol smiled as Thierswind released his hold on the sword.

'A very wise decision,' the wizard told him. He turned, staring off into the distance. 'The man we are hunting is near now, but moving again.' He pointed with a clawed hand, indicating the south. 'Let us hasten to relieve him of this burden he carries. Then we shall all gain what we desire.'

THE HANDSOME BANDIT was feeling a bit more himself now that he had put the cursed city of Mousillon and the dungeons of his former patron the Duc Marimund behind him. With most of the city cringing within their hovels in the aftermath of the dragon's attack, leaving Mousillon had been relatively easy. Just the same, he had paid a quick visit on Jacques, the old brigand who had led him to Marimund's castle, ensuring that he was not unduly harassed by the impoverished and desperate rabble dwelling in the streets. Perhaps Jacques had not known how Marimund's feelings toward Gobineau had changed. Perhaps his old friend really hadn't understood what he was leading the outlaw into. Still, Gobineau did not believe in letting any debt pass uncollected, and besides which, he'd needed some decent clothes and some travelling money after his stay in Marimund's dungeons. Jacques certainly wouldn't be needing them any longer.

Gobineau watched impassively as the rather plain looking serving wench brought the plate of mutton to his table. The inn prospered chiefly because of its location near the hunting grounds of no less than three local lords, and after a hard day of hounding boars and chasing stags, the knights were often of a mind to stop at the inn and sample its cellar. Fortunately, Gobineau saw no evidence that any of Bretonnia's chivalrous defenders were about this evening. If the rumours he'd heard were to be believed, they were probably out chasing after his dragon. After what he'd seen in Mousillon, Gobineau didn't think anyone would be hearing from any knight who found what he was looking for ever again.

The maid set the steaming mutton down before Gobineau, batting her doe-like eyes at him as she did so. The outlaw looked up at her, sucking at his teeth as he considered her charms. Not much to work with, he decided. His stay in Marimund's dungeon hadn't been long enough to lower his personal standards quite that much. He waved the woman away, paying her reluctant retreat little mind as he prepared to attack his meal with his knife.

'Ranald's cloak!' the thief cursed as he hastily withdrew the mutton from his mouth. He glared at the serving wench who was now timidly returning to his table, drawn by his outburst. With a violent motion, Gobineau hurled the plate at her. 'I said I wanted this cooked!' the outlaw roared. 'This is as cold as an eel!'

The serving maid knelt, retrieving the spilled mutton from the floor. 'But it was cooked,' she protested, cowed by the anger in the outlaw's voice. 'Any longer in the flame and it would have burnt.'

'Then burn it!' Gobineau snarled back. 'You mud-grubbing peasants might be used to eating your victuals raw, but I am accustomed to finer things!' He gestured at the girl with the point of his knife. 'Now take that back to the kitchen and see that it is prepared properly this time!' Gobineau let his furious eyes linger on the woman until she had retreated back through the door that led to the kitchens, then turned his gaze on the few other patrons scattered about the inn's common room, daring any of them to take issue with his harsh tones. Not a one cared to match the outlaw's eyes.

Gobineau turned his attention back toward the tankard of ale sitting on the table before him, one hand reaching up to scratch at his shoulder. Whatever cinder had struck him had certainly done its wicked work well. Examining it after liberating a horse from a peasant farmer a few miles outside Mousillon, the rogue had found his shoulder to be raw and red, as though someone had placed a hot iron there. The skin had peeled away and what lay beneath was wrinkled and slick with pus. Gobineau supposed that it was worry over this ailment that made him so irritable, there were enough diseases running rampant through Mousillon to make an ordained healer from the temple of Shallya shudder. The bandit desperately hoped that he had not contracted one of them.

A loud, bellowing voice thundering from the entrance of the inn snapped Gobineau from his worried thoughts, causing the thief's sword to leap into his hand, even as he dropped into a crouch that placed the bulk of his table between himself and the doorway.

'Jean Pierre Gobineau!' the voice roared. The rogue relaxed slightly as he saw the man who shouted his name. He was a tall, muscular brute with a full black beard where it was not interrupted by the criminal brand that graced his left cheek.

The bearded man strode across the inn as though he owned the place, his face showing that he took a great deal of amusement in Gobineau's reaction. The outlaw slowly rose, but kept his sword drawn.

'Hubolt,' the rogue greeted the newcomer, keeping his voice level and without either enthusiasm or hostility. 'I should have thought that ugly face would have been sitting in a basket by now.'

'Not for lack of trying on the part of the king's men,' Hubolt grinned back. 'I'd have imagined you knifed by some woman's outraged husband.'

'I still might if old friends see fit to shout my name across public places,' Gobineau retorted acidly.

Hubolt laughed at the outlaw's comment. 'Oh, you don't have to worry about that here,' the bearded man assured him. 'Not with this rabble. They wouldn't dare tell somebody about one of Hubolt the Black's friends tarrying here.' The big man paused, directing his gaze at the low-born patrons of the inn. 'They wouldn't dare,' he repeated in a deep growl. Those who had been observing the exchange between the two rogues hastily looked away, finding the wood grain of their tabletops of much greater interest.

'Still playing the brigand?' Gobineau inquired casually as he resumed his seat. Hubolt retrieved a chair from another table and sat down beside the other outlaw.

'Aye, and a bit of poaching as well,' Hubolt said. 'Still a fair bit of money to be made smuggling things into Mousillon too, if you have the nerve and the contacts.' There was a suggestive spark in the brigand's voice, one that Gobineau readily interpreted.

'Not for me, thanks,' the rogue replied. 'In fact, I've just come from there. I think I've seen enough of Mousillon to last me for some time.'

'Driven off by this dragon everyone is talking about, eh?' Hubolt laughed. 'They say it burned down half of Mousillon. Every knight from here to Quenelles seems to have taken it into his head to ride off and kill it.' The brigand laughed again. 'Ah well, while the cat's away chasing shadows, the rats have free run of the mill!'

'What if this dragon was more than a mere shadow?' Gobineau said.

Hubolt smiled back at him, as though waiting for the gist of the jest. Gobineau allowed the brigand several moments to wait. An idea was forming in the rogue's mind, a scheme so audacious it was worthy only of a man of his own boldness and cunning. But he might need to take on a few partners to make it work. Hubolt had been a tractable enough fellow in the old days, neither stupid enough to endanger his fellow rogues nor clever enough to worry about him usurping Gobineau's schemes for his own.

'Bah,' the brigand scoffed, taking a deep swallow of the ale in Gobineau's tankard. 'I've never seen a dragon, nor met anyone who wasn't a liar who had!'

'I've seen it,' Gobineau stated, staring hard at Hubolt, daring the larger man to call him a liar. 'I watched it smash Duc Marimund's castle into dust.' Hubolt was silent for a long moment, digesting this information.

'Then the knights will be coming back soon,' the brigand grumbled. 'Seems the good times are going to be short.'

'The good times are only beginning,' Gobineau contradicted him. 'Any knight that goes looking for that monster is only going to find his own death. I've seen it, seen what it can do. The only way those men are coming back is in caskets.' A sly grin manifested itself on Gobineau's face.

'These are times made for men bold enough to take what they want.'

Hubolt nodded his head. 'I can't say I'd miss the knights, but I also can't say I believe in this knight-slayer of yours. There may have been dragons before, there might even be one now, but in every legend I've ever heard, its always been the dragon that came out worst.'

Gobineau reclaimed his tankard, taking another sip of his ale. 'If you'd seen what I have seen, you'd know that there is a great discrepancy between legend and fact.' A cunning light gleamed in the outlaw's eyes. 'But let us tarry in the land of legend for a moment. What if I told you there was a way to call this dragon? A way to make it do what you wanted?'

Hubolt laughed again, grabbing back the tankard. 'I'd say you'd been drinking something a lot stronger than this swine-piss!'

Gobineau smiled back. That was the reaction he'd expected to hear.

'Ah, but there are some people who might not find the possibility so funny,' the outlaw stated. 'They'd take it very seriously indeed. Might do anything to keep a bad man from whistling for his dragon. They might pay anything too.' Suddenly Hubolt's face was entirely serious.

'You're saying a clever man might use these dragon stories to line his own pockets?' The brigand rubbed his hairy chin as he considered the prospect.

Gobineau leaned forward, lowering his voice into a conspiratorial whisper. 'We tell them that if they don't pay us, we'll call the dragon down on them. Burn their crops and their homes and their plump little children.'

'But what do we do if they won't pay?' the brigand pointed out. 'They'll need some convincing.'

'Why, we call up the dragon and burn down their village,' Gobineau said. 'Then the next village will require less convincing.'

'Call up the dragon,' Hubolt snickered. 'I like that, Gobineau. Of course, you mean that you have me and my boys
set a few fires in the middle of the night, eh? Burn 'em out
while everybody is sleeping and leave none to tell the tale?'

'Something like that,' Gobineau grinned back. He looked
away from Hubolt, watching as the serving wench emerged
from the kitchens with another platter of mutton.

'Sounds like a fine scheme!' Hubolt agreed. 'Especially
with all the knights busy chasing after their tails! Might
make a tidy profit before folks get wise.'

The brigand gave a sour look to the servant girl as she set
the plate down before Gobineau and hastily retreated.
'Where do we start?' he asked, returning his attention to the
outlaw.

'I was thinking we might start with Quenelles,' Gobineau
told him, eliciting a boisterous laugh from Hubolt as the
brigand imagined the preposterous magnitude of working
such a deception upon an entire city. Gobineau left him to
his laughter, attacking the blackened mutton with his knife.
Once again, he spat the meat from his mouth.

'May the Dark Gods rot your cook's soul!' the rogue
snarled. He rose to his feet, impaling the larger portion of
mutton on the length of his sword blade. Hubolt watched
in perplexity as Gobineau strode to the roaring fireplace that
rested against one wall of the room. The rogue thrust his
sword into the fire, letting the flames crackle and claw at the
mutton. For long minutes, he concentrated upon his task,
ignoring the whisperings and mutterings his actions evoked
from the peasants watching him. At length, Gobineau
retrieved his blade and marched with it back to his table,
sliding a blackened chunk of charred ash onto his plate.
Hubolt watched in morbid fascination as his friend began
to eat the almost cremated mutton.

'It's so hard to find people who know how to prepare
food properly these days,' Gobineau complained between
crunching mouthfuls of charred meat.

CHAPTER TEN

THE TRAIL THE bounty hunters followed was a grim one, a path
of ash and ruin, littered with the wreckage of human bodies.
The smoke that had beckoned them away from the south had
been rising from a small box canyon, the fire still chewing
away at whatever brush and twisted trees yet remained. The
floor of the valley was a blanket of ash, reminding Ulgrin of
the volcanoes that sometimes misbehaved in the southward
stretches of the World's Edge Mountains. Poking up from the
black cinders were broken bones and slabs of heat-ravaged
steel. The devastation was obvious, the power of the force
that had wrought it almost beyond belief. Brunner quickly
tired of the morbid game of counting helmets in an attempt
to decide how many knights had fallen here. Much of the
armour was so warped and blackened by the dragon's fire
that it was difficult even to determine sometimes if what he
thought to be a helm might not instead be a breastplate or a
piece of barding. The far end of the valley was heaped with
the bones and burnt carcasses of hundreds of cattle.

'Quite an appetite that lizard has,' Ulgrin commented, but even his jest was half-hearted, voiced to try and fend away the dread that was building within the normally stalwart dwarf.

They did not linger long in the valley, following still more distant columns of smoke rising in the east. For the rest of the day, the three hunters found themselves journeying from one scene of tragedy and ruin to another. Here a farmstead blasted into a crater, there an orchard, its trees stripped and barren in the aftermath of the dragon's flame. Once, they came upon what seemed to be a knight sitting beside the road. Ithilweil had dismounted to investigate the man when he did not respond to Ulgrin's hail. She would not speak of what lay behind the knight's visor when she lifted it, saying only that the warrior was dead.

THEY MADE CAMP that night beside a narrow gorge overlooking the River Grismerie. Brunner selected the ground because it made a good defensible position, the severe drop effectively forming a bulwark against attack from the south and the west. Unless of course the attacker were able to fly, such as a dragon. Of course, if that were the case, Brunner knew firsthand that even a castle was no stronghold against such a creature.

Ithilweil again stared out into the night, as though trying to cast her gaze far enough to see the creature whose tracks they followed. There was no faint glow upon the horizon, no thick pall of smoke marring the night wind. Ithilweil took that to mean that the dragon had settled down somewhere, perhaps resting after indulging its lust for destruction. But she knew that it would only be a matter of time before the wyrm roused itself once more and the fires burned anew.

'Ithilweil.' The elf turned as she heard Brunner call out her name. The bounty hunter was seated before the fire, still wearing his armour and weapons, having removed only his helmet. Nearby, Ulgrin sat on a mossy stone, chewing nervously at the pipe protruding from his beard. 'You gave a name to this monster. What more can you tell me about it? If Gobineau decides to call on it again, I'd like to know as much as possible about what we will be facing.'

The elf glided across the campsite, sitting upon the ground beside the fire. 'Much of what I know about him is rumour, the rest speculation.' Ithilweil paused, collecting her thoughts. 'The dragon is named Malok, a name that is heaped with horror and suffering.'

'Bah! Malok is known to my people as well!' interrupted Ulgrin. 'The name itself is from the old Khazalid. It means "malice", and you'll find that there is an entire page in the Book of Grudges with that gold-stealing lizard's name upon it!'

'Perhaps he had another name in the tongue of my people,' Ithilweil said, 'but if so, that given to him by the dwarfs soon displaced it. It is known that when war broke out between my people and the dwarfs,' the elf paused, expecting some surly outburst from Ulgrin, but he remained silent, 'the dragon served a prince of my people who had settled in the lands now known as the Grey Mountains. I can now imagine how that prince caused Malok to serve him, for surely he was one of the exiled renegade lords of Caledor.'

'It would figure that there would be elf sorcery at the back of all this,' Ulgrin grunted, spitting a blob of spittle into the fire.

'Then this prince was the one who created the Fell Fang?' Brunner asked.

'Or had it made for him,' Ithilweil said. 'But it would have been his will that made the artefact work, the strength of his own soul that bound the dragon to him. The Fell Fangs are terrible things, dominating the spirit of one creature by crushing it with the will of another. That was why they were denounced by the rulers of Ulthuan. And they are dangerous, even for the most strong-willed, for control is never assured. It is easier, less taxing to force a dragon to do something that is in its nature, but far more difficult to subdue its own urges. There was also speculation that the imposing of spirits might not be a one-way door as the Fell Fang was designed to be. It might be possible for the dragon's fiery spirit to bleed over into the body of the one using the artefact. In any case, control is tenuous at best, and once lost, the ire of the dragon will focus itself upon the possessor of the Fell Fang. For it will be able to sense the exact location of the Fang's user, however great the distance.'

'So, our reptilian friend might have had a fair journey when Gobineau called him to Mousillon,' Brunner observed. 'But next time the dragon will be closer, have less distance to travel and be there much sooner.'

'Yes,' agreed the elf. 'Without a powerful will to restrain him, Malok will find the Fell Fang, kill the one using it and probably level everything within a hundred miles. There are few among even the oldest and noblest of my people who would be able to restrain a creature like Malok, for his power and malevolence can only have increased through the ages. Among men, I don't think such strength exists. I am certain that if it does, it is not nestled within the avaricious dung heap that your Gobineau employs as his soul.'

'Leave it to elves to create something anybody can use but nobody can control!' Ulgrin swore, spitting again into the fire.

'What I still do not understand,' Brunner said, 'is how this elf prince ever lost control of Malok.'

'He used Malok against the dwarfs when there was war between our two peoples,' Ithilweil replied. 'The scars that so easily identify the wyrm were given to him during that conflict as the prince drove him against his enemies. The wound along Malok's belly was earned when the shaft hurled by a dwarf bolt thrower nearly skewered the dragon during the battle of Ilendril's Hill. Such was the potency of whatever runes the dwarf smiths placed upon the enormous spear that even a dragon, centuries later, still bears the scar. The other wound was inflicted during the scourging of the dwarf stronghold our chronicles named "Iron Peak", a jagged bolt of sorcerous lightning called down upon Malok by the high priest of the dwarfs.'

'Aye,' agreed Ulgrin, 'and well do we dwarfs remember that day, when the elf's pet monster gobbled up one of the oldest and wisest runesmiths in the kingdom.' Ulgrin ground his teeth together. 'That's a crime both the dragon and those who set him upon us will answer for one day.'

'But that still does not tell me how and why they lost control of the dragon,' Brunner interrupted, hoping to stem the brewing argument between elf and dwarf.

'It was decided to abandon the war after the Phoenix King was slain at Tor Alessi,' the enchantress stated. 'The war with the dwarfs was taking too high a toll, the killing far too senseless to endure any longer. It was decided to abandon the colonies, to return to Ulthuan. A great exodus of my people left the towered palaces and shining cities they had built for themselves here, to board the ships that would carry them back to the lands of their birth. The elf prince who controlled Malok charged his monster with guarding and watching over his people as they marched toward the shore. But protection and preservation was not a thing that came easily to Malok; the dragon longed to kill and destroy, as he had when waging war against the dwarfs. The ordeal of restraining Malok's rebellion would have taxed the prince day and night, until at last his control was lost. There is a tremendous pride within the fiery heart of a dragon, and Malok must have despised sharing in the stigma of the retreat. Perhaps it was this injured pride that at last enabled him to overcome the control of the Fell Fang. However it came about, Malok slew his master and then set about destroying every elf he could find, raining fire down upon the weary refugees as they slowly crept toward the sea.'

'Then at least the old lizard did some good,' Ulgrin muttered, clearly less than sympathetic to Ithilweil's tale of woe.

'Perhaps the records in the Book of Grudges are a bit too harsh on him.'

'It sounds to me as if this Fell Fang is more of a curse than a blessing,' Brunner observed. 'We may just be doing Gobineau a service by relieving him of it.' The bounty hunter stopped speaking as Ithilweil suddenly shot to her feet, frightened eyes scouring the darkness beyond the campfire. Brunner had enough experience with the sharp senses of the elves to know better than to question them. In an instant, he too was on his feet, the cruel length of Drakesmalice in his hand. A moment later, the horses and Ulgrin's mule began to stamp their hooves and voice their own unease as some faint scent offended them.

Ulgrin rose slowly, a sturdy hand axe gripped in each of his meaty fists. 'Any idea what has the animals upset?' the dwarf asked from the corner of his mouth. 'You don't think the lizard is hungry again?' he added in a subdued tone.

'No,' Ithilweil told him, 'but what is waiting out there in the night is just as much an abomination.' Brunner noticed the familiar quality of fear and loathing that edged the elf's voice. Shifting his grip on his sword, the bounty hunter lowered his left hand, unobtrusively palming a small object secreted beneath his vambrace.

A tall figure stalked out from the shadows. The intruder's heavy steps crunched into the dirt, betraying the fact that heavy armour pressed down upon his steel-shod feet. The faint smell that had alarmed the animals grew more pronounced, rising to such a stink that it carried itself to the much less discerning senses of Brunner and Ulgrin. It was a smell both warriors had encountered many times before – the rank stink of death, the vapour of an old battlefield. Both bounty hunters stepped closer to the fire, careful to keep their eyes averted from the flame and ruining their night vision. By degrees, a single baleful eye could be seen, twinkling from the dark shape as it reflected the fire, cat-like.

'A fine tale you spin,' a fell, pustulent voice hissed from the darkness, 'for a faithless elf slut!' Ithilweil visibly flinched as she heard the grotesquely distorted yet sickeningly familiar and hated voice. 'You said much that interested me,' the vampire continued. 'Enough so that I would have a few questions answered before I rip that lying tongue from your pretty face!'

'CORBUS!' ITHILWEIL BREATHED with horror. The enchantress retreated slowly, retracing her steps so that she stood beside Brunner. The bounty hunter took a step forward, lifting Drakesmalice so that the blade interposed itself between the enchantress and the vampire.

'There is reason enough for me to spill your life,' Corbus growled at Brunner.

The vampire knight strode into the circle of light cast by the campfire. Ithilweil gasped in shock as she saw the vampire's mutilated face. A pulpy mass of pus-hued filth was beginning to fill the warped, ruined socket, raw lengths of tendon and muscle had begun to reattach themselves to the vampire's shattered jaw.

The vampire smiled, displaying his fangs and further distorting his already mangled features. 'It will take many nights feasting on the thin blood of peasants to restore my face,' Corbus spat. 'How will you fare after I peel yours from your skull, assassin?'

Brunner kept silent, evaluating the foul knight of the Blood Dragons. Despite the hideous injury to his face, Corbus moved with a grace and strength that would put a professional dancer to shame, and he did so wearing a suit of heavy crimson plate armour that might have been the twin to that destroyed by Ulgrin's battleaxe. The thick Bretonnian broadsword clutched in the vampire's mailed fist was held against the creature's side, but Brunner was not deceived. He had seen the monster in action before and knew that with his inhuman speed, the vampire's unguarded pose was nothing more than an illusion.

'Kill him slowly, Brunner,' Ulgrin snarled. 'That scum owes me a battleaxe!' Despite the dwarf's bravado, Brunner noted that his fellow bounty killer was steadily backing away from the approaching vampire. He could not be certain if the dwarf was intent on his gear, intent on equipping himself with something more imposing than a hand axe, or if his mule and a speedy departure was Ulgrin's intention. The bounty hunter was unwilling to turn his gaze from Corbus long enough to make certain.

'Your filthy blood is not even worth taking,' Corbus hissed at the dwarf. 'Had you kept that foul tongue silent, I might even have allowed you to continue to defile the ground upon which you walk. Now I shall simply gut you like the vermin you are.' The vampire's burning eye turned away from Ulgrin, staring past Brunner at the enchantress sheltering behind him. 'From you I will hear more of this man who calls dragons. I am most eager to meet him.'

'The only one you meet this night is Morr!' Brunner roared, lunging forward, slashing at the vampire with the edge of Drakesmalice. With almost contemptuous ease, Corbus blocked the blow, the strength of the vampire's arm causing the bounty hunter's longsword to tremble. With his sword grinding against Brunner's own, the Blood Dragon's other hand closed about the bounty hunter's throat, undead talons clasping living flesh with a clutch of steel.

'You should have stuck to your tricks, assassin,' the vampire snarled. Corbus's jaw cracked as the vampire's mouth snapped open, far beyond the limits imposed upon it in life. The gleaming, wolf-like fangs shone like polished ivory in the flickering firelight as Corbus brought his ruined face toward Brunner's exposed neck.

'Who says I gave up my tricks?' Brunner managed to choke beneath the vampire's grasp. His left hand flashed forward, a white cloud billowing about the mutilated half of Corbus's face. An ear-piercing shriek erupted from the vampire's mouth as the creature recoiled, dropping Brunner to the ground. Greasy grey smoke steamed from the Blood Dragon's injuries, carrying with it the reek of burning meat. Brunner did not pause to recover from the vampire's brutal grip, instantly lunging forward, swiping at the monster with Drakesmalice even as his other hand removed an object from his belt.

Even in the midst of his agony, the skills and instincts of the life-long warrior exerted themselves and Corbus brought his own sword around in a parrying stroke that easily batted Brunner's blade aside. But with one hand still clutching at the sizzling wreckage of his face, Corbus left his other side exposed. The bounty hunter had put little force behind his feint with Drakesmalice, saving his energy for the true attack. The polished length of the wooden stake he had bought from a disgraced priest of Sigmar in the Tilean port of Miragliano dug into the vampire's side, sinking into the gap between the breast and back plates. The vampire shrieked again as Brunner drove the stake into his unclean flesh. The bounty hunter danced backward as Corbus lashed out at him with an ungainly slash from his broadsword.

The Blood Dragon staggered back, gasping and snarling as he fought against the pain assailing him. Corbus glared at the bounty hunter, his single remaining eye boring into Brunner's own. Then the undead knight lifted his broadsword once more, holding it as though it were a light-weight javelin being readied for a cast. Brunner's hand hovered near the butt of his pistol. He would have no chance of matching the speed of the vampire, but if the creature was as pained as it seemed to be, he might be able to exceed it in the matter of accuracy.

A loud crack and roar from the other side of the camp decided the question. Before Corbus could hurl his sword, the vampire was thrown back, his breastplate exploding as an iron bullet smashed into it. Having backed to the far side of the camp, the vampire was fortuitously poised near the edge of the gorge. The impact of the bullet was enough to knock him over the side. The vampire's wail of frustrated rage echoed from below as he plummeted down toward the banks of the Grismerie.

Brunner turned to find Ulgrin Baleaxe sitting on the ground, smoke rising from the wide-barrelled mouth of his huge rifle, a dwarf weapon known as a thunderer for the imposing noise its discharge created. The recoil from the weapon had knocked Ulgrin from his feet, landing him on his backside. The dwarf grumbled into his beard as he struggled to regain his dignity.

'Five gold crowns for the cost of powder, shot, and accuracy,' Ulgrin declared once he was on his feet again. 'To come from your share of the reward, naturally.'

Brunner shook his head. 'I don't think so,' he told the dwarf. 'Your throat would have been next on his list. Chalk it down to the cost of staying alive.'

Ulgrin snickered, leaning on the broad mouth of his weapon, then recoiling when he found it to still be hot. 'You don't get me that easy,' he said. 'That blood sucker would have been after tall-ears next. More than enough time for me to slip away if I was of a mind to.'

Mention of Ithilweil caused Brunner to look back at the elf. She still stood in the same spot to which she had retreated to avail herself of Brunner's protecting sword. As the bounty hunter stepped nearer, he could see the unfocused glaze in her eyes, hear the faint, musical words whispering through her lips. Carefully, Brunner reached forward, placing his hand on the elf's shoulder. Instantly, the melody stopped and Ithilweil's eyes regained their normal vibrancy.

'Thank you,' the bounty hunter told her, guessing at the purpose of her incantation. It had been more than pain dulling the vampire's unnatural speed and reflexes.

Ithilweil took several deep breaths, trying to restore her composure after her hasty spellcraft.

'It is always dangerous to draw upon the winds of magic when the sun is past and the dark powers are in their ascendancy,' she stated. 'But to allow you to be slain by that abomination would have been worse.' She gave Brunner an approving look. 'That was a clever trick, hurling salt into that monster's face.'

'I told you that I like to know about my enemy,' the bounty hunter replied. 'I've had dealings with such creatures before, and after my first encounter with one, I determined to learn their weaknesses.' He looked back at the edge of the precipice. 'By itself, the salt would only have pained him. But that wooden shaft I drove through his side was crafted for the express purpose of destroying his kind, blessed by the priests of Sigmar, if the good intentions of priests and gods have any merit.'

'Then that is the last we'll be seeing of that leech,' Ulgrin commented.

'Let us hope,' Ithilweil replied, a haunted quality of uncertainty in her voice. 'But I should feel much better if we were far from this place.'

'I don't think any of us would get much sleep knowing that thing's body is down below,' Brunner agreed, replacing Drakesmalice into its sheath. 'We'll risk a bit of night travel. Who knows,' the bounty hunter observed with grim humour, 'we may even find ourselves sharing the same inn as Gobineau.'

THERE WERE FIVE rogues in Hubolt's little mob, though Gobineau would not have put much stock in any of them should problems arise. Two of them looked old enough to be Hubolt's father, if any man had ever cared to accept that dubious honour. Another was young enough that Gobineau wondered if his chin had even considered sprouting hair yet. The other two were little different from the simple peasant rabble he'd shared the inn with the previous night, though they wore swords at their sides. None of these men had that ruthless, predatory air, the chill in their eyes that marked the veteran bandit. Whatever notoriety these men had garnered was due entirely to their leader.

Still, Gobineau knew such men were easily manipulated: lacking the proper experience or cunning to think for themselves, they were apt to follow most any command before questioning the intent behind it. No, Gobineau would have nothing to fear from such a quarter. Hubolt, however, might be a different matter. If he was reduced to allowing such men to call him captain, then the bandit must have fallen much farther than he had admitted to at the inn. There was no smuggling scheme with Mousillon, these men would be stripped and eaten five minutes after setting foot in that city. Probably not much thievery either, beyond some poaching and rustling. Hubolt would indeed bear watching, it would take only the tiniest spark of ambition to cause the man to think of better things.

The bearded bandit stared back at Gobineau from the fore-front of their small column. They were riding through a narrow strip of woods skirting the edge of a vast tract of farmland. After some discussion, the two had decided that Gisoreaux might make a more viable base of operations than Quenelles. Apparently the predations of the dragon had disturbed more than just the knights. There were tales that the wyrm's presence had driven twisted beastmen from their lairs deep within the Forest of Chalons. Hubolt was not willing to put such rumours to the test, and after seeing the man's company of rogues, Gobineau was inclined to agree with him. He'd not trust such men against a mob of children. Besides, if beastmen were roaming about the countryside near Quenelles, then the peasants would already have troubles enough to concern them than the threat of a dragon destroying their homes.

'Now, friend,' Hubolt said, his lips twisted into a grotesque leer because of the brand marring his face. 'We've yet to discuss the split for this scheme of yours.' It was a topic that had been suggested a few times. Gobineau noticed that Hubolt's demeanour was becoming more unruly the deeper into the country they rode. Perhaps the bandit was already starting to decide that he didn't need his partner? Gobineau had hoped to delay that eventuality a little longer. 'Since I have my five men to think of, perhaps I should receive the larger…'

Whatever percentage Hubolt was about to mention was lost in the strangled cry that rose from his throat. A red-feathered arrow protruded from the brigand's chest, its momentum knocking him from his saddle and spilling him into the road. Gobineau did not spare a second look for his erstwhile ally, but quickly scanned the road ahead. Emerging from cover were a half-dozen leather-clad archers, an armoured knight with a horned helmet mounted upon a great black warhorse behind them. However, it was the mounted man seated next to the knight that caused Gobineau's breath to fall short. How Rudol had found him was not quite so important as what the wizard wanted and was likely to do in the way of getting it.

Just the same, even as his instinct of self preservation stirred, another emotion began to assert itself. The desire to crush these men who dared to oppose him, to still their hearts and leave their burning carcasses smouldering beneath the sun. Gobineau caught himself just as he began to put spurs against the side of his horse, to initiate his mad and suicidal intention. With terror, Gobineau fought down the insane aggression that had flared up within him. He was not about to lose his life fighting knights and wizards. Not when there were others to fight his battles for him.

'Ride them down before they can fire again!' Gobineau shouted, drawing his sword and waving it above the neck of his horse like some Kislevite cavalry officer. Hubolt's vermin did not think twice, but dug their spurs into their own mounts and charged forward. Gobineau had to hand it to Hubolt, at least he had an eye for collecting morons.

The outlaw turned his own mount around with a savage tug on the reins. With any luck, the sacrifice of Hubolt's men would buy him enough time to put some distance between himself and the wizard.

RUDOL GLARED DOWN at Sir Thierswind. The knight had dismounted, prowling amongst the bodies of the men his archers had slaughtered, checking each one for the object the wizard had described for him so often since they had left the Chateau de Chegney. The wizard fairly burned with irritated frustration, enraged at this arrogant swordsman's stupidity. Rather than listening to the wizard, rather than hastening with all speed after the man who had escaped, Thierswind had insisted on searching the bodies of the slain for the Fell Fang, sending only two of his men in pursuit of the escaped man. Thierswind made no secret of his distrust of the wizard, suspecting Rudol's every suggestion and warning him that any deception on his part would be reported back to the viscount.

'It seems you were right,' Thierswind conceded as he rose from the last corpse. 'We should have pursued the man who escaped.' There was no note of apology in the knight's voice. Indeed, if anything, his tone was even more arrogant and hostile than before.

'And what will you do now?' Rudol sneered. Thierswind glared back from behind his helm.

'We question the one who is still alive,' the knight snarled back. Two of the men-at-arms dutifully lifted the injured Hubolt from the ground, the arrow still sticking from his chest.

'Who was the man that escaped?' Thierswind demanded. The bandit gave the knight a mocking smile.

Thierswind closed his armoured hands into fists. 'Tell me or…'

'Or what?' Hubolt wheezed. 'You'll kill me? You've already done that, so there's no reason to fear you now!' The bandit began to laugh heartily, enjoying the knight's impotent rage. But the laughter passed into a shriek of mortal agony as violet energy blazed into the arrow, searing through the wooden shaft into Hubolt's body. Seeing what was happening to their captive, the soldiers backed away. Sparks of energy rippled about Hubolt's body. Smoke rose from the stricken man, whose body twitched and shuddered as though seized by a fit. The magical lightning continued to stream into Hubolt until the man's body began to cook from the inside out, his screaming voice cracked with the shrillness of its tormented shrieks. Only then did the sorcerous attack subside, allowing the smoking corpse to topple to the singed earth.

Thierswind and his men looked with open horror upon Rudol as the wizard straightened himself in his saddle, the last flickers of power fading from his eyes. It was his turn to indulge in arrogance, now that he had shown the knight and his scum just who was in command of this little enterprise, that he could destroy each and every one of them with a simple gesture of his hand.

'We will do as *I* say now,' Rudol declared, daring Thierswind to protest. The knight did not rise to the lure, earning himself a reprieve from Rudol's wrath. 'The thief who has the Fell Fang knows we are after him. He will seek to lose himself in the nearest city. We will need to stop him before he can do so.'

'And how are we to accomplish this?' Sir Thierswind managed to ask. Rudol smiled at him indulgently, as though the knight were no more than an idiot child.

'My magic will tell me where the Fell Fang is, always,' Rudol stated. Then a broad smile began to spread on the wizard's features. 'Perhaps two men were enough,' he hissed. 'It appears that our prize is coming back to us.'

BRUNNER DISMOUNTED FROM Fiend, taking a closer look at one of the red-feathered arrows lying beside the bodies of the slain men. They had chanced upon a shepherd who recalled having seen Gobineau pass his fields, riding in the company of a half dozen men with ill-favoured looks. It was a simple matter to follow the trail of the riders, until it at last led them into a stretch of woods and the massacre they now gazed upon.

'Looks like our bandit met some of his fellows,' Ulgrin observed with grim humour. 'No honour among thieves, eh?' he hissed over at Ithilweil. The elf enchantress seemed distracted, out of sorts ever since they had come upon the ghastly scene.

'This was not done by a pack of rival bandits,' Brunner stated. The bounty hunter's voice was laced with such intense hatred that Ulgrin's hand instinctively fell to the small axe nestled beneath his belt.

Brunner snapped the shaft of the arrow he had been examining.

The dwarf wondered at the sudden change in his partner. What could there have been about a simple arrow that could get under the skin of so cold a character as the infamous Brunner? Ulgrin did not know, but suspected that such information might be of great interest and possibly of even greater profit.

'I see,' the dwarf commented, stabbing a finger at the charred remains lying in the middle of the road. 'Our dragon has taken up archery as a hobby.'

'This was not done by a dragon,' Ithilweil stated. 'That poor man was struck down not by dragonfire but by the darkest magic.'

Brunner looked at the corpse, giving it only the briefest of examinations. It was too large to be the man they were hunting. Beyond that fact, he had no interest.

The bounty hunter remounted his warhorse. 'I've seen a man who could work such sorcery,' he declared when he had regained the saddle. 'We are not the only ones hunting Gobineau.'

'Then someone else has claimed the bounty,' Ulgrin grumbled, immediately contemplating the expense of time and effort that he had wasted pursuing the outlaw.

Brunner shook his head. 'I don't think the wizard and his allies are interested in the bounty,' he told the dwarf. 'They are after the Fell Fang, as Ithilweil is.' He stared intently at the tracks leading away from the massacre. 'It looks as if they might have gotten what they were after too.'

'Then we must find them quickly,' Ithilweil told the bounty hunters. 'The Fell Fang in the hands of a fool who doesn't know what he has is bad enough, but it is much more dangerous in the possession of someone who actually thinks he knows what it is!'

Brunner stared back at the red-feathered arrows, remembering another time he had seen them sprouting from the bodies of fallen men. 'We'll find them,' the bounty killer said, confidently. 'Gobineau was with these men. It is likely he is now the prisoner of the ones who killed his comrades. That actually makes our job easier. Gobineau is an outlaw, a man so used to covering his tracks that it comes as easily as breathing to him. The men who have captured him are not, they are knights, trained warriors too arrogant to cover their tracks, too certain of their own abilities to bother about such things.

'We'll find them,' Brunner repeated. 'My concern is what will be waiting for us when we do.'

THE WANING LIGHT cast by the setting sun did little to disconcert the croaking ravens gathered about the broken corpse. The hungry birds had been drawn by the smell of death hovering over the lands in which the dragon now roamed. But there was little left in Malok's wake upon which to feed, only cinders and ash. So it was that the body lying upon the sandy bank of the Grismerie River provided a welcome meal for many hungry creatures. For long hours, their sharp beaks pecked away at the exposed flesh, trying to dig fresh morsels from beneath the coat of steel plate that encased much of the corpse.

One raven picked at the back of the face-down corpse's neck, throwing its head back and letting another sliver of meat slide down its gullet. But the bird had eaten its last: with the retreat of the sun, a new vitality filled the dead thing sprawled beneath the raven's claws. The bird croaked in fright, but as it rose to take flight, a powerful grip closed about it. The raven struggled to free itself even as its former meal shifted its body and rose from the sand.

Corbus glared at the scavenger, then lifted the struggling bird to his mangled, freshly burned face. The vampire's jaws clamped about the raven's body, swiftly draining it of the tiny amount of blood coursing through its veins. It was a pathetic meal, and did nothing to satisfy the vampire's growing thirst. But it would nourish the monster, give him strength to find other, more satisfactory prey.

The undead knight threw the broken bird from him, then closed his hands about the wooden shaft protruding from his side. It had been a near thing: the treacherous assassin had nearly killed him with his dishonourable deceits. The salt had badly burned his already mutilated face, but the stake had come near to destroying him. Only the mail he wore beneath his plate armour had prevented the bounty hunter's blow from piercing deep enough to penetrate his heart. To come so close to destruction when he was so near to redemption was a thought that made Corbus seethe with fury. The assassin would suffer for the indignities he had heaped upon him. By the oaths he had sworn to the Blood Dragons, Brunner would be a long time in meeting his end.

The vampire's jaws distended to utter a long painful howl as, with a tremendous effort, Corbus ripped the stake from his body, casting it into the swift moving waters of the Grismerie.

CHAPTER ELEVEN

GOBINEAU CURSED AGAIN the fickleness of Ranald, god of thieves. Things had seemed to be going so well for him. He'd escaped from the vengeful Duc Marimund and the blighted city of Mousillon, left the notorious bounty killer Brunner buried beneath an entire castle, and made the rather profound discovery that the hoary old elf artefact actually was able to do what myth claimed it could do: summon dragons. Gobineau had just decided on a course of action to exploit his discovery when misfortune had again reared its ugly head. The wizard Rudol had found him, no doubt by some sorcerous means. At first Gobineau had counted himself lucky yet again, making good his escape while Rudol's men slaughtered the sorry remains of Hubolt's bandit gang.

But things had taken a bizarre turn then. Two of Rudol's men had ridden off in immediate pursuit of him, determined that no one should escape the massacre. Even so, their horses had been chosen for war, while Gobineau's had been selected for speed. It should have proven an easy matter to elude his pursuit. Then the same compulsion that had nearly claimed him when the ambush had been sprung came over him once again. Instead of fleeing, Gobineau had turned his steed around, charging headlong into his pursuers. One of the men he had struck down with the edge of his sword, but the other had exploited the demise of his comrade, slashing at Gobineau's horse and causing the injured animal to hurl the outlaw from the saddle. Gobineau had struck the ground hard, and before he could recover his wits, the remaining soldier had disarmed him and bound his hands.

The outlaw had considered that his luck might have been restored when he was brought back to Rudol and the wizard did not kill him outright. The conjurer had immediately relieved Gobineau of the Fell Fang. The outlaw viewed the theft with a surprising degree of relief, something working on a primal level within his soul taking joy in the absence of the enchanted artefact. Then things had started getting worse. First Gobineau learned that the men aiding Rudol were soldiers in the service of the Viscount Augustine de Chegney, a man infamous for his cruelty and villainy. Then he had learned why Rudol had not killed him as the wizard began interrogating the rogue regarding Gobineau's experience with the Fell Fang and how the talisman was employed. For all of his knowledge of legend and lore, the wizard knew far too little about the treasure he coveted.

Gobineau shuddered as he considered their present destination, and the reason Rudol continued to suffer the outlaw to live.

SIR THIERSWIND RODE at the head of the small column of riders, the wizard Rudol beside him. Though the knight towered over the wizard, everything about him dwarfing the thin sorcerer, there was no mistaking the subdued air that hovered about him as he spoke with his companion.

'Why do we not simply return to the Chateau de Chegney?' Thierswind asked once again.

Rudol gave the knight a thin, irritated smile. The professional warrior was becoming even more obnoxious now than he had been with his pompous ego intact. Thierswind kept asking the same question over and again, as though Rudol might change the answer.

'We must ensure that the Fell Fang will do what it is supposed to do,' the wizard told him. 'The viscount would not be terribly forgiving if we presented him with an artefact that does not work. I would rather not trust to his forgiveness if such a thing were to happen, would you?' Rudol turned his attention back to the road ahead. 'We shall find the dragon, and make certain that it will obey the will of he who holds the Fell Fang. Only then will the viscount hear of our success.'

'The bandit,' Thierswind said, gesturing to the centre of the column where the bound outlaw rode the horse of the man he had killed. 'Why keep him alive?'

Rudol was beginning to understand why a suspicious despot like de Chegney trusted a man like Thierswind to command his troops. The man had probably never had an original idea in his life.

'He used the Fang,' Rudol stated. 'He knows how it works firsthand. I have been learning all that he knows, but it is always possible that he is holding something back. The nearer we draw to the dragon, the less keen our prisoner will be to keep things from me. After all, whatever happens to us will happen to him as well.'

Rudol stood upright in his saddle, stretching a claw-like hand forward at the darkening twilight. 'On the horizon!' he shouted. Visible in the distance was an expanse of jagged hills and low mountains. The creature they were looking for was there, Rudol could sense it. Since gaining possession of the Fell Fang, he found that his geas spell had persisted, now attuning itself to the monster bound to the artefact's power. Just as he had been drawn to the Fang, so now the Fang was drawn to the dragon. 'The Massif Orcal! We will find our dragon there!'

* * *

Brunner rose from the path, wiping the mud from his breeches before climbing back into Fiend's saddle. There was no question about it, the men they were hunting had turned south. It made little sense, he knew these men were in the service of Augustine de Chegney. By rights they should be heading east, toward the Grey Mountains and the viscount's domain. Instead they had turned toward the Massif Orcal. There could be only one reason: the wizard was running the show now. And the bounty hunter had a very bad feeling he also knew why Rudol might be so interested in the mountains. It had been several days since they had last seen any sign of the dragon, no new pillars of smoke rising from cremated towns and villages. Ithilweil had offered the possibility that Malok was resting, waiting until the Fang goaded him into activity once more. It was a theory that fit all of the facts, and every tale he had ever heard regarding dragons claimed they preferred to make their lairs in the mountains.

'They are heading for the mountains,' Brunner told his companions.

Ulgrin's face lit up and he grinned beneath his beard. 'Good! Should prove easy to ambush them then!' The dwarf rubbed his hands in anticipation of a swift conclusion to the hunt. His enthusiasm dimmed when he saw that he was the only one pleased by the news.

'The wizard,' Ithilweil said. 'He must know where Malok has gone. With the Fell Fang in his grasp, there are spells he can use to divine the location of the dragon's lair.'

Ulgrin spat into the dirt. 'Well, that collapses the shaft then! There's no way we can go up against a dragon *and* a mad wizard!'

Brunner shook his head. 'Maybe we won't have to. If the dragon is sleeping, we might not need to worry about it.'

'Which just leaves us with a mad wizard to deal with!' Ulgrin protested. 'And even if the dragon is sleeping, all this Rudol lunatic needs to do is blow on that damn elf whistle and the thing will be down on us like a cave fly on filth!'

'We'll just have to make sure he doesn't get the chance to use it,' Brunner told his fellow bounty hunter. 'But if your courage has deserted you, then Ithilweil and myself will see this thing through.'

'Are you saying this wench has more stomach than I do?' Ulgrin growled. Before the dwarf could continue his tirade, the person in question span around in her saddle, looking back down the road they had been travelling upon. Ithilweil's eyes scanned the darkness, her ears listening to the sounds of night. Brunner and Ulgrin both became silent, watching the elf with keen interest.

'What do you see?' Brunner asked at last, his pistol in his hand.

'Nothing,' Ithilweil admitted. 'But I heard something, a rider, some distance away. And there is a foul scent on the wind.' She looked straight into the bounty hunter's face. 'A smell of death.'

'The vampire,' Ulgrin groaned. 'We can't fight a dragon *and* a mad wizard *and* a vampire!' he exclaimed, ticking each adversary off on his fingers.

'No, we can't,' agreed Brunner, dropping back down to the surface of the road. He strode over to his packhorse and removed a torch from one of the sacks fixed to its harness. 'So why don't we see if we can't persuade our friend back there to join our side.'

Sir Corbus strode out from the night like some nightmare visitation. The vampire was, if anything, even more foul in appearance than he had been when he had attacked the bounty hunters' camp. The monster's face was still scarred and mangled from the salt Brunner had cast into it and the bullet that had broken its jaw. Great gaping holes in the monster's flesh showed where carrion crows had been at work and the putrid ruin of the vampire's destroyed eye was missing entirely now, leaving his socket an empty pit. The vampire knight led a tired-looking draft horse, a hastily secured replacement for the animal he had lost following his fall from the cliff.

Brunner stood his ground in the centre of the roadway, waiting for the vampire. In one hand he held a lit torch, the other was closed about a clay jar filled with lamp oil. Some legends held that vampires could be destroyed by fire. The bounty hunter earnestly hoped that Corbus had heard the same legends.

Ithilweil and Ulgrin were hidden behind the trees. The elf had slipped into the trance-like state that characterised her enchantments, already working to disorient the vampire's mind with her spellcraft. Beside her, Ulgrin stared down the barrel of his thunderer, a double charge of powder and an extra load of shot crammed down its barrel. The dwarf was determined that Corbus would not shrug off his next shot so easily.

THE VAMPIRE GLARED about him, his broken face twisting into a sneer as his unnatural vision easily spotted the dwarf and elf hiding off the road. Then the Blood Dragon turned his attention back to the man facing him. The wolf-like fangs glistened in the flickering light cast by Brunner's torch.

'I had expected you to keep on running like the craven cur you are,' Corbus hissed. 'This will make things much easier.'

'I wanted to speak with you,' Brunner told the monster. 'I have a proposition to discuss.'

'Keep your lies to yourself!' the vampire snarled. 'I've already had a taste of your treachery!' Corbus waved an armoured hand before the ruin of his face. 'Nothing you have to say will keep me from my vengeance!'

'Then revenge means more to you than finding the dragon?' Brunner asked. It was a dangerous gamble, to weigh this creature's fury and hate against his need for drinking the blood of a dragon and purging himself of the curse that ran through his polluted veins. But, as the vampire heard his words, Brunner could see the indecision shining out from his eye, see some of the ferocity drain from the vampire's body. Good, the bounty hunter thought, I have his interest.

'I can find the man who carries the Fell Fang on my own,' Corbus growled. 'I don't need you.'

'But you do,' Brunner corrected him. 'The man who stole the Fell Fang isn't alone. There are others with him.'

'One or twenty, no man can stand against me!' the vampire knight boasted.

Given the horrendous toll he had taken from Marimund's enemies in Mousillon, Brunner was somewhat inclined to give Corbus the benefit of the doubt.

'One of them is a wizard,' the bounty hunter informed Corbus. This seemed to deflate a bit of the vampire's self assurance. Even a creature like him was ill-at-ease around sorcerers and had a healthy dread of the unnatural powers such men could call upon.

'How can I trust you to honour any truce we make?' Corbus demanded, his voice dripping with suspicion.

'Because I have no desire to face a wizard either,' Brunner confessed. 'And he has allies now. I'd rather balance the scales a bit more in my favour.'

The bounty hunter could see the vampire considering his proposal. 'All I want is the bandit; the dragon is your affair,' Brunner told Corbus. 'If the wizard wins out, then neither of us will get what he wants.'

'There is still a score to settle between you and I,' the vampire warned.

'It can wait until the wizard is dead,' Brunner promised, his tone as menacing as that of the vampire.

Corbus considered his words, then nodded his head.

'You have my oath,' Corbus told him. 'Until the wizard is dead,' he added.

Even with the vampire's oath, Brunner maintained his caution. 'They are heading for the Massif Orcal,' Brunner informed Corbus. 'They are sticking to the main road, but there are other paths I know of that might allow us to reach the mountains before them.'

The vampire nodded his head. 'Then I shall continue to follow your trail,' he said.

Corbus turned his horse around, walking the animal back into the darkness. 'I shall meet with you an hour after sunset until our agreement has run its course,' the Blood Dragon stated. 'Look for me in the night.'

Brunner kept his eyes fixed on the vampire's back as the creature withdrew. His every instinct cried out for him to destroy the foul, loathsome creature, to oppose it with every ounce of his strength. But the bounty hunter had learned long ago to subdue his instincts. As long as the monster was useful, he would continue to make use of it.

The sound of Ithilweil and Ulgrin emerging from their hiding places caused Brunner to turn.

'I still say that this is a dangerous thing you contemplate,' Ithilweil told the bounty hunter. 'Corbus is determined to kill you. A creature like that does not change its ways.'

'Yes,' Brunner agreed, 'but at least our intention to kill each other is out in the open. No surprises there. Better than watching our backs all the way to the mountains waiting for him to strike.'

Ulgrin began unloading his rifle, dumping the powder onto an old blanket so he could return the explosive to his powder horn. The dwarf looked up from his labour. 'Just so long as that blood sucker knows I'm not splitting the reward with him!'

Sir Thierswind removed his helmet, staring with thinly disguised anxiety at the masses of craggy rock looming up on every side. The Massif Orcal was a barren, desolate place, a blighted region almost devoid of life. Scraggly pines clung to some of the upper heights, and equally sickly-looking brambles crept about the lower slopes, vainly trying to wrest moisture from the thin layer of soil that powdered the rocks.

This was a miserable region, shunned by the men of Bretonnia. There was no game to be hunted here, no mineral wealth to be wrested from the mountains, no fertile land to claim and build upon. Only orcs and goblins called this place home, foul remnants of the once great hordes that had been scoured from the lands of Bretonnia during the founding of the kingdom. The ruined battlements of old watchtowers and keeps built long ago to guard against the threat of greenskins sometimes loomed into view, slowly crumbling away upon some distant hilltop, forlorn reminders of a time when the goblins could still sometimes muster great armies to despoil the lands of Quenelles and Bastonne. Indeed, the path upon which the wizard led his allies was too even and regular to be any accident. Thierswind guessed that they travelled upon the remains of an old road built to facilitate the movement of troops between the watchtowers.

There had been no sign of life since entering the mountains. Not a bird or beast made its appearance known to the riders; the only sound that disturbed the silence was the ever present clop of their horses' hooves. Thierswind would almost have welcomed the shrill war cry of a goblin or the bull-like bellow of an orc, but whatever had frightened the animals seemed to have likewise kept the greenskins in their caves.

It was growing dark once more when Thierswind noticed the smell – the thick, cloying, acrid musk that permeated the air. It was the same smell that had clung to the lands the dragon had despoiled, the scent of the old wyrm's scaly body.

Rudol looked over at the knight, reading the apprehension in the warrior's face. 'Yes, it's close now,' he told him. 'Ready your torches,' Rudol called to the other soldiers. 'We ride until we find the wyrm!' The wizard's words did little to encourage the men, who grumbled fearfully but made no move to obey. The brief flash of energy crackling within Rudol's eyes, however, lent the men-at-arms a certain eagerness and vigour in producing flaming brands to light their way. None of them had forgotten the ghastly and unnatural death of the bandit Hubolt.

They rode onwards for several hours, following the narrow road as it wound its way between the jagged rocks, through the wind-swept valleys that slithered in the shadows of the mountains. With every step, the unease of man and beast alike began to build. Men muttered to themselves, holding holy icons close to their hearts. Horses snorted and refused to advance until spurs were dug into their flanks. Only Rudol seemed oblivious to the growing aura of dread, his face lit by an expression of feverish anticipation that caused all who gazed upon him to cringe.

At last, the narrow road opened into a broader expanse. Thierswind could see similar roads emerging from several other valleys to merge before a stretch of land as flat and featureless as a tabletop. The flat stretch was bordered on three sides by craggy mountains, and on the fourth by a deep chasm nearly a hundred yards wide. Beyond the chasm, the road continued, rising across a small hill and disappearing over its top. The chasm itself was spanned by a narrow bridge, just wide enough for two horsemen to ride across side by side. Thierswind knew that no human hand had ever built the span. It was too delicate, too wisp-like, to have been crafted by the same race that had produced the ponderous castles and fortresses of Bretonnia. The knight had seen the bridge leading into the city of Parravon, which was reputed to have been built by elves, and the span he now gazed upon reminded him of that one.

'Across the bridge,' Rudol said. 'What we are looking for is on the other side.' Given the degree to which the musky stench of the dragon had increased, Thierswind was inclined to believe the wizard's statement. Rudol looked over to the man-at-arms holding the reins of Gobineau's horse. The wizard leaned close, sneering into the outlaw's face.

'Perhaps there is something you'd like to say?' Rudol asked. Gobineau shook his head, eyes wide with fear. The wizard withdrew. 'Keep him close,' he ordered the soldier. 'I want him near me at all times.'

The passage across the bridge was an especially unpleasant one. The drop was prodigious. One of the soldiers had flung his torch into the abyss to test its depth and the light had been a long time in reaching the bottom. Thierswind imagined that its end might lie at the very roots of the world. It was a possibility the knight did not like to dwell upon. He was thankful when Mannsleib rose into the night sky, the pale moon bathing the ruinous landscape in soft silver light, allowing him to make out the road ahead in greater detail. He could already see Rudol and the foremost of the men-at-arms on the far side. The wizard was pointing angrily back the way they had come. Thierswind looked back over his shoulder, surprised to see four riders emerging from one of the valleys. The knight cursed: whatever mischief the newcomers might portend, there was nothing he could do about it until he gained the other side, the bridge being far too narrow to turn around on.

The knight was nearly the last of his party to reach the far side. Looking back across the chasm, Thierswind could see that the newcomers were already on the bridge and making their way across. He looked over at Rudol. The man's face was twisted into an angry scowl.

'The bounty hunter thinks to meddle in my affairs again!' Rudol spat. His stormy eyes fixed upon Thierswind's. 'Cut that scum down!' the wizard ordered. Thierswind nodded, removing his great helm from where it was tied to his saddle and settling it over his head.

The prospect of battle, far from agitating the knight, had a profoundly calming effect. Dragons, wizards and hoary old artefacts were things beyond Thierswind's understanding. Sharp steel and spilled blood were arenas of knowledge in which he was far more comfortable. He would dismiss the unease, the doubt and fear that had been plaguing him with the blood of these interlopers, whoever they were.

Thierswind led his soldiers back onto the bridge, moving with such haste as they dared muster to meet their foes. The knight had always found combat to be an invigorating experience, a purifying ritual that purged soul and mind. He felt his confidence swell. Was he not a champion of Augustine de Chegney, the most feared lord in the Grey Mountains? Had he not been tried by the fires of battle time and again and always emerged victorious? When he returned from dealing with this rabble, it would be time to remind Rudol that a wizard was just as human as anyone else and that two feet of steel would spill his guts like any other man.

BRUNNER WATCHED THE soldiers return to the bridge, galloping across the narrow span with as much speed as they dared. The bounty hunter's fist closed about the hilt of Drakesmalice, his knuckles whitening beneath his gloves. He recognised the colours these men wore, the heraldry that belonged to Viscount Augustine de Chegney. More, he recognised the bull-horned helm of the knight riding at the forefront of the soldiers. Sir Thierswind. It had been at the end of another life that Brunner had last laid eyes on the knight. Now it was time to settle that score and send de Chegney's dog to yap at the gates of Morr's dark realm.

Beside him, the vampire knight Sir Corbus grinned with the ghastly ruin of his face. For the vampire, battle was the only thing left of his former life, the only way he could experience again what it was like to truly be alive. Brunner could sense the eagerness boiling within the monster as Corbus drew his sword.

'The knight is mine,' Brunner cautioned the vampire. Corbus gave the bounty hunter a savage look. 'Consider it a term to our agreement,' the bounty hunter added in a voice too chill to brook argument. Perhaps there was still enough humanity left within the vampire to remember what it was like to feel honest human hate.

Corbus gave Brunner a grim nod, then put the spurs to his steed, charging forward at a reckless speed. Brunner hissed a command into Fiend's ear, urging his own horse to keep pace with the vampire.

Behind them, Ithilweil and Ulgrin hung back, understanding that any adversaries who made it past Brunner and Corbus would be their problem.

Corbus was the first to reach their enemies. The vampire's blade flashed in the moonlight as the monster drove it with hideous force through the neck of his enemy's horse, slashing deep into the animal's flesh and removing the hand gripping its reins. The fury of the stroke caused the dying animal to topple, pitching over the side of the bridge and carrying its screaming rider into the abyss. The vampire did not delay for even a second in considering his enemy's death, but leapt from his saddle, crashing down upon the stonework of the span. Corbus snarled up at the approaching riders, licking blood from the slaughtered horse from his face and hands. The riders paused in their approach, horrified by the ghastly sight. Even Brunner hesitated, seeing first hand how very close the vampire had been to losing control of his bloodlust during their long ride through the Massif Orcal. Now the monster acted without restraint, glorying in his bloodthirsty assault.

One attacker was not as timid about fighting the vampire, however, and Brunner urged Fiend forward to block the man's attack. If anyone on the bridge would cross swords with Thierswind, it would be Brunner. Drakesmalice crashed against Thierswind's sword of blackened steel, a metal cry not heard for many years. The knight tried to batter away the bounty hunter's stroke, but found that the angle of his attack was ill-suited to such a parry.

'You should have hunted easier prey,' Thierswind snarled. 'This one belongs to the viscount.' The knight slashed down at Brunner, but found Drakesmalice once again between his blow and his target.

'Leave it to de Chegney to send a jackal like yourself to steal another man's property,' the bounty hunter snarled back. He returned Thierswind's attack with one of his own, the edge of Drakesmalice deflected by the knight's thick armour.

Thierswind snorted disdainfully at the bounty hunter. 'You face your death, scavenger. I've put fifty men in their graves, one more will not trouble me.'

'How many of those were women and children?' Brunner retorted, his blade lashing out once more. Thierswind allowed it to glance from his vambrace, snarling back at his antagonist. *Good,* the bounty hunter thought. *Puncture that pompous arrogance of yours and you throw all your skill and training right out the window. Nice to see that some things never change.*

RUDOL WATCHED AS the battle on the bridge unfolded. Brunner seemed to have picked up a rather motley group of allies. The two hanging back were a dwarf and some woman, one with more than a little touch of the power about her. The armoured warrior who had ridden forward with Brunner was amazing, a whirling engine of slaughter and destruction. Rudol had seen men work some incredible feats when gripped by the juice of Crimson Shade, but the bounty hunter's ally put even such impressive moments of brutality to shame. His first stroke had nearly decapitated a horse, and since then he had accounted for another of Thierswind's men, ripping the soldier from his saddle and tearing out his throat with his teeth. Thierswind himself was beset by the bounty hunter, seemingly unable to deal the man a deciding blow while Brunner managed to land minor strikes against the knight's legs and arms. It was an old trick that the knight should have recognised, a tactic designed to sap the strength from his limbs, but Thierswind seemed lost in some mindless frenzy.

Rudol smiled. It was about time he ended the show anyway. The outcome of the battle was inconsequential, no one would be leaving the bridge alive in any event. The outcast celestial wizard began to draw the power into his body, feeling the magic energy writhing through his veins. Yes, indeed, it was time to end this.

'Get a firm grip on his horse,' Rudol ordered the only soldier remaining on his side of the chasm. The man-at-arms dutifully strengthened his hold on the reins of Gobineau's animal. Then the wizard raised a claw-like hand, gesturing toward the bridge. In response to the words of power whispering from his mouth, a fierce gale howled across the span. Rudol watched as men and beasts struggled against the gale, fighting to retain their footing upon the narrow strip of stonework. The first to fail in the struggle was one of Thierswind's men. Toppling from his saddle, the wretch fell screaming into the chasm, his cry strangely distorted by the shrieking tempest. The others seemed to have better sense, dismounting as the wind began to grow. Rudol could see the animals racing for the far side of the span, abandoning their masters to the sorcerous storm. One of the animals crashed against the woman he had noticed earlier, causing them both to fall onto the edge of the bridge. Inhumanly nimble, the woman just managed to grab hold of the horse's reins as she was pushed off the bridge, hanging above the abyss. A valiant effort, but it would not avail her. The storm was going to grow much worse before it expended itself.

The wizard looked aside at his remaining lackey and his prisoner. 'Come along,' he said. 'There is nothing more to be done here, and much to be done on the other side of the hill.'

CHAPTER TWELVE

THE UNNATURAL WIND continued to howl across the ancient
bridge. Brunner had forsaken the saddle to crouch against
the stonework, presenting the clawing tempest the smallest target. Through eyes tearing with the effort of staying
open under the snapping gale, the bounty hunter took
stock of his situation. The only horse he could see still on
the bridge was one a dozen yards behind him, lying prone
upon its side. The other animals were even now galloping
away into the shelter of the narrow valleys. Brunner could
see Ulgrin Baleaxe crouched low in the saddle of his mule,
trying vainly to turn the frightened animal about before
dwarf and steed vanished down one of the valleys. On the
bridge itself, he could see the bodies of two of Thierswind's men slowly being rolled by the gale, the broken
soldiers sliding inexorably toward the edge of the span. Of
their killer, there was no sign. The vampire knight Sir Corbus had vanished as completely as dew on a warm
summer's morn.

One other form stirred upon the bridge, however. Brunner could see the armoured shape of Sir Thierswind struggling to his feet. So intent upon punishing the bounty hunter for his caustic insults was the arrogant knight that he tempted even the sorcerous windstorm called down by Rudol's foul magic. The steel-clad warrior swayed unsteadily as the wind clutched at him, but, with slow, faltering steps, he began to make his way forward.

Brunner watched Thierswind advance, drawing his pistol as the knight drew closer. The knight paused for an instant as he noted the motion, then uttered a snarl of contempt, raising his sword and striding forward once more.

Firearms were rare in Bretonnia, and its warrior nobility despised them as being unworthy of their profession even more so than the longbow. Brunner had profited greatly in the past by the lack of knowledge Bretonnians often displayed toward foreign weapons. No doubt Thierswind reasoned that a gun was no different from a bow, that its shot would be cast aside by the tremendous wind just as an archer's arrow would be diverted from its mark. The bounty hunter smiled. Over a long distance, the knight's assumption might have proved correct, but with every step he took toward his enemy, the chances of the bullet going astray diminished considerably.

THIERSWIND GLARED DOWN at Brunner, the knight's body swaying in the gale. He lifted his blade, intending to end the life of this miserable commoner vermin that had dared to insult his honour and that of his lord. He could see the bounty killer lifting his crude pistol and snorted contemptuously. If the man expected him to show fear before that toy of his, then he was sorely mistaken. If he'd had any confidence that the weapon could have stopped the knight, he would have used it long before now. Thierswind took another tottering step forward and prepared to deal the coup de grâce to his prone adversary.

* * *

THE FAMILIAR CRACK and roar of the pistol was lost in the howling gale. The acrid black smoke of the discharge was blown back into Brunner's face, forcing him to shut his eyes against the foul-smelling smog. When he opened them again, Thierswind had slumped to his knees, hands clutching at the gory wound smoking at the centre of his belly. The knight was no longer able to resist the wind, but fell to his side, sliding remorselessly toward the edge. Desperately, he clutched at the lip of the span with one hand while the other tried to hold his injury closed. Brunner slowly rose to his own feet, his body buffeted by the clawing tempest. Step by careful step, the bounty hunter made his way to the knight's side. He lifted Drakesmalice, displaying it to the wounded knight, waiting until he saw Thierswind's eyes widen with recognition.

'When you get to the gates of Morr,' Brunner shouted above the shrieking wind, 'be sure to prepare a place for your master!' With a savage downward stroke, he brought the edge of Drakesmalice slashing into Thierswind's hand. Such was the strength of the blow that the armoured digits were severed, tumbling away over the edge of the chasm. Thierswind screamed in horror as he lost his grip and his body began to slowly slide across the bridge once more. The sound of the doomed knight begging the bounty hunter to save him struggled to oppose the howling winds and the cold hate that filled the eyes of the bounty hunter. In the past, pleas for mercy had gone unheard by Thierswind, now his own fell upon deaf ears.

Brunner sank down to his knees, his body swaying and rocking in the wind and watched as Thierswind at last fell into the abyss, his final scream drowned out in the shrieking gale.

THE WINDSTORM AT last dissipated and Brunner rose to his feet. Except for the fallen horse he had noticed earlier, the bridge had been cleared by the wizard's magic. Brunner turned his eyes toward the far side of the chasm. It was fortunate indeed that Rudol had not tarried to ensure the potency of his sorcery. The bounty hunter was determined that the wizard would not get the chance to try again.

Just as he began to sprint toward the far side, a cry sounded from behind him. Brunner turned and raced to the source of the sound. He leaned over the crippled horse and gazed down into the chasm. Below, the reins of the animal wrapped about her arm, Ithilweil swayed in the lingering breeze. The elf's face was even paler than usual, and the arm wrapped within the coils of the leather reins was twisted, either broken or dislodged from its socket by the sorcerous gale. Brunner returned Drakesmalice to its sheath and began to slowly, carefully pull Ithilweil upward. The elf did not cry out, but Brunner saw her face contort with pain as pressure was put on her damaged arm. Yet once she was safely back on the bridge, her thoughts were not concerned with her own injuries.

'The wizard,' she gasped as Brunner set her down against the fallen horse. 'Did you get him?'

Brunner shook his head. 'No, he escaped over the hill just after the storm started,' he told her. 'Ulgrin's mule got away from him, took him back into the valley. I don't know what happened to Corbus.'

Ithilweil seemed to digest this information for a moment, then turned her penetrating eyes back on Brunner. 'You must take me to the wizard. We have to stop him before it is too late.' She reached upward with her uninjured arm. Brunner accepted it and lifted her to her feet, letting her lean on him for support.

'How do you know it isn't too late already?' the bounty hunter cautioned her. The elf's answer was a grim one.

'Because we are still alive.'

THE WIZARD STOOD in the bowl-like depression that lay sprawled beyond the hill, glorying at the awesome sight lying before him. He had seen the dragon from a distance and so knew what to expect in theory. But he had failed to appreciate the true enormity of the creature, the immense power that emanated from its body even in sleep. The crimson scales were as thick as armour plate, the claws that tipped each of the monster's feet looked capable of tearing apart mountains. Rudol stared intently at the reptilian face, the long snout with its rows of jagged fangs, the leathery lids concealing the wyrm's ancient eyes. A sound like a bellows rasped through the reptile's flared nostrils as the dragon slumbered.

Rudol looked down at the crescent of ivory clutched in his hand. The fools in Altdorf would regret their mistake. He would make them pay, level their puerile institution and cast their charred corpses into an open pit while the entire city watched. He would show them who was the great wizard and who was the frightened fool. Rudol turned his eyes back toward his remaining companions: Gobineau and the soldier he'd kept to guard the man.

'You stand at the crossroads of history,' Rudol told them. 'You stand witness to the moment when Rudol claims his destiny!' The wizard's triumphant cackle was diminished as he saw the powerful warrior in the crimson armour emerge from the rocks behind Gobineau.

Rudol's confidence began to waver as he recalled the ferocious power the knight had displayed when butchering Thierswind's men. With a speed that was almost beyond belief, the vampire sprung forward, falling upon the last soldier like a lion pouncing upon a goat. The doomed man managed a single cry of horror as the vampire gorged himself on the soldier's blood.

Rudol turned, lifting the Fell Fang to his lips. Whatever unholy force gave such strength and ferocity to the red knight, it was about to be consumed by an even greater power.

* * *

ITHILWEIL AND BRUNNER rounded the hill just in time to see Corbus pounce upon Rudol's sole surviving guard. As the vampire attacked, Brunner could see Gobineau running for the far side of the bowl-like depression, striving to put as much ground between himself and the vampire as possible. Then the bounty hunter's attention became riveted on the immense reptilian shape sprawled about the base of the depression. While he watched, the dragon's claws began to flex, the steady breathing became uneven, and Malok began to stir.

Ithilweil stabbed a slender finger at the black-cloaked source of the dragon's discomfort. Rudol had lifted the Fell Fang to his lips, urging Malok from his slumber.

'You must stop him!' the elf shouted needlessly.

Brunner cast one last look at the fleeing Gobineau, then began racing toward the wizard, Drakesmalice clutched in his hand. Ithilweil watched the bounty hunter hasten to put an end to Rudol's magic, then forced herself to enter the trance-like state that would allow her own magic to play its part in the conflict. It was madness, what she was contemplating, even the most powerful mages in Ulthuan would have found what she was going to try difficult, if not impossible. To try and influence the will of a dragon, to disorient and confuse a mind so ancient, was a thing on such a scale as she had never dared imagine before. But she also knew that if she failed, then all of them would be dead in a matter of seconds.

RUDOL LAUGHED AS he watched Malok stir, removing the Fell Fang from his lips and shouting triumphantly at the mammoth beast. 'Yes! Yes! Awaken my pet! Hear your master's call!' The massive shape contorted its body in a long, serpentine stretch, then swung its head around to face the wizard. The leathery eyelids slid open, the huge yellow orbs behind them staring intently at the cackling conjurer. The dragon's long tongue slid from between its jaws, tasting the air and the scent of the sorcerer. Rudol gloried in the moment as the dragon became aware of its new master. Then he turned around, glaring back at the hill. The red knight had cast aside the carcass of the soldier and was now rushing down the hill, his pale face streaked in blood. Behind him, Rudol could also see the bounty hunter, Brunner, likewise charging down the hill. Still further distant was the slender figure of the young woman from the bridge, wisps of magical power billowing around her as she worked some spell of her own.

The wizard's lip curled in contempt. 'Kill them, Malok!' he cried. 'Kill! Kill! Kill them all!' His voice swelled with the fury and outrage that filled him. These vermin thought to come between himself and his destiny; now they would become the first victims of his new power.

AHEAD OF HIM, Brunner could see the mammoth reptile begin to move, its head swinging about to regard Rudol with serpentine eyes. The bounty hunter could feel terror gnaw at his stomach as he watched Malok sluggishly stir into motion, but another emotion overwhelmed his fear and lent a new speed to his legs. His mind became clouded with darkling thoughts of the future. His eyes shifted their focus from Malok to the red-armoured Sir Corbus, the knight's sword clenched in his mailed fist. During the long nights riding toward the Massif Orcal, the vampire had repeated over and again his intentions, the dream that relentlessly drove him onward: to drink the dragon's blood and purge his body of the loathsome thirst that plagued him.

Brunner redoubled his efforts, lunging toward the vampire. Drakesmalice flashed toward the knight's back, striking the monster in the small of his back. It was a telling stroke, but the sturdy armour worn by Corbus held and instead of sinking into undead flesh, Brunner's sword merely scraped across the steel plates. Corbus spun about, dropping to his haunches, his broken face snarling up at the bounty hunter like some feral beast.

'He's no good to me dead,' Brunner hissed at Corbus, his longsword slashing at the vampire's face.

Corbus raised his own blade, blocking the bounty hunter's blow.

'Treacherous maggot!' the vampire roared as he repelled Brunner's attack.

'My word is only as good as who I give it to,' the bounty hunter responded. The mangled visage of Corbus seemed to glow with the fury boiling up within him. But the vampire was not so lost to his anger that he did not notice Brunner's other hand swinging around. With incredible speed, the undead knight sprang backwards, beyond the cloud of salt the bounty hunter hurled at him.

Corbus hissed at his enemy, every muscle in his body coiling for the next attack. The bounty hunter had used his last trick, now he would become the last victim of the unholy thirst raging through the vampire's veins, the last supper before Corbus claimed his redemption. He tensed his body, like a tiger preparing to pounce.

Just as the vampire leaped, a gigantic crimson claw smashed into the ground before him, throwing Corbus back as the earth exploded beneath the dragon's strength. Brunner leapt from beneath the dragon's other claw as the monster brought its leg crashing down upon him. Broken fragments of rock pelted the bounty hunter as he rolled away from the reptile's assault.

Malok glared down at the bounty hunter, his yellow eyes narrowing with annoyance as he saw his prey elude his attack. With a growl, Malok slashed out at the man once more, his claws cutting across the ground like steel rakes, digging deep furrows in the rocky terrain. Once again, Brunner managed to leap from the path of the dragon's assault.

Malok continued to savage the ground as he alternately slashed at Brunner and Corbus, always missing his

intended prey. Rocks exploded beneath the dragon's crushing blows, the earth trembled beneath the pounding force
of his attacks. There was no doubting the deadly strength of
those claws, and it would only take a single misstep to be
smashed into oblivion beneath them. Yet it also seemed to
Brunner that Malok's attacks were somehow clumsy, as
though the dragon were not able to focus completely upon
his prey. He risked a look back up the hillside, seeing Ithilweil standing near its top, as still as a statue. That he had
not already been crushed beneath one of Malok's massive
claws was due to her subtle magic disordering the dragon's
mind, of this he was certain.

Brunner dodged another of Malok's strikes, jumping
back as the ground where he had been standing exploded
into grey dust. Their section of the depression's floor was
rapidly becoming choked with rock dust, a grey curtain that
was beginning to obscure vision. If it was difficult to avoid
the dragon's attacks now, the bounty hunter did not even
want to consider how much worse it would be when he
could no longer see them coming.

The sound of rattling armour caused Brunner to spin
about. The dark figure of Sir Corbus emerged from the
clouds of dust, his blood-stained armour now grey from
the dust clinging to it. The vampire's mangled face twisted
into an evil leer and with an animalistic snarl, he charged
at the man who had broken faith with him.

Before Corbus could reach his prey, Malok's claw slashed
downward, crushing the vampire beneath it. With his
attention fixed upon Brunner, Corbus never saw the blow
that hammered him into the rocky earth. Malok lifted his
scaly paw from the crater he had pounded into the ground.
Corbus hung from one of the black-tipped claws, the
vampire's belly impaled upon the talon, the bright red
blood of his recent victims spilling from the grotesque
wound. Malok shook his claw, like a man wiping something from his finger, flinging the broken vampire across

the depression as though he were nothing more than a crushed insect.

'Yes, Malok!' Rudol shouted, his voice cracking with the delirious ecstasy filling him. No one would stand against him now. 'Destroy the other one, Malok! Destroy Brunner!'

Malok's reptilian head swung around once more, the snake-like eyes gazing down upon the black-garbed wizard. The dragon had almost forgotten this little shouting rat. But now he had drawn the dragon's focus back to him. Malok glared at Rudol, a low growl rumbling from his chest.

'Malok, do as I bid you!' Rudol roared at the dragon. 'Kill the bounty hunter!' The wizard felt anger well up within him when the dragon did not move. 'I am your master, do as I command!' To emphasise his authority, Rudol held out the Fell Fang that his gigantic slave might know the uselessness of resisting his commands.

The dragon's head drew back, the scaly mouth opening in a hiss of hatred and disgust. Malok recognised the ancient talisman, remembered the long years he had suffered the elves to dictate where and what he would destroy. But this fool had no such power over him as the long dead elf prince who had once tried to control him. Nor would the wizard ever have the chance to gain such knowledge.

Malok hissed down at the threatening wizard and for the first time, doubt crept into Rudol's eyes, quickly followed by a horror that rose from the very depths of the man's soul. Rudol waved the Fell Fang before him, as though it were a protective charm. 'Malok, do as I say! I am your master!' Rudol cried, but now his shouts were those of desperation, not command.

The dragon drew back then swatted the wizard. The enormous scaly paw struck Rudol with the force of a lightning bolt. The wizard's enchanted cloak flashed for a moment, then faded into dull black, its magic unable to deflect an attack of such magnitude. Like a broken rag doll, Rudol was flung aside, every bone in his body cracked and splintered by the dragon's assault. His corpse struck the rocky side of the depression, then crumpled against the ground like a wilted weed.

Malok threw back his head, roaring with triumph. The maggot who had disturbed his sleep was no more, the vermin who thought to enslave him was destroyed. The dragon's roar shook the craggy mountains that surrounded the depression, causing tiny rockslides to trickle down their gnarled faces.

The dragon exulted in his victory for only a moment, then swung his head downward once more. There had been others here who had earned his wrath. Now they too would join the foolish wizard in annihilation.

BRUNNER WATCHED AS Malok hurled Rudol across the depression. In that instant, the bounty hunter could see the Fell Fang locked in the death grip the wizard's hand had fastened about it. Cold ambition filled him, and the bounty hunter began to sprint across the depression, racing through the very shadow of Malok, intent on gaining Rudol's body.

The dragon noticed the movement, once more glaring down at the bounty hunter. Brunner watched as Malok lifted one of his feet and slashed down at him like an angry cat swatting at a mouse it has grown weary of playing with. There was none of the clumsiness that had plagued the wyrm's earlier assaults, only by the merest of margins did the bounty hunter escape from beneath the smashing blow, throwing himself flat against the ground just beyond the dragon's strike. The earth behind him exploded, throwing up large chunks of rock that battered the bounty hunter's body. Brunner felt a rib crack as one jagged rock smashed into his side.

The bounty hunter rolled painfully onto his back, fighting to block out the pain assailing him. His eyes glanced momentarily at the hilltop, and saw that Ithilweil had gone. Whatever sorcery she had worked upon Malok, the dragon was now free of her enchantment. Brunner looked back at the crimson-scaled monster, watching as death glared back at him.

Malok hissed as he gazed at the broken man, lowering his head and flicking out his tongue to taste the sweet smell of fear rising from his prey. All the crude beasts of the world knew fear when they stood in the shadow of death, and dragons had ever been the very incarnation of that shadow, the prophets of doom and destruction.

As Malok leaned closer, a battered figure leapt upon the dragon. With his armour ravaged and crumpled, with blood and the black filth that coursed through his veins continuing to drool from the gaping hole in his belly, Corbus lunged at the dragon. Even with his body crushed and mangled, the vampire's inhuman strength and unholy desire spurred him onward. Corbus's leap found him poised upon Malok's shoulder. The undead knight lifted his sword high above his head, then sent it stabbing down into the blackened scar beneath him.

The dragon roared in pain as the vampire's sword bit into him, twisting his head and shaking his body in a desperate effort to dislodge Corbus. The knight held firm, however, sinking against his sword, fastening his fangs about the broken flesh torn by his blade. Like some hideous tick, the vampire began to drink. Malok continued to roar, stomping about the depression in a maddened effort to remove the sucking parasite. At length, the dragon's struggles met with success, one of the horns on his head striking the feeding vampire and ripping him free.

Corbus struck the ground hard, feeling his shoulder disintegrate against the rocky ground. But the vampire had little concern for such injuries, his mind focused on the fiery sensation surging through his diseased body. He could feel the dragon's blood burning and gnawing at the corruption within him, feel it scouring the loathsome thirst from him. Never more would he feel the foul desire to feed, to fatten himself upon the blood of others. He would become a man once more. No, more than a man, for the strengths of the vampire would still be his, all of the power of the Blood Dragons and none of their weakness. He would be a god.

The vampire howled his rapture into the night, but the cry of victory was short-lived. Malok's mammoth claw smashed into Corbus, crushing him back into the earth and pinning him beneath it. The dragon glared down at the trapped vampire, then drew back his head. Since becoming a vampire, Corbus had forgotten what the sensation of fear was like, but the undead monster remembered it now. His remaining eye widened with horror as Malok's head shot downward once more, jaws agape. Orange flame exploded from the reptile's mouth, engulfing its foot and the monster pinned beneath it. The scales of Malok's paw resisted the dragon's flame, the vampire trapped beneath it did not. Corbus shrieked as he was consumed, as his body was annihilated by the dragon's breath, reduced to ash in the batting of an eye.

SLOWLY, PAINFULLY, BRUNNER tried to crawl away. He knew it was a vain struggle, but perhaps Corbus would distract the dragon long enough for him to effect some manner of escape. The sudden blast of heat that washed over the bounty hunter as Malok expelled his fiery rage told him that whatever distraction Corbus might have presented, the vampire would be one no longer. Brunner looked back as Malok lifted his paw from the blackened crater that marked the grave of the vampire. The dragon's horned head swung around to stare at him, the reptile's yellow eyes narrowing as they fixed upon him. With tremendous strides that caused the ground to shudder, Malok stalked toward the wounded man.

Then, abruptly, the monster froze, Malok's eyes becoming unfocused, almost dazed. Brunner could see the dragon's muscles twitching beneath his scaly hide. The bounty hunter also became aware of a light, a fiery brilliance emanating from where Rudol's body had fallen.

Ithilweil was standing above the wizard's broken remains, the Fell Fang clutched in her hands. Waves of heat and light were pulsing from her body as she blew into the hollow crescent of ivory, a strange and ghostly melody rising from the ancient artefact. Brunner watched in morbid fascination as the elf strove to increase the pitch of the haunting music, as she blew ever more deeply and forcefully into the Fang. As she did so, the waves of heat boiling from her increased as well and the bounty hunter could see her clothing and hair begin to catch flame, as though ignited by a fire emanating from within her. The bounty hunter recalled the words she had spoken long ago, warning him that only the strongest of wills could effectively use the Fell Fang, that any lesser spirit trying to employ it would be destroyed, consumed by the very power they tried to wield.

Brunner began to crawl toward the elf enchantress, knowing as he did so that he would be too late. Ithilweil's clothes had burned away completely now, exposing a body that had become blackened and charred. Brunner could see the scaly skin that now clothed the woman split, could see tiny wisps of fire and smoke rising from the cracks in her flesh. The magical energies the elf was drawing upon were consuming her as surely as a lamp consumed oil.

Above him, the transfixed bulk of Malok stirred. The dragon uttered a low growl, then unfurled his wings. The bounty hunter covered his head as the dragon fanned the air with his mighty pinions and rose into the darkened sky. The immense crimson shape rose into the night, circling the small depression once before turning, flying off towards the south. Brunner watched the dragon depart and as Malok faded from view, so too did the awful heat and light pulsating from Ithilweil. The bounty hunter saw her smoking body collapse to the ground, like a puppet whose strings had been cut. Brunner forced himself to his feet, ignoring the pain in his side and ran to the fallen enchantress.

She was no longer recognisable as the beautiful elf woman who had journeyed with the bounty hunter from the cursed city of Mousillon. Her skin was burnt and blackened, and her eyes had had all the life and vision seared from them by the intense heat of the energies she had tried to command. Only the faintest spark of life clung to the ruin of her body.

As Brunner reached her side, Ithilweil spoke to him. 'I had to use the Fang,' she gasped. 'It was the only thing left to do. I knew the rituals, the proper way to make it work.' She groped desperately at Brunner's hand, her blind eyes seeing only darkness. Brunner reached down and gently took her charred hand in his own. 'I knew it would destroy me,' she said. 'I knew that I was not strong enough.'

'But you were,' Brunner told her. 'The dragon is gone.'

The ruin of Ithilweil's once beautiful face twisted into a thin smile. 'All I did was to heighten a desire that was already within Malok's mind. The dragon wanted to return to his home, and that is where I sent him. If the desire had not already been there, I could not have placed it there.' A shudder shook the dying woman and her grip upon Brunner's hand tightened. 'It has consumed me, Brunner. I had to feed my soul into the Fell Fang, had to use my life to fuel its power, to overcome Malok's will.' Ithilweil shuddered again, then lifted her other hand. Brunner could see the Fell Fang, unmarred amid the burned flesh. The elf held the artefact out to the bounty hunter.

'I cannot destroy it now,' Ithilweil told him. 'You must do it for me.' The enchantress seemed to sense the doubt that flared up within the bounty hunter. 'Don't let your hate rule you Brunner, or it will destroy you. That is the lesson my people learned far too late. Your pain has taken enough from you, don't let it take everything.' The elf was gripped by another shuddering convulsion. 'Promise me you will destroy the Fell Fang,' she begged, her words fading into a whisper.

'I will destroy it,' Brunner told her as Ithilweil's body grew slack, as her last breath sighed past her charred lips. The bounty hunter held onto her hand a moment longer, feeling the strength fade from her tortured flesh, then he rose to his feet, pausing to remove the Fell Fang from her slackened grasp.

Brunner stared at the carved ivory tooth, studying the runes and inscriptions crawling across its surface. He thought again of Malok, of the dragon's sinister gaze and awful power, of a rain of fire and of castles falling into dust. Brunner's fist tightened about the artefact and with a savage motion he thrust the fang beneath the loop of his belt.

'I will destroy it,' the bounty hunter told the uncaring night. 'When I am through with it.'

GOBINEAU CONTINUED TO make his way through the narrow, jagged valleys. The outlaw was under no illusions that his situation was desperate. Alone, lost within the goblin-infested Massif Orcal, his hands bound, the rogue decided that his situation was just about as bad as any he had ever faced. Still, he knew that things could have been much worse. He could still be back at the depression with Rudol and Corbus and the dragon Malok. None of them were creatures Gobineau cared to be near, much less all three at once. The roars and screams and rumblings sounding from behind him told the thief that flight had indeed been the wisest course to pursue. Let them kill each other; when it was all over there would be a decided drop in the number of Gobineau's enemies.

As the bandit rounded a corner in the narrow fissure, he suddenly felt his breath flee his body as the solid mass of a

steel axe slapped into his mid-section. Gobineau fell to his
knees, wheezing with pain. Through tear-stained eyes, the
outlaw watched as his attacker glared down at him.

'Well, well, well,' Ulgrin grinned. 'This must be my lucky
day. The notorious Gobineau, and all trussed up like a
birthday present. I'll have to remember to thank my ancestors for favouring me with good fortune.'

Gobineau opened his mouth to speak, but Ulgrin drove
the flat of his axe into the man's stomach again, spilling
him to the ground.

'Be a good boy and keep quiet,' the dwarf told him. 'We
have a long ride ahead of us, and I intend to make it in
record time. There's a purse of gold waiting for me and a
piece of old rope waiting for you when we get to Couronne.
It would be a shame to waste them.'

Ulgrin Baleaxe kicked the outlaw until he regained his
feet, then pushed him towards his mule. The dwarf hesitated a moment, glancing from one side to the other, then
smiled again. No sign of Brunner. Ulgrin allowed himself
to imagine his erstwhile partner resting in the belly of the
dragon and his smile broadened. He was hardly going to
split the reward with a dead man, was he? And if Brunner
did turn out to still be among the living, well, he'd just have
to hope he could catch up to Ulgrin before he reached the
Bretonnian capital.

The dwarf started to whistle an old miner's work song as
his mind began to spend two thousand pieces of gold.

EPILOGUE

ELODORE PLEASANT QUIETLY withdrew from his master's presence, his head nodding vulture-like as he retreated back towards the heavy oak doors that loomed against the entryway. He had served the Viscount Augustine de Chegney long enough to read the volatile nobleman's dark moods and knew when the man's temper was about to explode. At such times, it was healthy to be as far away as possible.

The viscount sat upon his throne, scowling down at the object the messenger had brought him, fury and fear striving for mastery of his features. It had been several weeks since the wizard Rudol had come to him, fuelling his ambitions with wild tales of dragons and the power to command them. Since that time, there had been no word from the sorcerer and the soldiers de Chegney had sent with him. Then, Sir Thierswind's horse had returned to the castle – riderless. Within one of the animal's saddlebags had been found the object that was the cause of de Chegney's ill humour.

It had been wrapped in the blood-stained black cloak Rudol had been wearing, a large flattened object roughly the size of a soup bowl. As soon as he laid eyes upon the leathery, crimson plate de Chegney knew what it was. Rumours had already reached him of a monster, a gigantic dragon ravaging the lands to the west, decimating entire companies of knights and leaving dozens of villages burning in its wake. At first the rumours had excited him, as he connected them to the wild tales Rudol had spun and he had seriously begun to believe the wizard might be able to deliver what he had promised. Now they filled him with dread.

The object was a reptilian scale, such as might be plucked from the hide of a snake, only far grander in size and toughness. That it had come from the dragon, de Chegney did not question for a moment. But it was the symbol carved into the tough leathery scale that caused fear to gnaw at the Bretonnian's stony heart. De Chegney had not seen that sign in many years, but it was as familiar to him as his own coat-of-arms. It was a crude representation of a drake rampant, rendered in the stylised manner of the Empire. When de Chegney had last seen that symbol, it had been upon the coat-of-arms of his vanquished adversary, the Baron von Drakenburg.

He'd thought the baron long dead, worked to death beneath the hot desert sun by Arabyan slave masters. Such was the fate he had condemned his old enemy to in the aftermath of his victory. But as he stared down at the symbol carved into the dragon scale, de Chegney knew his enemy had survived. He could feel it in the very pit of his soul. The horse, the wizard's cloak, and the scale were all part of a message: *I live. I know what you were hunting. The power you sought is mine now and it will come for you.*

De Chegney rose from his throne, letting the scale fall to the floor. The nobleman began to pace the empty expanse of his great hall, his footfalls echoing from the stone walls.

He realised now what it must be like for the prisoners rotting within his dungeons, certain they were doomed to die but never knowing the hour when the executioner would call their name.

ABOUT THE AUTHOR

Exiled to the blazing wastes of Arizona for communing with ghastly Lovecraftian abominations, C L Werner strives to infect others with the grotesque images that infest his mind. First joining the ranks of the Black Library's authors in the pages of *Inferno!* magazine, C L Werner continues to pen tales of bloodshed, carnage and horror. He is the author of three novels detailing the career of Reiklander bounty hunter Brunner and the novel *Witch Hunter*. When not engaged in his ongoing schemes to become warlord of the American Southwest, he can usually be found watching old Christopher Lee films from his DVD collection. Rumours that C L Werner is the illegitimate offspring of the monster Rodan are mostly untrue.

Check out the action-packed

WITCH HUNTER

BY C L WERNER

A nameless horror stalks the district of Klausberg,
leaving a trail of bloody destruction in its wake. Can
Witch Hunter Mathias Thulmann end the vile curse
and put an end to this reign of terror?

ISBN: 1-84416-071-8

Buy it now from **www.blacklibrary.com**

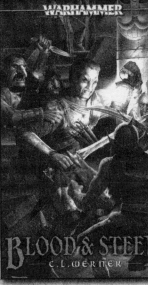